ABOUT THE AUTHOR

Sue is a keen onomast, bibliophile, numismatist, philatelist and writer. She worked for the BBC at Caversham, then lived in a converted cave in Spain with her husband Peter, until she realised she loved England and the awful English weather more.

Sue's first love is writing poetry, her second is writing books (fiction and non-fiction), her third is star-gazing and listening to beautiful music.

Sue's book of poetry, *The Long Wave*, was published by Austin Macauley in December 2022.

SUE McGREGOR

Song of the
Nightingale

AUSTIN MACAULEY PUBLISHERS™
LONDON • CAMBRIDGE • NEW YORK • SHARJAH

A CIP catalogue record for this title is available from the British Library.

ISBN 9781398492226 (Paperback)
ISBN 9781398492233 (ePub e-book)

www.austinmacauley.com

First Published 2024
Austin Macauley Publishers Ltd®
1 Canada Square
Canary Wharf
London
E14 5AA

DEDICATION

For Kate & for Rob

CHAPTER ONE

If you could fly over the Doure valley, you would see Nefton
Hebb's farm, nestled in undulating countryside, verdant and
lush, the farmhouse an ancient building, low and mellow in
the afternoon sun. Of course, Nefton (known as Neft) is no
longer with us. He passed away of an undiagnosed illness
– maybe he caught something from the farm animals or
even from the soil. No one knew. On closer inspection, his
farmhouse and farm buildings were in a poor state of repair:
the two barns still standing, a linhay and bothy, needed
attention; only the brick stables, a sign of more prosperous
times. If only Neft had had money or if only Neft had had a
business head on his shoulders... But he didn't, and consequently, he left his wife, Anella, with a farm in good heart,
but its buildings decrepit. He left no money to speak of, but
then, he left no debt either.

So here's his wife, widowed young with no family. Her
parents long gone and the in-laws fading away one after
the other, leaving their only child, their son, and his barren
wife. A dismal end to a family well known and respected in
the district. Anella Hebb, a wife but never a mother, living
a farming life, but not a farmer, the owner of Haswell Farm
but with no money to run it. 'Haswell', meaning 'the spring
or stream where hazels grow': a lovely but unremarkable
part of the valley, two hundred and fifty-two acres which
Nefton had struggled to manage.

The house itself, like most farmhouses, had an endless
assortment of small rooms, each with a specific purpose.
You first came into the boot room and off, there was the

kitchen, a large, comfortable, scruffy room, always in use. Many doors led off. There was the dairy, the still room, the pantry, the larder and the log store, next to which was the coal shed, so that in the winter, you didn't have to go outside in the cold to get your fuel. Then there was the laundry room, the apple store, the gun room, the garden room and two empty storage rooms that the in-laws hadn't managed to fill. The kitchen was the heart of the house, the eating room and various sitting rooms hardly ever used. They were forlorn, dusty and neglected. Upstairs was the same: many unused bedrooms, cold and unloved and box rooms and lumber rooms and attics full of old abandoned beds and furniture that Neft's parents insisted would come in handy one day, but of course, never did.

Well, they did, but only the day after you threw them out.

So what happens to a barren wife, widowed and alone? She drops into a well of deep despair. She cries. She eats little. She slopes around all day in her dressing robe, she neglects herself and the farm animals. She doesn't bother to keep herself clean and tidy and she doesn't bother with the house either. What's the point? She sits at the kitchen table in the evenings with a bottle of wine (of which she's drunk too much), railing against a husband who had the temerity to leave her in this pitiful state. How could he? This state of grief, unhappiness, worry and resentment can last for ever, but Anella realised she would, at some time, have to re-surface from this pit of misery. Maybe it was money or the lack of it that rallied her. One can't live on tears, more's the pity.

It happened then. A visit to Neft's solicitor. A strange and nervous meeting. Anella sitting in his office, in her dark two-piece suit, wearing proper heeled shoes and with her only handbag on her lap. It became all too apparent that there was very little money indeed. The solicitor, a dry, spare man, peered at her over his glasses with a slightly disapproving air. He advised Mrs Hebb to sell up, buy a little town house somewhere; a bijou residence by the sea, so bracing. Maybe a boarding house – she could take in paying guests. His suggestions filled Anella with gloom. So Neft wasn't good with money, but he left no outstanding financial commitments, no debts, nothing hidden and what he did have, the farm and house, he left to Anella.

Leaving the solicitors' office, she spotted Mr Graves, who owned the farm adjacent to theirs – well, hers now. She asked if she could cadge a lift home. He laughed at this request. In their valley, a cadger was someone who went from farm to farm, selling goods. He hadn't quite finished his business, he said, but if she didn't mind waiting, he would be glad of her company on the journey home.

It was late afternoon by the time she got home, so it was a quick change back into old clothes and boots and out to see to the animals; not many animals now, only pigs, goats, chickens and bees, and the two dogs, of course. She would check the bees on the morrow. It was too late to let the hens out in the field now, so she threw handfuls of grain in the run to distract them while she collected the eggs.

In order to get the pigs back up from the lower field, she stood and banged a bucket, calling them, "Here, piggy wiggy wiggies," and they came charging up. She had to make sure she was standing against the sty wall, otherwise they would knock her over, such was their eagerness for the scraps of food. The dogs rounded up her few goats and they were safely penned for the night, and then it was back to the house to feed herself and the dogs.

Kicking her boots off and her outer garments, Anella stood in the kitchen, her back against the door, hands behind her, holding onto the door handle. She looked around at the shabby, well-used room, the morning's washing up still in the sink, the dirty wine glass from the night before on the wooden draining board, the battered kitchen table and the grubby tea towels hanging on the rail. The old range was glowering gently in the chimney alcove, keeping the room warm and friendly. All this was hers now. She felt a glimmer of excitement. Thie semi-derelict farmhouse, with all its unused and useless rooms, belonged to no one else but her. She went through the rooms with a curious sense of owner-ship. Every room had its fireplace, but the house was never really warm. The washing room, where countless farmers' wives had scrubbed smocks and washed linen bedsheets and then across to the still room, unused this year because of Neft's illness. There was still plenty of cider and mead that he'd made from the previous summer, she couldn't see herself drinking any of it. So many rooms.

For Anella, this was a strange and lonely day. No one left but her. She had been Neft's all in the beginning, but as year followed year and no babies arrived, she'd fallen out of favour. He became morose, a man of few words. They had an empty marriage, an empty house, empty nursery, empty perambulators; sometimes her sense of failure was overwhelming. Neft made it clear that the fault lay with her, and she never doubted his blame. It was her fault, but it was too late now to dwell on such matters. She shrugged her shoulders. Neft was gone and all his clothes and posses-sions would have to be packed up. It would be a hard matter to address, but it would have to be done and another attic would be filled with trunks and boxes of stuff, still smelling of him, still having that air of ownership, as if Neft would come into the room and ask what did she think she was doing?

The week following her visit to the solicitors was a week of introspection. Anella traipsed around the farm, doing only what had to be done, constantly thinking about what should be done regarding her situation. Did she want to leave the farm? No, but the thought of a little house in the village or by the coast was a good thought. She would make friends, do a little entertaining, hold musical soirees. She imagined herself, cool, sophisticated, charming with a group of guests, well connected, people of regard in society – and then, reality set in. Really? Did she honestly believe this sort of cultured event would take place under her roof? Get away, she told herself, you're being ridiculous. Consequently, if she decided to stay put, certain decisions would have to be made regarding the farm. She could do some of the work, but not all. The heavier work was a man's job, so a man or men would have to be found and money would have to be found to pay them. Unless they lived in, she thought. With a disused bothy and a near derelict linhay, both these buildings could be bought back into use

That evening, sitting lonely in her cluttered kitchen, Anella made the decision to stay at the farm and try to bring it back to its former glory. If the farm itself was in good order, who knows? Maybe one day, if she decided to sell up, it might sell for a better price, then she could buy a better house as a result.

The following morning, Anella traipsed over the fields to see Mr Graves. He was a typical blunt-faced, jovial farmer with a similar smiley-faced wife and four grown sons. Without preamble, Anella asked if he would be interested in renting some of her fields. And without hesitation, he said, yes, he would. His sons were of an age, he explained, where they needed extra work. Extra work meant extra money. The deal was done there and then, not only for a monthly sum, but for an amount of flour and grain also. They shook hands, and it was agreed: Anella would consult her solicitor to draw up a contract, to be signed by them both as promptly as circumstances would allow.

As she was in walking mode, Anella crossed to the lane

and went down to the village. At the back of her mind was the seed of an idea that there was a widow, like her, with a large family; two of the sons older, she thought. Maybe they would want work. Yes, they did. The widow was Mrs Bosworth, living in a hovel of a cottage, with six children: twins Clem and Clance, sixteen; Maisie, fourteen; Polly, twelve; and two "littlies", as she called them, Alfie and Ollie, soon to be attending the village school. The boys were eating her out of house and home, she said, and she had two daughters also. Would they be of any use? Anella had to smile. No, she said, but perhaps later on, Maisie, if she hadn't gone into service, could come and work in the house – would that be any good? Mrs Bosworth was in transports of delight. When would Mrs Hebb want the boys to start? They were "on the roads" today, but such work was intermittent and unreliable. They wanted full-time, permanent work because they needed the money to give to their mother. Anella explained the boys would live in at the farm and the deal was this: they would have one day free a week, together; they would take over the bothy; they would be fed and watered; no pay to start with, but yes, eventually, as things improved, there would be wages. In the meantime, Anella would supply them with eggs and milk and butter to bring home on their day off. Mrs Bosworth almost clapped her hands in joy. What a relief. Two boys gone, more room for the rest of them, the biggest eaters off her hands and the promise of work for her eldest daughter. What a day. She couldn't wait for the boys to come home to tell them the good news.

It was arranged then, that the boys would come over on the morrow, get themselves acquainted and settled in and start two days later, on the Friday. Mrs Bosworth was a very happy lady, and so was Anella.

There was so much to do when she got back to the

farm; goats to milk, eggs to collect, pigs to let out, butter and bread to make. Hopefully, these would be the last few days when she would have to tackle everything on her own. Tomorrow would be a new start.

The following morning, Anella woke weary. A night of dreams – with Neft deeply disapproving of her actions yesterday. He'd made her trudge back to Mr Graves, it was raining and – No! Mr Graves would not rescind the contract. His four sons chased her off their property, she fell in the mud and lost her boots; she was climbing a spiral staircase, they were chasing her, getting nearer and nearer; she was looking over her shoulder, she was afraid – and she jumped awake, hot and sweating. It took a few minutes to realise she was safe and it was just a dream. She couldn't sleep properly after that and, consequently, Anella was up and about early, so it was down to see the bees before it became too warm.

She let the pigs out to the lower field, freed the goats from their pen and fed the chickens, released the dogs from their shelter and made her way back up to the house. She was pleased to see the twins just arriving. They didn't seem to have bought much with them but one had a sack on his back, very mobile; hopefully he had ferrets in there. Now that would be handy!

"Morning, boys. I'm Mrs Hebb. Which one of you is Clem, which one Clance?" The two boys looked identical, both tow-headed, pale-skinned and not particularly strong by the look of their build. Anella's hopes wavered slightly. She sent up a silent prayer: "Let this work, please."

"I'm Clem, Ma'am, this 'ere's Clance, but it don't matter much, ma'am, we'es answer to either." They gave each other a quick sideways glance, as if to say they had misled quite a few people in the past.

"No worry about getting your names wrong then, is

there? Right, come with me, I'll show you the bothy. It needs a good clear out. Put the stuff you find in the barn, unless you can use it, of course. Once you've emptied it and cleaned it out, come to the house and we'll get the beds down and anything else you might need."

They had stopped in front of a ramshackle little building, the bothy. "Well, this is it," Anella waved a hand. "This is your new home, it's up to you to keep it clean and tidy. You'll find brooms and brushes in the barn; come over to the house about 10-ish for tea." Anella took out her fob watch; she must get on.

The boys looked at her, perplexed. "Please Ma'am, we've no way of time telling." Clem shrugged his shoulders.

"The stable clock will strike the hour. Listen out for it, or you'll be drinking cold tea. When you've done, have a walk around, get your bearings." She turned away. "I'll expect you to be prompt. You have a lot to do today."

She was off, back to the kitchen. There was bread to make, butter to churn, a cake to bake, the goats to milk.

The dough was made and proving, a cake was in the oven, so it was down to milk the goats, the dogs, Tam and Ella, following her. Their home was here in this field: a wooden structure, inside filled with clean straw, covered in an old blanket – one of Anella's mother-in-law's, years old, but still of use. The open side of the doghouse faced the hedge away from the prevailing wind. The dogs spent much time here; it was their job to guard the chickens from the foxes and to stop the goats from escaping. The goats' aim in life was to eat their way through the hedge and find freedom and it was the dogs' aim in life to stop them, and on the whole, they did a good job.

Three nannies, three kids; it would be nice to have a few more, mused Anella. *Maybe I could save up some of the egg monies and buy another doe. Do I buy a nanny in kid or do I buy a Billy? Mmmm, a Billy would be hard to handle when the does came into season,* she thought and, *Oh, the smell!* She wrinkled her nose in distaste. No, it would be better to buy a pregnant doe and a wether. He would alert Anella to the nannies coming into must. Not much milk today, but with the boys here now, they could remove the kids at night so that Anella would have the best part of the milk in the mornings. They would have to create another set of pens. Again, she thought, so much to do, but that practical side of her came to her rescue, as it so often did. It will all get done, eventually.

Picking up the milk pail, it was back to the kitchen, to the dairy, to pour off some of the fresh milk into yesterday's, to make the butter. The whey she would strain off and give to the pigs. The remainder would be split: some milk for the house, some to make her cheese.

In the house, Anella rescued the cake from the oven, divided the dough to make loaves and put the kettle on for tea, and shortly after 10 o'clock, the boys were in. Anella showed them the water pump over the kitchen sink and they were splashing and washing, enjoying the sheer novelty of having running water inside the house. The huge old teapot was placed on the table, along with a jug of goat's milk, a bowl of sugar and the rescued seed cake. The twins couldn't believe that they could eat the cake and it wasn't even Sunday. When Anella saw the twins demolish the cake, she was secretly glad she had agreed with Mr Graves about the flour and grain arrangement. They guzzled mug after mug of sweet tea and were then ready to resume work. They had made great headway with the bothy even in such a short space of time, so while they were still busy, Anella was upstairs, sorting through boxes in the attics. The boys needed bed linen, blankets, pillows, curtains, pots and pans, cutlery and candle holders. She'd have to give them a few of her beeswax candles, she thought and they would need to stack up with logs. She sat back on her heels, thinking maybe it hadn't been a bad idea not to throw anything out. She grabbed a few towels and added them to the pile and then went downstairs, to get the bread out of the oven.

By the end of the day, the boys were proud to show Anella the results of their hard work. The beds were in and made up, there was a fire in the grate, a pair of gingham curtains at the newly cleaned windows. It was touching to see the boys so pleased over what they had achieved on their first day.

Seven o'clock found the three of them back in the kitchen for supper. Anella had made a pigeon pie and mashed a mound of potatoes with a generous knob of goat's butter. There was a bowl of foraged greens and a jug of gravy and the cob loaf that she had baked earlier. The twins fell on the food, not bothering too much with conversation; they obviously hadn't had a decent meal for a long time. She sat and watched them wolfing their food. *Yes*, she thought, *this will work. They're alright, these two; we'll work well together.*

"Boys, in the morning, we don't let the hens out 'til mid-day. I like them to lay first. Don't want them laying away. We collect the eggs, take them into the village. We have regular customers, I'll give you the list and how much you have to collect. A few customers take the goat's milk also. We have breakfast at eight, lunch at twelve and our main meal at six. We're late today," she said, looking at the clock. "The pigs: check the styes every day, the pens will need swilling down. Let them out to the lower meadow first, I'll show you. The goats: top field for them, next to the chickens. The dogs go too, that's their job; they keep the goats from escaping and protect the hens from predators. The woodland needs clearing; all wood needs to be stacked in one of the barns. They both need clearing, by the way, and the orchard needs doing. Once the orchard is done, we can put the pigs in there, they can eat the fallen fruit. Hedging and ditching is done earlier in the year, March time. Which one of you has the ferrets?" Clem raised his hand. "Good, there's plenty of meat out there, partridge, plover, pigeon, rook, hares, rabbits, deer – it's all there, all you have to do is catch it! At the right time of year naturally," she added. "Chicken, too, but I'll let you know which hen. Where are they now?" she asked, meaning the ferrets.

"I've roughed up a pen in barn," Clem nodded.

"Good. The more rabbits you catch, the better we eat and the better it is for the land. I'll show you the fields Mr Graves rents. If you wish to bathe, there's the river. It's shallowest by the ha-ha and it's private there. Up in High Field, there's the waterfall. It's lovely on a hot day. I used to take the washing there in the summer. It's not anything dramatic, you'll see it on your walk round, but it's lovely. Plenty of fish there, too. The most immediate job is clearing the barns, then clearing the woodland, then planting, then repairing the linhay... Oh, it goes on and on. Sorry, boys, you must be so tired. Do you have a clock? Can you tell the time? No? Well, that will have to be remedied, but the stable clock strikes the hour. I'll see you in the morning."

Off the twins went, exhausted by all the hard work and the good food they had eaten that day in quantities they were not used to. And so the day ended. Over time, a new routine was set for the boys and the days began to fall into a pattern. Change was happening, and tidiness and order began to prevail. The farm looked a little less neglected – they were repairing the linhay, after a fashion – and both barns had been cleared and tidied. It was Clem's habit now to go out ferreting most mornings, and what he bought back was cooked and eaten at the end of the day.

CHAPTER TWO

Clearing the woodland was the biggest job to be tackled and they needed a heavy horse, so Anella visited Mr Graves to see if he could help. Such an obliging man; yes, of course. One of his sons and a horse could come end of next week for a couple of days. Anella tutted, not being rude, but with impatience.

"Oh I'm sorry, Mr Graves, you must think me terribly rude. It's just I've got the bit between the teeth now and I just want to get on. At last, we're making headway. Things are looking so much better and clearing the woods will make such a difference."

"Go up and see the Major at Chilworth House. He has a man and heavy horse, does clearances for others. I'm sure he'll oblige you. If not, you'll have to bide your time. Let me know and we'll sort one of the lads out for you."

The following day, Anella walked up to Chilworth House to see Major Eade Jameson and it occurred to her that maybe she should have made an appointment. The house and drive were rather imposing. *Oh well, too late to worry about that now*, she thought. *The Major can say yes or no.* Heaven knows what he would think of this dowdy farmer's wife come begging favours. There was a grounds-man sweeping the gravel who stared at her keenly as she approached the front steps.

"Eh lass," he called, "if you've come for position, it's round back. Staff entrance, like." He nodded his head towards the double front doors. "These not for us. Come with me, I'll tek you."

"No, no, sorry, I've not come for a place, I've come to see the Major. Would you know if he is in?"

"No carriage called for, so master's in." He turned to resume work. "Sorry, Missus, thought you was applying for the job." He doffed his cap and Anella nodded.

Now she began to have doubts. What were her chances? *Ah well,* she bit her lip, *I can only ask.* She tugged at the bell pull and could hear it echoing through the house. She waited. It seemed a long time before the door was opened by a tall, imposing footman. He assessed Anella within a few seconds and said she had come to the wrong door; if she had come for the post, then she should go round the back.

Anella was beginning to lose patience. Did she look so down-at-heel that she could be mistaken for a servant?

"I've come to see the Major on business. I haven't made an appointment. My name is Mrs Anella Hebb of Haswell Farm." She looked at him directly, affecting a confident and superior manner, and she could see him falter under her gaze. He opened the door wider and made a small, sweeping gesture to invite her in. She followed him in, through a large empty hall to a comfortable, airy room, warm and inviting; a crackling fire, many small tables and a large, imposing desk, each wall covered from floor to ceiling, with books, books and more books. Anella gazed in wonderment: how wonderful. Beautiful, leather-bound books, probably never looked at, so perfect were they. She thought of her shelves of dog-eared books at home, much-loved, well-used, battered from constant use. She would rather have them, than these, she thought. Into this reverie came the Major, faultlessly but casually dressed. Anella noticed he was sporting a cream cravat. He was a tall man, dark-haired, of uncertain age, broad-shouldered, with an air of authority about him. Anella's heart sank; she'd met people like him before. They were usually arrogant, overbearing, so sure of their high position in life. She gave an inward sigh. *Never mind,* she said to herself, *it'll have to be Mr Graves.*

"Mrs Hebb. Good morning. We haven't met before, have we? You farm? Busy time of the year for you, I expect?" He gazed at her quizzically.

Anella was nervous. She took a deep breath. "Major Jameson, I farm Haswell Farm, just a few miles down." She indicated with her head. "I'm recently widowed. My husband was poorly last year, so virtually nothing was done on the farm. Now I find there is more heavy work than I can cope with. Mr Graves tells me I might be able to hire a man and horse from you. Is that possible?" It was difficult to assess how this request was going down. It didn't look too promising.

The Major walked across to his desk, sat down and rubbed his chin. There was a few minutes silence. Anella stood there. He suddenly looked up. "Mrs Hebb, sorry, pardon my rudeness. Please, take a seat." He nodded to the seat opposite and suddenly stood up, as if he was going to assist her to sit down.

'Grief, thought Anella. *Do I look that decrepit?*

"Mrs Hebb, I have Buchanen, he's the man for you. He can be a bit intimidating, he's short on social skills, but he's a good, hard worker. You mustn't be put off by him. Tell me when you need him to start and we can get something arranged. It's a brave undertaking of yours; a woman on her own in farming is a rarity."

Anella shrugged her shoulders. "I have little choice. The farm is now mine, I have to do something with it, I can't just let it go."

He nodded, "No, I agree. I'll tell you about Buchanen. A few years ago, he suffered a catastrophic head injury, lost his memory, changed him really. He has no memory of certain things; now and again, something will trigger in his brain and he will have total recall of certain events which can be upsetting for him. On the whole, he's a good man; quiet, hardworking. He's always better for working outside with his horse."

Now it was down to business and it was arranged that Mr Buchanen would come over later in the week to see what needed to be done with a view to starting the following Monday. Anella was enormously pleased and thanked the Major profusely. *Goodness,* she reined herself in, *don't be too effusive.* Neither of them had mentioned payment, but Anella had indicated she would pay upon completion. She would have to go to the bank and withdraw some of the little monies she had left. Mr Buchanen could stay overnight in the linhay if needed until the work was done and Anella secretly sighed with relief that the boys had done rudimentary repairs on it. When she got home, it would be back upstairs to the attics to sort out another bed and bedding and bits and pieces to make it comfortable.

"Well Mrs Hebb, let's hope Buchanen can sort things for you. He's a good man, he'll be no trouble."

Major Jameson stood up, so Anella stood also, realising their interview was over. They shook hands and said polite goodbyes. As Anella wandered down the drive, she realised she was no further forward than if she had agreed to Mr Graves. Sometimes she was just too impatient. Major Jameson watched her departure from the library window and shook his head. A woman farming – whatever next? He gave a wry smile. It might be interesting to get the factor in to assess the widows farm and property. She wouldn't last long and when it went up for sale, he could be first in with an offer, that's if it could be a useful add-on to his estate. Food for thought. he rubbed his chin. In the meantime, Buchanen would do his best for her.

CHAPTER THREE

The following week passed quickly enough. Anella took the twins out on the egg round to meet her customers, most of whom they knew vaguely anyway. It didn't take the boys long to cobble together a handcart which made transporting and delivering the eggs and milk a lot easier. The linhay was finished, and the boys helped get a bed in there and a few bits of old furniture and a couple of old candle sticks and, again, some of Anella's precious beeswax candles.

On Monday, making the bread and having got a cake in the oven, there came a knock on the kitchen window and Anella realised it was Mr Buchanen. She opened the door and there he was, filling the doorway, tall, broad-shouldered, shabbily dressed, unruly dark hair tied back in a queue, a length of string tied around his left wrist. Unshaven. Unwashed too, probably, thought Anella. She wasn't sure he would do, but then, she mustn't offend the Major. After all, she did ask for him, didn't she?

He respectfully touched his forehead. "Buchanen, Ma'am, here for your clearance. The Major sent me."

"Mr Buchanen. No horse?"

"Back of stables, Ma'am."

"Right. I'll find one of the boys for you. Come and see the linhay, you'll be staying there. I just want the copse cleared and all the wood stored in the barn. We can log it later. And the orchard, that needs clearing. It's in such a state; can't let the pigs in there until it's done."

She showed him the linhay and barn and then, she followed him round the back. There was his enormous shire horse, the size of a house. It was standing patiently enough, but as Anella approached, it gave a warning stamp. Anella decided to go no nearer. Just then, Clem appeared. He'd been expecting Mr Buchanen. They were introduced and Anella returned to the kitchen again, to rescue a slightly charred fruit cake and get the bread in. She was kept busy making a rabbit stew with dumplings for dinner and, in honour of Mr Buchanen, she made an apple and blackberry crumble with bottled fruits from last autumn. Clem's ferrets were earning their keep and keeping the rabbit population down nicely. She heard the stable clock chime and knew the men would be in shortly for tea, so she filled the enormous kettle and got it on and put mugs, milk and sugar on the table along with the still-warm fruit cake, plates and a great bread knife. Within minutes, they were in, splashing noisily at the sink and making a mess and lots of chat between the twins. Mr Buchanen didn't have much to say, but he drank his tea and, as with the boys, munched his way through a goodly portion of the cake. Things were going well, they said and in a short space of time, they were back outside to resume work, leaving Anella to get on with her woman's work in the house.

Later in the afternoon, Anella took a quick inspection of the barn and was amazed at the quantity of wood that had already been bought back up. It was a very satisfying sight. The twins were seeing to the animals and Anella found Mr Buchanen sweeping the end stall; he was doing this for the shire. For some reason, this annoyed Anella. She should have had this done already by one of the boys, but it had been overlooked. But still, permission should have been sought. She was cross that she felt annoyed, cross that she felt guilt. She knew she wasn't being reasonable, but she just couldn't help it.

And so the week passed; the boys and Mr Buchanen

seemingly getting along well. He was still morose, of few words and brooding, but that was his nature. Clem and Clance spoke of him with respect and they were awed by the regard in which he held his horse. Its well-being and comfort came before his; its food and water came before his. Every evening there was grooming, every evening checking of hooves; and only when all of this was completed did Buchanen deign to come into the kitchen for supper.

There was no doubt that supper time was becoming the best part of the day. Work done, hands washed, the men sat down at the table, looking forward to a meal they had provided for themselves. Whatever meat they ate, nine times out of ten, the boys had caught it, stripped it, gutted it, but it was Anella who did the most important job of all. She turned it into the best meal, stew or pie with fresh bread and potatoes and foraged greens. There was always cider or mead, and Anella could always make a bread pudding or an egg custard. If a goat's cheese was ready, that was bought out too, along with a couple of store apples. After a meal such as this, even Buchanen would join in the conversation. There was always much discussion between the twins as to what they were going to do long-term and what needed doing the following day. The kitchen was cosy, the stove fire glowing gently in the alcove, the kettle puffing away on the hob. The men liked it because they were replete with good food, comfortable in the warmth of the room. Anella like it because the kitchen came to life; there was noise, chatter, clutter and mess to clear. Neft would have been astonished and probably quite angry at the sitting around at the table after the meal was done, it was not something he ever did. Anella sent up a silent apology. "Sorry, Neft, this is the way it is now."

The following Monday, Buchanen went back to Chilworth House and Anella felt obliged to visit the Major.

There was no disparaging footman this time; she was cordially invited into the library and only had to wait a few minutes before the Major appeared.

"Mrs Hebb, good morning. Nice to see you. How did you get on with Buchanen? He's a good man, isn't he? He tells me you keep goats? You must let me know if you need him in the future, there's plenty of farms hereabouts that need him, so he's always busy." He looked at her inquiringly.

"Major, I can only thank you. He was invaluable. He's a man of few words but he got on well with my boys. I think they learnt quite a lot from him last week and they got a lot of work done. By the end of the week, they were good friends. I would like to have Mr Buchanen again some time."

"Your boys? And how old are they?"

"Sixteen, growing and eating, but full of ideas for the farm."

Good grief, thought the Major, *at what age did this young woman start breeding?* She looked far too young. Still, the working classes, bred like animals, didn't they.

Realising there was some misunderstanding here, Anella was quick to point out that although she referred to them as her boys, they weren't, in actual fact, hers. "No, no. They're Mrs Bosworth's two. I needed help, she was only too glad to get them off her hands; boys that age usually have huge appetites."

Yes, and not only for food, thought the Major.

"I thought you looked rather young, if you'll pardon me. Now, Mrs Hebb…"

Anella jumped in, "Yes, about payment."

The Major put a hand up, "Mrs Hebb, don't let's talk about payment yet, at least not until the end of the month, because there's something else I want to talk to you about. The village school is under my domain. The children who attend are my workers' children. No one has to pay. It is my school on my land. I want my next generation of workers to be educated. I want them fit and healthy. For that reason, I want the children to have a cup of milk every day, maybe cold in the summer, hot in the winter. Now Buchanen tells me you keep goats and I wondered if you could supply the school. There's normally about fifteen children, Miss Sorrell, the mistress and Miss Garton, her assistant, but if you could provide for twenty, then that would be ample. What say you?" he inquired. "Would it be manageable? I thought we could come to some arrangement – my bill for Buchanen with your bill for the milk. What do you think?" He saw Anella's hesitation. "Don't give me an answer now, think about it. I can send up drinking vessels for the children, all you do is supply the milk, Monday to Friday. I'd like to think we could still supply the milk even when the school is closed for harvest and Christmas, but I haven't got that far yet."

Anella was thoughtful for a minute. This was rather sudden, but what an opportunity. Could she supply milk for that many? Never say no, she said to herself. "Well, I'm sure something could be arranged, Major; this is a bit of a surprise, but we can come to some sort of agreement, I'm sure." She was thinking; no more *laissez-faire* attitude over whether the kids stayed with their respective mothers. That would have to stop. "When would you want this to start?"

"Maybe in a couple of weeks?" he looked at her inquiringly. "It would have to be delivered regardless of the weather, every day. You would be alright with that?"

"Yes, surely. We can manage that."

"Come and see me on Friday, Mrs Hebb, and we'll finalise things. This is good, everybody benefits."

He smiled. Anella smiled back at him warily; she was

beginning to like this man, and not only because he had offered her a business opportunity.

"If you have a few minutes, we'll go and see cook now and get her to sort the mugs for the children."

He opened the library door and made a sweeping gesture with his hand. She followed him down to the bowels of the house to the cook Mrs Harvey's territory. There was much bustle and heat here and noise and clattering of pans, which all came to a sudden halt when the staff noticed the Major. He held his hands up by way of apology.

"Sorry to interrupt, I know you're busy and I shouldn't be here, but this is Mrs Hebb, she's going to supply the school with milk and needs mugs. Sort it out, can you? And get one of the stable boys to take them over."

He smiled at them all and said he would see Mrs Hebb back in the library and with that, he left and Anella stood there feeling rather like a spare part.

"I'm sorry, I didn't realise..."

"Don't you fret, lass, that's typical of the Major. I'll get Daisy. Daisy!" Mrs Harvey called, and from another room, diminutive Daisy appeared in an overlong apron with her sleeves rolled up and looking hot and flustered, flour on her apron and hands. "Daisy, take Mrs Hebb to the store, she needs mugs for the children at the school."

"The major said one of the stable lads would take them up for me. We won't need them until next week. Is that alright? I'm sorry to be a nuisance, I didn't realise the Major would be in such a hurry."

"That's typical of him," declared Mrs Harvey. "We'll sort it. Go with Daisy now and make your choice, and I'll get them sent. Good day to you, Mrs Hebb."

An hour later Anella was back in the library. The Major had had tea sent up and he was pouring a cup as she came in.

"Ah, Mrs Hebb. Tea?"

"Yes, please. I'm parched."

She thanked him as he handed her a cup. This was rather unusual, wasn't it? She sat there, thinking, how strange was this? Did the Major often take tea in the library? She felt rather flattered. They both started speaking at the same time and the Major stopped and bowed to indicate Anella speak first.

"I was just going to say thank you. For giving me this opportunity." She replaced her cup and stood up. "Shall I come up on Friday?"

"Of course. Yes. Maybe you'd like to have a look around the farm or the estate? Or even the school? Meet the children and Miss Sorrell. The parson will be there, I expect. I'll take you. What do you think?"

"Do you know, I would like that very much. What time, roughly?"

"Tennish? I'll have the gig ready. I'll see you Friday." And he reached out to shake her hand.

"Good day, Major."

"Ma'am."

He saw her to the door personally and then watched her as she walked down the drive. He bit his lip. She was a genuinely nice woman; he liked her but wasn't sure as to why he actually liked her. This business with the school milk – well, it was just an excuse, really. He was thoughtful. *Let's just see where it leads*, he said to himself. She had stopped halfway down the drive to talk to Buchanen and still the Major stood and watched. He sighed. Too much time on his hands, he thought. But this woman was a bit of a free thinker, like him; but he had the authority, she didn't. He could do anything, she couldn't. She was only a woman, widowed and in farming. *Mustn't encourage her too much*, was his final thought.

Arriving back at the farm, Anella was surprised to see a nanny goat tethered in front of the bothy. Clance appeared from the barn.

"What's this?" inquired Anella.

"Ma'am, you know where Granny Oates lives?"

"No."

"By the beck. Coming back from the eggs, there she is."

"Granny Oates?"

"Nay. T'nanny. Just there she was, not tethered, just there." He shrugged his shoulders. "So us called Granny Oates like, called and called. Knocked on the door like, no one, so I peeked in, som'at not right, I could tell, so I popped into Mother's on the way back and told her. She was gonna go up and take a look, but goat, well I couldn't just leave her there, so's us bought her back. Don't want her escaping, I think she's in kid. Just making her a pen in the barn, keep her safe like 'til we know what to do."

Anella helped Clance with the bedding and went to get some twigs and browsing matter, which she lobbed over the barrier. Clance had got water. He wiped his hands on his trousers. "She's a good 'un, Missis."

"Clance, keep quiet about her, tell no one. If anyone asks about her, well, all well and good, but if no one asks, we'll say nothing."

"Right-oh." He tapped the side of his nose in a gesture of secrecy. "Granny Oates had nobody, so we'll care for her goat."

"Yes," replied Anella, "we'll look after her goat."

CHAPTER FOUR

The days were falling into a regular pattern, so with the twins off on farm jobs, Anella decided to tackle the eating room. It was never used and was full of dusty, unused, unloved "stuff" that had to go. The sideboard was full of moth-eaten napery, serving dishes, discoloured cutlery, pewter candlesticks and old china. It was daunting, but once started, it felt good to clear it all out. Dusty wineglasses and decanters and a tantalus were taken into the kitchen for washing and old sepia pictures taken down. They had to go. Then she was brushing down the curtains, sweeping the floor; she even cleaned the windows, abandoning the job in hand to rescue the apple cake from the oven – she was becoming a past master at retrieving cakes just in the nick of time. She placed it on the kitchen table along with the cottage loaf she'd made earlier. The boys would be in soon, so the fresh goat's butter came out with the sugar and jug of milk. She was hot and sweaty now, so decided to put the kettle on and make her way up to High Field and pick some wildflowers for the newly cleaned eating room.

Coming back with armfuls of rosebay willow herb and cow parsley, she waved to Mrs Bosworth trudging up the farm track.

"Morning" she called. "Have you come to see the twins?"

"No, Ma'am, not really. 'Tis you. Just to let you know, Granny Oates. You know, she was a couple of days gone when the boys found her?"

"Oh no." Anella wrinkled her nose in distaste. "I'm so sorry. Not nice for the twins."

Mrs Bosworth nodded, "Well, the funeral is on Friday, tennish. Won't be up to much. There won't be a wake – no family, see? Someone will take over her hovel, handy there by the beck." She rubbed her nose with a grubby handkerchief.

"Do you want me to tell the boys?"

"Oh no, lass, they won't want to go. I just thought I'd let you know."

"Well, I feel I ought to pay my respects; I have her goat in my barn. It's the least I can do. Mrs Bosworth, come up to the house, have a cup of tea, the boys will be in. I'm having a bit of a clear out, so you'll have to ignore the mess. Come."

Mrs Bosworth was intrigued and honoured. She'd love to see inside the farmhouse, so she accepted, with alacrity and followed Anella into the warm kitchen. It was cosy: the kettle puffing away merrily on the stove and the boys in, as usual making a wet mess at the sink and over the floor; they were chattering away busily, only stopping in surprise at seeing their mother there. Anella made tea and cut the still warm cake and then, on impulse, asked Mrs Bosworth to see the dining room.

"I'm having a big clear out, as you can see. Heavens, I don't know what I'm going to do with all this stuff. It has to go. You wouldn't know anyone who could get rid of it for me, would you?"

"Well, I could take it for you. Get it out of your way. I could sell it for you, I'm sure someone would like it. If you're alright with that, we'll get the boys to bring it down to me?" It was a question delicately put by Mrs Bosworth; she had seen a few items that appealed to her and she might be able to make a bit of money. Of course, she didn't actually have a dining room herself, but…

While they were sorting through the clutter and deep in conversation, Clem came in. He stood and watched silently for a few minutes and then coughed politely.

"What, Clem?" Anella asked.

"Erm…" He indicated with his head. "There's a gentleman in the kitchen. A Major somebody."

"What? No, surely not."

Anella was shocked. She was at a loss. What was he doing, here in her shabby old kitchen? She clutched the neck of her dress.

"Mrs Bosworth, whatever are we going to do?" She was seriously nonplussed.

"Ay lass, 'tis only the Major, no worry. He's probably come to check your buildings. The estate do mine every so often."

"Oh no, I know he hasn't come for that. Go back, Clem, offer him a cup of tea – oh, and a slice of cake. I'll be in."

She glanced in a mirror and patted her hair.

"Oh dear, what am I going to do? Why is he here?" She stepped warily into her kitchen, Mrs Bosworth following.

"Major." She put on a false smile. "I'm sorry, you're catching us at a disadvantage."

He looked totally out of place, immaculate in jodhpurs and riding boots, his usual cream cravat and crop in hand. He didn't look half as discomforted as Anella.

"Mrs Hebb, sorry to arrive on spec, but I thought I should tell you. Friday, ten o'clock, the parson's doing a funeral, so our school visit will have to be delayed."

"Oh yes," piped up Mrs Bosworth, "that's Granny Oates. It shouldn't take long though, she's got no folks."

Anella looked at Mrs Bosworth in surprise; she wasn't intimidated by the Major's presence.

"Well," Anella was at a complete loss, "I was just going to pay my respects."

"Mrs Hebb, shall we just make it later in the day? After lunch, say, about two-ish?"

Anella nodded; the Major could see she was acutely

uncomfortable but was unaware that it was he that was the cause. "I must go. Mrs Bosworth, will you come? I think I need a word." He smiled a farewell at Nell and the boys and escorted Mrs Bosworth out.

Anella followed the boys outside a few minutes later, and was taken aback to see Mrs Bosworth just off down the drive. The Major came over to her.

"Mrs Hebb, just wondered if I could take a look at your goat empire? Have to make sure you can supply."

Anella bristled with indignation "Pardon? Do you not think I'm good for my word? I have four goats, capable of producing eight, ten, sixteen pints of milk a day. I think that's more than enough for the school's needs. If you doubt my word, Major, I see no point in continuing this arrangement."

She was cross, and the Major knew he had annoyed her. He held his hands up in supplication

"Mrs Hebb, sorry. I have this ability to act first, think later. Mr Buchanen told me about your goats." He shrugged his shoulders. "I thought I'd come out for a ride and let you know about the funeral. I'm sorry. Tell me what you've got here."

As a distraction, it worked; and Anella was off, showing him around the farm. Pointedly, the goats were first on the agenda They looked extraordinary fat and sleek, and in fact, Anella felt pleased and proud showing the Major round. He kept his distance with the bees; he didn't quite trust Anella when she said it was safe to go near. He took her word for it, but he was impressed.

"I'll bring you up some honey later in the year; you'll like it, wildflower honey." She smiled.

Major Jameson was quite taken aback. Mrs Anella Hebb was a very attractive lady, and she was completely unaware of it. Now it was him that was discomforted; he was embarrassed and not sure why he suddenly felt ill-at-ease.

Anella was proudly pleased. Everywhere she showed the Major was clean, swept and tidy; the boys, on a daily basis, were doing a good job.

"Well," the Major shook his head. "Don't you feel you're doing well, Mrs Hebb? It can't be easy, on your own."

He chewed on his lip. He had completely under-estimated this lady and felt rather guilty, thinking of that first time she came to ask for his help. Immediately, he assumed she would fail and he could snap up her failing farm for a low price. He wasn't comfortable with these thoughts.

"Well," he said again, and stuffed his hands in his pockets. "I must be on my way. Will you walk back up with me?"

Anella nodded, her equilibrium recovered. They returned to where the Major's horse was still tethered.

"Shall I call for you Friday then? Two-ish? he inquired as he mounted his horse.

"Yes please, Major, I shall look forward to it." She gave him a shy-ish smile. She wouldn't admit to herself – something was about to brew, she knew it.

He doffed his hat.

"Good morning," and he gave her such a smile, Anella's heart skipped a beat.

CHAPTER FIVE

Come Friday, Granny Oates' funeral was predictably a very poor affair. Only a handful of people were in attendance. It had a profound effect on Anella. The vicar, a thin, bespectacled man, just wanted the service over. There was no money to pay for anything; these paupers were a nuisance. What a shame, thought Anella; no one to grieve for her, no one to care, no one of her line left, gone for good. It made her think of Neft. The last of his line and of herself, the last of her line. Barren. It must be quite common, she thought, and it made her very, very sad.

She walked home in a sombre frame of mind and had a good cry when she got home. She made a quick lunch for the boys, then went upstairs to change into something less severe to go to the school. Major Jameson was prompt, picking her up at two and immediately noticed Anella's forlorn frame of mind. He didn't know why she was so serious, but tried, unsuccessfully, to cheer her up.

"Mrs Hebb, are you not in the mood to visit the school today? We can always put it off."

"Oh Major, I'm sorry, I'm so sorry. I've been to Granny Oates' funeral. I didn't know her, but there was no one there for her. That's why I'm sad. It's upset me muchly and I don't really know why it should bother me. After all, we all die alone. Oh, just listen to me. I'm just maudlin, I suppose." She wiped away an errant tear. "Oh dear, I'm sure I'll cheer up when I see the children." She sighed and felt guilty that she had subjected the Major to her sentimental wanderings.

She looked at him and gave him a brave smile. His heart flipped.

"Mrs Hebb, not to worry. You're about to meet the future generation, and if they don't fill you with hope AND dread, nothing will. Brace yourself, those children give no quarter."

He turned to smile encouragingly at her. Oh dear, the Major's considerate smile had a funny effect on her and her spirits lifted. She was looking forward to meeting them all and Miss Sorrell.

And what an afternoon. Besieged by children. They were definitely children to be seen and heard. They were excited and chatty and not in awe of the Major. They knew him; he was a regular visitor. Under Miss Sorrell's guidance, they had such a lot to show them. Their schoolwork, drawings, their nature table, such noise and pride in their achievements. It was a busy, interesting and tiring afternoon, and the Major suggested they go back to Chilworth House for tea before he took her home.

They went straight to the library and the Major was immediately collared for business by the factor. He apologised to Anella and promised to be back in a few minutes. As she was on her own, Anella browsed the bookshelves. All beautiful, tooled leather, probably never read, never even opened; but one little book caught her eye. Not pretentious like the rest. She excitedly pulled the slim volume from the shelf. She couldn't believe her eyes *The Feminine Monarchie* or *The History of Bees*. One of the first books on beekeeping, printed in 1623. How wonderful. She was completely captivated and could hardly drag her attention away when the Major re-entered the room.

Before he could speak, she said, "Major, did you know you had this book?" She held it up for him to see. "Doctor Butler. Probably the first beekeeper to record his findings.

He says, 'Be no stranger to your bees. You must be chaste, cleanly, sweet and sober, quiet and familiar and they will love thee and know thee from all others' – just like a marriage, don't you think? I envy you this book, Major. I know of the doctor, but I've never seen his work before." She clutched the book to her chest as if reluctant to let it go. A silence. "Sorry, got quite carried away. I was just looking at your books while I was waiting."

The Major gave a low chuckle and shrugged his shoulders "Actually, no, I didn't know. I'm not an apiarist. Not many of these books ever get read. No time."

He was interrupted by a maid, bringing in a tea tray. She was thanked and she bobbed a curtsy and left. The major eyed the tea. "Well, Mrs Hebb, how about a cup of tea?"

"I would love one. Would you like me to pour?" She stood up.

"Yes, you pour and you can take that little book for your efforts."

Anella, apart from being pleased, was horrified. "Oh, no, I couldn't possibly. I'm sorry, I really shouldn't have just helped myself to your books, so rude of me." She shook her head as if to say she didn't know why she did such a thing.

"Mrs Hebb, pour the tea, please, I'm so dry. Those children could talk the hind leg off a donkey."

She obliged and they sat in companionable silence for a few minutes, the Major stretching his long legs and resting his head on the back of the chair. This amused Anella. It suggested a comfortableness in her company, and she wished she could be the same. She finished her tea and stood up.

"Well, Major, I think I must be off. Work to do."

He sprang up. "Well, if you must go, I must take you." He rang the bell and within minutes, a footman appeared. "Have the gig bought round, will you, Thompson?"

"Major, I can walk home, it's quite alright. The fresh air will do me good."

"No, no, it's my pleasure." The thought of letting her go unaccompanied was unthinkable. "And please, take the bee book." He saw her face. "Borrow it, then. You can always return it. I think we have a few books about beekeeping."

She gave in and nodded her head in thanks.

It was a very pleasant sensation having the Major help her up into the gig. Anella noticed he waved the footman away. The journey home she was dreading. What could she talk about? What could she say that would be of interest? Better be the school and the children and the milk, but suddenly they were waved down by Mr Buchanen.

"Mantel? What's to do?"

"Mrs Hebb." He touched his forehead respectfully.

"Eade, something's happened. I've remembered my name, my whole name. Mantel Buchanen O'Kyan. A little bit of memory has come back."

"How? Why? When did this happen? Anything else?"

"Yes. I'm descended from Anselan O'Kyan. Irish. Chieftain. That's it, but it's all good. At last I know who I am."

Eade reached down and shook his hand. "Not long now, Buchanen, not long now. We'll get you back where you belong. We must talk later. Just taking Mrs Hebb home."

The major put his hand up in salute and Mr Buchanen watched them disappear down the drive.

Anella turned to the Major. "He's a brave man, isn't he? How dreadful not to know who you are. Why, he might be someone of importance in Scotland."

"He is, we know. He's got an estate up there somewhere."

"Oh dear." Anella felt embarrassed. "I treated him rather like a servant when he came to me. I wasn't aware."

"Don't worry, Buchanen is a gentleman. You know, since his accident, I believe he's just glad to be alive. In his way, he's quite content. He wouldn't work for you if you had upset him."

"Well that's a relief, but it's a reminder that 'man looketh on the outward appearance'. I must not be so judgemental in future." Eade looked at her shrewdly and Anella caught his glance. "I'm sorry."

He laughed and patted her hand. "Your humility does you credit."

They discussed the school milk on the way home and the costings, and it was agreed delivery would start the following week and continue until the school broke for the harvest. Arriving in the courtyard, Clem was there. He ran over.

"Mrs Hebb. Granny Oates' nanny."

"No!" Anella was inordinately excited. "Oh Major, you must come and have a look. This is a new addition to our herd. Is she alright, Clance?"

"Clem. Yes, she's fine; lovely kid, very pretty. Keep your distance, tho', Mum's pretty feisty."

They walked into the barn.

"Oh!" Anella was in transports of delight. "Oh Clem, she's just lovely. I'm so pleased." She turned to the Major. "There's a few more pints there every day, Major."

He nodded his head by way of an apology and wisely said nothing. He was quite content to stay leaning on the barrier and watching the interaction between Clem and Anella. There was no apparent hierarchy between them, just an easy friendliness and it seemed to work well. Eade would have to remember this.

They turned to go, and Anella said, "Major, I would invite you in, but I can imagine the state of my kitchen, the boys having had the run of it today and me not being there."

He laughed and touched his forehead. "I'll be off, save you any embarrassment," and they walked back to the gig.

"Shall you be up next Friday? We can finalise the milk contract and then we're clear."

She nodded. "I certainly will. Thank you, Major, for your help." A moment of seriousness suddenly.

"My pleasure Mrs Hebb; after all, everybody benefits. I look forward to seeing you next week. Good day."

And he was off at a spanking pace, Anella standing on the drive, watching him go, the gig and horse smartly turned out. It was a lovely afternoon, that time of day when the birds stop singing and all is quietness, except for the rustling of the trees. Anella stood and let the days pleasantness wash over her, the slow realisation that, actually, she was happy. No money, but no money worries either and the future, with the boys working the farm, was full of hope – and the Major? Who knew? He was an intriguing man.

CHAPTER SIX

A copy of the contract arrived on Monday, signed by Mr Graves, which was good. It meant he would start paying rent at the beginning of the month.

Anella gave the kitchen a good bottoming that week; the table and the draining board scrubbed until they were white. The rugs were lifted and beaten, the floor swept and washed, items of clutter removed and boxed up for Mrs Bosworth. She might be interested, you never knew, and Anella walked out to pick a bunch of wildflowers. Arranged in a jug and placed on the newly cleaned table, she stood back and looked with satisfaction at her homely warm kitchen. As usual, there was bread in the oven and a honey cake made with a few spoonfuls of last season's honey. A pigeon pie was waiting to be baked, along with an apple crumble made with fruit from the apple store; past their best, but still edible. She knew that whatever she cooked, the boys would fall on it like starving animals. They appreciated everything she baked. She sighed with satisfaction; it gave her a nice feeling.

The new doe was turning out to be a prodigious milker – what a stroke of good fortune and what an asset she would turn out to be; and so the week progressed. On Friday, it was a warm, cloudy day, perfect for walking to Chilworth House. Anella had paid a little more attention to her outfit than usual, wearing one of her better dresses, a deep plum in colour with a pie crust frill and a neat little black bolero jacket with a silver broach on the right-hand revers. Neft had given her this broach on their first anniversary, when he still loved her and believed there would be a baby sometime.

Well, there was no baby and the broach had spent many a year in a box in a drawer and, Anella decided, it either had to be worn or sold. There was no one to leave it to. It was pretty and as it was a lovely day; it was right that it should be worn. As was the way with Anella, as she walked, she turned over in her mind the numerous jobs still to be done. The year was progressing, and a cockerel would have to be purchased later on to increase their stock. Once he'd done his job, he'd be for the pot. The early pears were ready and perfect and she would have to dip each stalk in wax to keep them fresh before laying them down in the apple store. The boys would take sixteen weaners to the market the following week; two to be kept back for themselves. That would be a tremendously busy time for Anella. Maybe Mrs Bosworth would come and help.

She was returning the bee book today; there was never any shortage of conversation once Anella started on her bees.

The Major was waiting for her in the library when she arrived, casually but immaculately dressed, a loose-fitting tweed jacket and cream cravat – always he wore a cravat.

"Mrs Hebb, good morning. Nice day for walking?" He indicated a chair for her to sit, but before doing so, she held up the book *The Feminine Monarchic*.

"I've bought your book back, Major. It's a very interesting little journal. Thank you."

He shrugged his shoulders, as if to say it's of no consequence, and they got down to the final details of the milk agreement. The tea tray arrived, as was usual now, and talk turned to mundane matters, except when Anella inquired after Mr Buchanen.

"We were at Bussaco together. My horse was shot from

under me. Physically, we were in a very poor state, they were expecting us to die. There were a few of us, dysentery was rife, the sickness fever was everywhere. We were transferred to an English vessel and, actually, Mr Buchanen improved. He didn't die, and neither did I. Once we got here, Chilworth, I realised the estate was very run down. Buchanen was making plans to go back home to Scotland, before eventually returning to Portugal, but fate intervened. Ironically, he came though military action unscathed bodily but the sustained a catastrophic head injury here, on my estate. He had the unofficial post as woodward, but unfortunately, he was hit by a falling tree."

The Major turned abruptly to look out of the library window. The shame of what happened never left him. It was an accident, no one was to blame, but Eade, the Major, bore the burden of guilt on his shoulders.

"Mr Buchanen suffered complete memory loss and considerable damage all over. He was in a bad way. He had a terrible head injury, but when he eventually came round, he couldn't speak. Gradually, things improved; but his mind, well, it was very strange. Here's a man who can remember how to tie his bootlaces, how to use a knife and fork, how to write… We had to tie a bit of string around his left wrist so he could recall with which hand he wrote. We kept putting the quill in his right hand and he couldn't do anything. His left hand, well, of course, it turns out he could write with that. The string is just an aide-mémoire really, but he won't take it off. He'll come good over time and, eventually, he'll go home to Scotland. When he's ready. It's up to him, really. There's always this stillness in him. One day, all his memory will come back, I'm sure but every day, little things jog him. Sometimes it doesn't make sense. He's living at the dower house, it's been empty for years. I have a lady who does for him and cooks; he's alright there. He's free to come and go and work elsewhere whenever he wants. He's always better for working outside with the horses. He's a good man, Mrs Hebb."

"Yes, I'm beginning to realise that now. When he told us his full name, Mantel Buchanen O'Kyan, son of an Irish chief, I felt I should curtsy. I must never be so judgemental. When he came to me, the boys worked well with him, they respect the way in which he treats his horse. He seems to be a very lonely man, Major. I must let him know, he can always come to the farm whenever he wants to. I hope one day he will be a contented man, his memory fully restored."

The Major stood up. "Mrs Hebb, one moment. I've sorted out a couple of books for you. I thought you might be interested; they haven't been looked at for years."

He picked up two little books from a library table and handed them over to Anella. *Handling Bee Swarms* by Anton Janscha and Doctor Edward Bevans' *The Honey Bee*.

"Oh." She closed her eyes momentarily as if receiving an especial benediction. "Major, I can't thank you enough. How wonderful; you have these books and you didn't even know."

He inclined his head by way of an apology. "Mrs Hebb, later on in the year, we have the Harvest Festival. You must come. I'm sure the children would like to see you. After the service, we have a harvest supper for everybody, villagers and children. We distribute all the food. We always have an enjoyable day. It will be a good harvest this year. You'll enjoy it."

"Can we all come? The boys, I mean?"

"Of course. Everyone comes to the harvest festival. It's a celebration."

"Major, we must come then, I would love it. Now, I have to go." She picked up the bee books. "Don't worry, I can see myself out." She gave him a lovely smile.

"Mrs Hebb, I can take you home in the gig." He didn't want their conversation to end.

She waved her hand in dismissal. "No, no, I want to walk. It's a beautiful day. Thank you so much." She held out her hand. "I'll see you next week?"

He shook her hand and escorted her to the main door. She left, and the Major went back to the library and watched from the window. He always watched her leave. She was clutching the two books to her chest. What was it about this woman? In status, she was below him, but he admired her. It irritated him that he was attracted to her. She spoke to him as an equal. As he felt compassion for Buchanen, so he felt benevolence and something more towards Mrs Hebb. He bit his lip. He'd invited her to the festival. He looked forward to her visits. Something would have to be done.

The milk deliveries began and were received with much pleasure by the children and the school mistresses; and every week, Anella visited the Major in the library. Ideas were batted back and forth between them; maybe the school could keep chickens, perhaps the children could grow vegetables, ought'en there to be a school library? Could there be a trip to the big house so the children could see what job opportunities would be available to them – not just household staff, but carpenters, smithies, gardeners, even better jobs for the girls? These meetings were enjoyed by them both and sometimes, weather permitting, they would take a stroll around the estate and the Major would tell her of his plans and ideas for the future; sometimes Mantel would join them. He was as full of ideas as the Major, and sometimes there would be friendly banter back and forth. On one particularly enjoyable day, the Major invited her to stay for supper. She would have loved to, but felt she had to refuse, knowing the twins would be expecting her return and a meal on the table.

"Well tomorrow, then," he insisted. "Buchanen and I are a dull old pair, it would be nice to have a bit of company."

Mantel nodded in agreement. "Mrs Hebb, it would take the pressure off me, if you would. He's incredibly boring sometimes." He winked at her.

She considered. "What time, then? No, sorry, I can't. How will I get back?"

"Mrs Hebb, I will take you home, of course I will. It will be my pleasure. I'm sorry you had to even think about it." The Major took her hand. "We'll see you tomorrow." He gave a little bow, took her hand and kissed it! Oh! Anella was astonished.

"I'll send Thompson in the gig to pick you up, about seven-ish. Will that suit?"

Yes, she agreed, that would suit nicely.

Consequently, the following day was busy. Bread had to be made, a currant cake baked, butter churned and goat's cheese made. She did a jugged hare and prepared wild vege-tables and mashed a great heap of potatoes and made an egg custard. As there was such a glut of eggs, she pickled easily a dozen, and come morning break, she sat with the boys in the kitchen, satisfied with a good morning's work. They were incredulous that she was to dine at Chilworth House and were delighted that they were invited to the harvest celebrations, not being church attenders.

That afternoon, she went upstairs to rest and then sort out a gown to wear. She went as far as to wash her hair. She sorted out a trim little dress of royal blue, scoop-necked, puff shoulders and long-sleeved. A nipped-in waist and full skirt. Pretty. She looked at her reflection in the mirror and liked it. She wore a loop of opera pearls – her mother's – and little pearl earrings to match. She pinned the little silver broach on the left of her shoulder and then tackled her hair. What a mess, she thought. Try as she might, she was unable to pin it up tidily and it kept escaping in tiny, curly tendrils. Eventually, she gave up. Nothing would tame it, so she let it be, but put in her purse, her comb and a few clips so that, if need be, she could tidy it up once she arrived. Dabs of her own rose perfume on her wrists and throat, and she was ready and waiting in the kitchen, with the boys at the table eating jugged hare and mopping the gravy with great chunks of bread and promising her they would leave the candles alight and the fire in for when she came home, and did she want them to stay up for her? Of course, she said no, but she was touched by the twins' concern for her. A few moments later, the gig arrived and both boys escorted her out and Clem actually assisted her up into the carriage. They stood there and watched her go and Anella felt a glow of happiness. *Those boys*, she thought.

She had a lovely evening at the House with the Major and Mr Buchanen. It wasn't as formal as Anella was expecting. There were only the three of them, and the conversation was easy and relaxed and the food was wonderful. Anella thought herself to be a good cook, but this food was on a different level. The Major was captivated, she was lovely. Soft brown hair, falling thickly from its pin, no artifice, just so natural. It was a lovely evening and, all too soon, it was time to take Mrs Hebb home, so he rang for the gig and blankets in case it was chill. She said formal good nights to Mr Buchanen and took her leave. Not surprisingly, Mr Mantel Buchanen O'Kyan watched this intriguing lady disappear down the drive with Eade and knew where tonight's events would lead. It was not for him. He shook his shoulders and a sadness overtook him. Mrs Hebb was not for him, then, but there was someone out there for him, of that he was sure.

Driving home, it was a clear cloudless night with a gibbous moon. Anella could hear an owl hooting and a vixen screeching somewhere in the surrounding fields. Turning into her drive, she asked the Major to stop. She tapped his arm and pointed up.

"Please, stop. Look." She leaned back to view better the night sky. "Look, see there, that's the Milky Way. Isn't it amazing?" She couldn't see the Major's face, but she hoped he was impressed as she was. He was silent, just looking. "I know a few of the planets, do you?"

The Major looked at her. "Anella, I've never really looked up before. I just thought they were all stars. I've slept under the stars quite a few times."

"No, there's planets, stars, orbiting satellites, moons." She suddenly started quoting a poem:

"There's Aurora Borealis, those Northern flashing lights,
There's Venus and Mars Planets and stars
And silent satellites…"

"Satellites?"

"Well, moons, really. The planets have orbiting moons. There's so much up there, meteors, shooting stars. If you look up long enough, you'll see a shooting star, maybe two or three on a good night. I like the night sky. When I was a child, my papa would drag the mattresses outside and we'd sleep under the sky. There was so much happening up there, some nights, it was impossible to sleep. Mama taught me to sing, Pa taught me about nature, frogs and spawn, caterpillars and moths, bugs; I think he would have liked a son, but hey-ho, he made do with me and he taught me such a lot, and not all the girly stuff either. He had a telescope…" She shook her head. "Sorry. Pa was an inspiring man. I think if he was alive now, he would be disappointed in me. I haven't quite lived up to his expectations."

"Mrs Hebb, Anella, I think he would be very proud of you right now. You have so much knowledge, I'm impressed."

"A lot of people would say, 'What's the point of educating a girl?' but my goodness, we have brains every bit as good as a man's and it's so easy to learn, don't you think?" She stopped, bit her lip to stop herself saying any more.

The Major shook his head and looked up, at the same moment Anella jumped up.

"Oh! Look! A shooting star, Major! Oh! Eade, how astonishing! We were just talking about shooting stars and there is one!" She found that incredible. "Well, told you. There's always so much to see up there."

She was inordinately pleased, and so was the Major. Anella had called him Eade and she hadn't even realised.

"Well, what a night. Who'd have thought it?" The Major chuckled. "The things you can learn on a simple drive home." He clicked the horse on, then stopped. "So we've got the sun and the moon, stars, planets and satellites?"

"More or less," she answered eagerly.

"Mmmmm, not sure it's my thing, but I'm impressed, I didn't realise you were so knowledgeable."

"Oh." She was disappointed, slightly. "Oh well, never mind. One day, I'll teach you about the night sky. It's fascinating, honestly. It will captivate you."

He thought, *Not as much as you, Ma'am.*

He clicked on the horse. "Best get you home."

Only a few minutes later, the Major was helping Anella alight from the gig and she was pleased to see the twins had lit lanterns outside to offset the darkness. They hadn't closed the kitchen curtains and light streamed out. In a spontaneous gesture, Anella invited the Major in.

The boys were sitting at the kitchen table with mugs of tea.

"Major, you've met Clem and Clance?"

"Certainly have, but not sure which one's which." He smiled a greeting at them both.

The boys stood. "Well, I'm Clem, he's Clance, but it don't matter; we answer to either."

"They catch girlfriends out that way," Anella joked. "Major, can I offer you alcoholic refreshment?"

He had to laugh at her formal question.

"Mrs Hebb, I would very much enjoy an alcoholic beverage. Maybe a whisky if you have it?"

Anella was relieved she had sorted the eating room a few weeks ago. The decanters and glasses were out on the sideboard, cleaned, with no dust! She poured him a generous measure and they sat at the kitchen table, Anella realising that this was a novel situation for the Major. He had certainly never sat in his own kitchen at home.

He was reluctant to leave, but eventually, even he realised he had to go. He mentioned to the boys that it would probably be a regular occurrence from now on that Mrs Hebb would be dining at Chilworth on a Friday. The twins accepted this, but Anella was a little indignant, but not wanting to spoil the atmosphere, kept quiet. She saw the Major out to the gig and stood in the semi-darkness, saying nothing, suddenly shy. She thought, she hoped, he might attempt, a kiss but he didn't. Giving a little sigh of disappointment, she turned away.

"Mrs Hebb." The major took her hand and held it. "Thank you," and he brushed a kiss on her hand. Anella shivered and, traitor that she was, said she looked forward to next Friday!

CHAPTER SEVEN

The following day, a groomsman arrived with flowers and fruit from the Major. Grapes and a pineapple, peaches and bananas. The twins had never seen fruit like it. They knew of apples, pears, plums and damsons, but this? Anella put it all in a big bowl, so it was on the table to be eaten at any time. The pineapple was a puzzle: how to get into it caused much head-scratching, but when Clance, in desperation, chopped it in half with a butchers' knife, the boys discovered its sweet interior.

It became the norm then that Anella's Fridays were spent at Chilworth with the Major, and the following day, fruit and flowers and the odd book on beekeeping would arrive, much to Anella's delight. After a few weeks, the Major again suggested that Anella attend the Harvest Festival, so she did. The church had been decorated in great fashion. Centrepiece was a huge golden baked sheaf of bread – a work of art. It was truly magnificent. Surrounding it were loaves of bread, cakes and jars of chutney and jams; there were duck eggs, chicken eggs, even pheasants' eggs and on a marble slab were some of Anella's goat's cheeses, some of her pickled walnuts, apples and pears. There were great bunches of horseradish and watercress from the stream. It was surprising to think there could be need when so much of nature's bounty was free.

A rousing sermon and everyone's favourite hymns, "We plough the fields" and "All things bright" and "All thanks to Thee our God". At the end of the service, the children helped the Major and the vicar distribute all the food and gifts. It made a sunny, autumnal day a day of golden kindness and the poorer villagers went home, knowing they had food for the next few days. There was also later, the village feast. About four-ish, people started gathering on the lawn. There were long tables covered in white cloths with jugs of wildflowers and bowls of seasonal fruit; candles in glass jars had already been lit and a four-piece band was playing lively music. Out came the food; great pies, square and round and decorated in such a manner to indicate what was inside, tongue, steak and kidney, rabbit or chicken and great mounds of baked potatoes. Elderflower cordial for the children and small beer and cider for the adults and then, of course, the sweet pies, apricot or apple, the crumbles and charlottes and jugs of thick cream.

Mrs Bosworth was there with her daughters and the two littlies and Anella was there with her twins.

What a lovely day, but it wasn't finished yet. There was dancing, the old, traditional country dances that everyone knew without ever having learned, and the people watching clapped their hands to keep the dancers in time. Anella was pleased to see the twins dancing, Clem with a village lass and Clance with Miss Garton, the assistant schoolmistress. Eventually, the day came to a close and the musicians packed away their instruments and the villagers slowly made their way home and the servants, as if they hadn't had a busy enough day already, started clearing the tables. The children, full, sleepy and tired, were given the table fruits to take home and the Major arranged, very kindly, to take the Bosworth family home and the twins to be dropped off at the farm, which left him alone with Anella. Together they walked up to the house where Mr Buchanen joined them. They had their meal, a much-reduced affair, in the small eating room, a more intimate arrangement. Mr Buchanen was full of amusing anecdotes which had Anella almost crying with laughter. How could such a deep, morose man be so funny?

As was usual now, the Major took her home and it was a still, quiet night. A barn owl flew silently overhead. Anella looked up at the night sky and pointed out the constellations that she thought she recognised. She bit her lip. She wasn't being entirely honest here, a lot of what she was saying was guesswork.

"Did you enjoy today, Mrs Hebb? It was good, wasn't it? The locals enjoy it. We have a similar festivity at Christmas; a party for the children, a dance for the villagers. In fact, we always have a small house party, nothing much, you should come. The school mistresses always attend and the vicar and his wife, my sister and husband and the four children and Mr Buchanen, of course. Usually, there's about sixteen of us." He stopped then, realising he was prattling on. "Shall we see you as usual on Friday, then?"

Nell hesitated. The Major had given her a lot to think about. Already, in her mind, she was forming a polite refusal. She didn't fancy trying to mix with those above her social station. She was a farmer's widow and that was that; although she was surprised that the school mistresses would be there. That was food for thought.

"Yes Major, I look forward to it – and today was lovely. I think I might have a bee book to return."

The Major touched his forehead by way of a salute. "See you on Friday, then," was all he said, before flicking the reins and trotting smartly away. Anella stood and watched him disappear into the darkness. A curious man, the Major, but interesting also.

The following Friday found Anella walking up the drive to Chilworth House, wearing her tweedy blue suit and her beret set at a jaunty angle, secured by her silver broach. As seemed the way lately, she met Mr Buchanen. He had no horse with him today. He doffed his cap respectfully.

"Ma'am."

She nodded and noticed he still had a piece of string tied around his left wrist.

"Mr Buchanen, you had that piece of string round your wrist when you came to us. What's it for?" She didn't want to appear rude, but she wanted to know why he still wore it.

"I write with this hand. Sometimes, when your memory's not working properly, you forget. Now, Mrs Hebb, your broach is jogging my memory. How did you come by it? I think I'm right in saying it's a Luckenbooth broach."

She touched her beret. "My husband gave it to me for our first anniversary. I don't know how he came by it; it has great sentimentality for me. It reminds me of Neft." She fingered the broach lovingly. "How do you know it's a Luckenbooth broach? What does it mean?"

"It's Luckenbooth because, originally, it was sold from a booth in Edinburgh." He shook his head "Don't ask me how I know that, I just do."

"Mr Buchanen, well done! Maybe you've bought one at some time? How incredible that you should remember, just like that! How exciting. Now you have to figure out when you bought it and for whom."

"Aye, that will come, I can't rush it, it happens in its own good time, bit by bit. You up to see the Major? I'll probably see you later, then," and with that, he doffed his hat and returned to work.

She was shown into the library and within minutes, Thompson bought in a tea tray. No Major, though. Thompson coughed politely and announced that the Major was here, just come back from a farm inspection with the factor and he wouldn't be long.

Anella poured herself a cup of tea and waited and

eventually, the Major appeared, not his usual immaculate self, but windblown, smelling of the outdoors, of chill, autumnal days. He was wearing a rough, tweed jacket and muddy riding boots.

"Major, I've been here ages. The tea is probably cold."

"Oh, so sorry, you know how it is. Better pour me a cup of tea quick and put a splash of whisky in to make it drinkable." He laughed.

She poured his tea and handed it to him, minus the whisky. She didn't know where the decanter was. He pulled a face and shuddered.

"Bloody awful stuff, tea no good without whisky. Now Mrs Hebb, I know I've mentioned it before. Christmas?" He saw her hesitate. "I've told my sister Eliza about you; she's looking forward to meeting you. We have the children's Christmas party here in the hall. I know Miss Sorrell and the children particularly want you to be present. I know you were a bit doubtful when I asked, but I'm really hoping you've made up your mind to say yes."

"Major, I don't think I can." She saw the disappointment cross his face. "I believe your guests will be far above my station. I could come for the children's party, but that's all."

The Major was disappointed. He crossed the room and actually took her hand. "The school mistresses will be here, my sister; not the great and the good of the county, only us. My sister is keen to meet you. Mr Buchanen will be here. You know the vicar."

She still hesitated. There was a lot of lip biting going on as she tried to come to a decision.

She shrugged her shoulders. "I wouldn't be comfortable. I'm farming. A farmer's widow. I haven't got the right clothes." What an admission to make!

There was a silence between them. Anella swallowed. "I

would like to come, really, I would, but I feel I just can't. It wouldn't be right."

The Major let her hand go and moved away. He gazed out of the library window. "So, you refuse our offer of hospitality?" He pursed his lips and inclined his head.

"OH! No! Please don't say it like that! You make me sound very rude and ungrateful." She was hesitating now, the Major could tell.

"Well, I have to admit, I'm not used to people turning me down." He turned towards her. "Mrs Hebb, please."

She was wavering; she took a breath. "Alright, Major, you win."

The Major was so overjoyed, he came straight over and kissed her on her cheek.

"Major!" She held her face as if she'd been slapped. He was quite unrepentant and poured himself another cup of tea with a splash of whisky by way of celebration.

There followed general conversation and social niceties, but both of them knew, a line had been crossed. Anella finally had to admit the Major was becoming an important factor in her life. It made her unsure.

And the Major – he was secretly delighted. He'd caught this woman, hooked her, now all he had to do was land her and make her his wife. His wife! Confirmed bachelor that he was, his aim now was to get married and it was the Widow Hebb he had in his sights.

Anella refused a drive home, preferring to walk in the chill air and noticing the leaves, twirling and blowing around her feet as she walked. Autumn was here and this was the time of year she loved best.

Major Eade Jameson watched her every step from the library window; she triggered certain feelings that he hadn't experienced for a long time. She was completely unaware of how attractive she was, and he liked that. He was looking forward and hoped she would enjoy Christmas with him at Chilworth. Who knew what was coming?

CHAPTER EIGHT

There was much making do and mending at Anella's over the following few weeks. The twins were good at improvising and took great pride in creating something out of nothing. Clem was making goat-proof pens in the barn and Clance was re-building an old glass house. He wanted to grow exotic fruits. The baskets of fruit arriving every week from Chilworth House inspired him. He wanted to grow pineapples. The fact that he didn't have a heated green house, he didn't have any knowledge – yet – didn't stop him. He had nothing but his own energy and enthusiasm and although Anella shook her head in disbelief, she said nothing to discourage him. She had no doubt Clance would achieve his aims; nothing deterred him.

Then there was three days of pigging. Two pigs had been kept back, each about 100 lbs in weight. Mrs Bosworth came to help her and the boys as there was so much to do. They made black pudding and sausages. Nell made brawn with the pig's cheek. She boiled the tongue and roasted the ears until they were crispy and they ate those as they worked as a tasty snack. Mrs Bosworth and she were making pork pies when Mr Buchanen arrived. What luck! Another helper and he was hauled into helping out without preamble. Nell was roasting the pigs' trotters for them all later, but in the meantime, legs of pork, the hocks, shoulders and sides had to be salted for hanging. She braised the kidneys and made a wonderful liver and apple casserole and much, much later, they all sat round the table, Mrs Bosworth and her two girls; they had been so handy, the two littlies and the twins, she and Mr Buchanen. What a feast they had. Bowls of mashed swede with black pepper and lashing of goat's butter and potatoes grown by the twins and the last of Neft's mead and cider. They sat there for a long time, everybody too full to move and Anella felt a wave of happiness, tinged with sadness too, that the house was busy and noisy and messy and smelly. It had never been like this in Neft's day. She liked it.

Anella had arranged for Mrs Bosworth and the children to come and stay at the farm over Christmas. Whether she stayed at Chilworth House just for the day or stayed for the length of the Christmas period, she wanted her farmhouse to be full and jolly. She asked that fires be lit in some of the bedrooms, especially hers just in case she came home. She'd made a Christmas pudding and there were jars of mincemeat in the pantry. She'd told the twins they could cull two hens; they would know, better than her now, which ones to take, and with the school closing for the holiday, there would be plenty of milk to make butter and cheese.

December was almost upon them and Nell spent many a day altering or adjusting her dresses. They were all of an age, but exceptional in quality; they were sponged and pressed and she added a bit of lace or a ribbon here and there, and she was satisfied with the results. She cleaned her hats and shoes, packed and re-packed as she didn't really know what to take. In the end, she took everything, eventually standing back and looking at the valise, the suitcases, the travel bags. She was ready for the off on the 23rd of December and the carriage arrived early afternoon, with two footmen, who showed no surprise at the amount of luggage she was bringing with her. Sitting in the carriage bowling along, her spirits lifted. She was going to meet new people, experience a new way of living and entertaining. She must put all her reserve behind her and relax and enjoy socialising with the

Major and his friends. She had a rare opportunity to wear some of her nicer clothes and the jewellery left to her by her mother. Deep down, she felt a swell of excitement and anticipation and didn't like to admit to herself, the Major! He was the reason she was feeling this way. If nothing came of it, nothing was lost; she hoped she wouldn't embarrass herself, that was all.

It was a very cold and grey day and the sky presaged snow, but nevertheless, it was an exhilarating drive. Anella, muffled with warm winter clothes and covered with a travel rug, was warm and cosy, only her cheeks revealing how cold it actually was. Before long, she was standing in the vast hall, divesting herself of shawl, scarf, hat and gloves to a patiently waiting maid, who told her her name was Tilda and that she would be her personal maid while Anella was a guest. That really surprised Anella: a maid of her own. Goodness, Tilda would be witness to all of her clothes and underwear. Gracious, it didn't bear thinking about!

The hall, when Anella had a chance to look, was exuberantly decorated with great boughs of holly and ivy, lots of red berries and red ribbons and candles, hundreds of them, everywhere. A great fire burned in the grate and long tables were being set, for this is where the children would eat and play their party games. There was an air of excitement and Anella was standing there, taking it all in, when the Major appeared.

"Ah Mrs Hebb! I'm so glad to see you. Hope you haven't been here too long on your own?" He took her arm. "Can we forget the Mrs Hebb? It is Christmas, after all. You call me Eade, I'll call you Anella – or Nell? Which do you prefer?"

"Either will do. I'm looking forward to meeting all your guests, Major. Eade, sorry." She blushed.

He gave a little bow. "Come on then, they will be

delighted to meet you," and he escorted her into a reception room, seemingly full of people.

She realised straight away, she would be more plainly dressed than most of the ladies present, but she inwardly shrugged. They would think she was a dowdy farmer's widow, which, she thought, with a smile, was exactly what she was.

She noticed a smiley, friendly lady attending the teacups firstly.

"Just in time," commented Eade as he saw the tea being poured. "Anella, this is my sister, Eliza, she's good at pouring tea, the gentleman sitting nearest the fire is her good husband Harold and any wild children you spot running around at the moment, are hers. There were four last time I counted. Eliza, this is my good friend, Anella."

Eliza, tall, with curly hair, like her brother in looks, was warm and friendly and didn't appear too differently dressed to Anella, which made her feel much more comfortable.

Before they could converse, the Major had whisked her away to meet Mr Bussey, an incredibly old and wizened gentleman, sombrely dressed but with a smile that lit his face. There was his son, Edward, tall and thin, quite a nice-looking young man; he greeted Anella politely and then the Major, steering her towards the larger group, introduced her to Mr and Mr de Hass, Emery and Calenna, and their daughter, Merissa; she was dark-haired and petite, pale-skinned and brown eyed, very young and practising her flirting skills with a fan and fluttering her eyelashes at Eade. Anella felt a little tremor of jealousy, but didn't have time to dwell on it, as Eade was introducing her to Lady Helena Westcott and her daughter Daphne. Anella had to restrain an urge to curtsy before passing on to the vicar and his diminutive wife and Mr Buchanen. She inwardly sighed on seeing Mr Mantel Buchanen O'Kyan. If Eade had to leave her side for hospitality reasons, she would have him to fall back on. That was a relief.

Eliza approached them with cups of tea.

"Anella, my brother's spoken a lot about you. How did you meet? Harold and Eade were at school together. Both rowdy lads, but my Harold settled down to a domestic life; my brother didn't!"

"Mrs Erskine..."

"Eliza, please."

"Eliza, I met your brother through the school, really. He wanted the children to have a milk drink every day; I own a farm nearby, I keep goats and he asked me if I could supply them. Such a generous kindness. The children really benefit, healthwise. The Major is a very good man."

"That is typical of Eade, thinks he's Lord Bountiful, but yes, he is kind-hearted..."

They were interrupted then by the children rushing into the room, breaking all the rules. They were not allowed downstairs, but it was nearly Christmas, and they were going to attend the children's party later and they were very excited. Eliza clapped her hands to capture their attention. She indicated to her offspring she wanted them to attend to her and they obediently came over to their mother.

"Children, this is Anella, you will address her as Mrs Hebb." She turned, "Mrs Hebb, meet my family. This is Ellis, our eldest, he's twelve and home for the holidays. He's going to sail the world when he's older." Ellis extended his hand to shake but was very shy. Next was Adam, nine. "He needs taming," said Eliza, "a bit like his uncle." He glanced at Anella, and she could tell he was the cheeky one. "Now, the girls: this is Florrie, her Papa calls her Flower, and this is her big sister, Freda. Freda is sorely afflicted by her younger sister, but she is very, very patient with her."

The girls were pretty: Florrie, dainty with pink cheeks

and brown tumbling hair; Freda very much like her mother, with pale freckly skin and reddish hair.

"Now, let me see, if Ellis is twelve, you," Anella said to Freda, "you must be ten?"

This made Freda crow with delight. "Nooooo, I'm SEVEN!"

Anella affected great surprise, "Seven? Why you're nearly as tall as your Mama! So how old is Flower? Mmmmmmm, let me guess, is she five?"

Freda pulled herself upright to make herself look even bigger and she confided to Anella, "She's only a baby, really, and she does everything WRONG! I have to do it all!" She raised her eyebrows in such a dramatic manner that Anella was hard pushed not to laugh. "And she's only four."

"Well, I think she is very lucky to have a big sister such as you to look after her." Anella smiled, just as Eade came over.

"Anella, the children's party starts around four o'clock. We dine at eight. I've called for Tilda, she will take you to your room. Give you chance to have a bit of a rest, get yourself sorted. My sister must call her nanny and get her children under control or they will wear themselves out before the party begins."

Anella excused herself and followed Tilda upstairs to her room. It made her gasp when she saw it. It had the most beautiful views over the gardens and lawn. There was a cheerful fire crackling in the grate and vases of hothouse flowers, decanters of port and brandy on her dressing table, along with her personal items. Her gowns were hung up and many candles were lit.

"Oh Tilda, this is lovely. Thank you so much. You can probably tell, I'm not used to being a house guest. Will you help me with my dresses? You will probably know better than me which ones I should wear when. Not that I've got anything very dressy. I just want to wear what's appropriate. I hope you don't mind me talking to you like this?"

Tilda bobbed "Not at all, Ma'am. We can get you accommodated, don't you worry. There's no need to change for the children's party. Some of the ladies will change and then change again for supper, but there's no need. What had you in mind to wear tonight?"

"The blue."

Tilda went to the robe cupboard and bought out the blue dress. It was of a nubbly fabric with a dull sheen, wide-necked to show off Anella's creamy shoulders. She planned to wear her mother's opera pearls and matching earrings.

"Leave that to me, Madam, I'll sort it out, make it fuller. Are you going downstairs now? Would you like me to brush your hair?

"Oh Tilda, what luxury, I would love you to brush my hair, though there's not much we can do with it, is there?"

"We'll see." Tilda picked up the hairbrush and deftly, with broad sweeps, swept Anella's thick, dark hair up in a chignon and clipped it up with a sparkly clip.

"That didn't take long, did it, your ladyship? Your hair is lovely, so easy to style. We'll do it again later, before supper. This little clip has been left in the drawer for a long time, might as well use it. I'll be here for you when you come back up."

Tilda bobbed a curtsy and left Anella alone for a few minutes. She poured herself a small port and drank it back in one before venturing downstairs. Goodness, the house was like a maze, so many rooms; only one wrong turning before she found the stairs, and she could hear the excited chatter of children and much disturbance as she descended. The school children recognised her immediately and rushed over to her. "Miss, Miss, Miss 'Nella!" They hopped and skipped around her and eager hands grabbed hers as she walked over to their teacher, Miss Sorrell.

"Good evening. Are things going to happen soon?"

Miss Sorrell gave a wry laugh. "Straight away." She clapped her hands loudly, "Children, quiet please. The Reverend will say a prayer, so it's hands together, eyes closed, let us pray."

There was complete silence and then a long prayer of thanks for the good works of the Lord, their generous bene-factor, the Major, the earth's bounty and how he expected to see them all in church on Christmas day… He would have carried on, but a discreet cough from the Major reminded him that the sooner the children's party was over, the sooner the adults could enjoy their evening. The vicar might be a man of the cloth, but he was also a man of the table. He liked his food and the wine that went with it.

And so the evening began, with noisy children's games, much hand clapping and singing of nursey rhymes until Miss Sorrell clapped her hands and requested the children attend the table.

"Hands together, eyes closed. Silence, if you please. Repeat after me: 'For what we are about to receive, may the Lord make us truly thankful. Amen.'"

There was much scuffling of shoes and scraping of chairs and happy chatter from the children until the baize door opened dramatically and a line of servants paraded out carrying platters of food. Mounds of mashed potatoes and jugs of gravy, cabbage and swede and carrots and the famous Christmas pasties, filled with beef and onions and a hot sauce, known by only a secret few adults as to what it was. One each. Only at this party did they have a whole pasty to themselves. Then it was pudding time, the highlight of the meal. Many candles were taken away, so the room was quite dark and in came the flaming CHRISTMAS PUDDING.

There was much cheering and shouting when this appeared and, covered in custard, it went down a treat. This feast was washed down with elderflower cordial. Afterwards, the children sat at Miss Garton's feet while she read them the age-old story of the birth of Baby Jesus, the shepherds and three wise men. Miss Sorrell stood in the background enjoying a quiet cup of tea. There was much yawning and thumb-sucking at this stage but there was still presents to distribute, one for each child, not to be opened until Christmas morning, and an apple and orange for everybody. Then it was coats on, boots on and out to the waiting carriages that the Major had organised to take them home. There were "Ooooohs" and "Aaaaahs" from the front porch. Much to their excitement, it was snowing. Nothing could be more perfect.

All the house guests dispersed after the children's party and the servants swooped on the chaos in the great hall; within a short space of time, all evidence of the festivities had been cleared away and it was back to its usual welcoming elegance.

Upstairs in her room, everything had been laid out for Anella: her pearls and comb on the dressing table, her dress hung with its freshly crimped lace at the neck and sleeves and a corsage of white and lemon flowers waiting for her to use. Seeing everything ready sent a little shiver of anticipation through her. She told herself to take advantage of this time, she might never get another opportunity to live like this. She might not be as wealthy as the other guests, but she was every bit as good. That's what she told herself; now all she had to do was believe it.

She washed in the warm water that had been left in her room and felt much fresher, when there was a knock on the door and Tilda entered.

"Madam, you've washed?"

Anella nodded.

"Ma'am, I want to show you this room." Tilda beckoned for Anella to follow her down the corridor a little way and opened a door like all the others. Anella gasped in surprise. A small room with a small, glowing fire. The room was empty except for a hip bath and a wooden airer draped with large towels. There were shelves with bottles of lotions and soaps and drying powders. It was cosy and sweet-smelling.

"This is your bathing room, Madam. If you let me know when you wish to bathe, I will get it ready for you. The fire is always kept in, there are always fresh towels."

"Oh Tilda, I'll tell you now, I'll wish to bathe tomorrow before supper. How heavenly; but what if any other guests wish to use it?"

"No, Madam," Tilda shook her head, "This bathing room is only for you. There is another one further down for general use. It's such a good idea, don't you think, Ma'am?"

Anella sighed. "Tilda, I think this is wonderful – and it's all for me, just me! I can't wait to have my bath tomorrow. Too late for tonight. I'd better get ready, but I'm going to spend a lot of time in this room, I can tell you. What bliss."

Back in her bedroom, Tilda helped with Anella's toilette. She brushed and brushed Anella's hair until it shone and expertly twisted it up, much tighter this time, in a neat bun at the nape of her neck, secured with the sparkly pin. A little pink powder was applied to Anella's cheeks and lips and a blackener painted onto her eyelashes to make them more noticeable and finally, the blue dress was laid on the floor for Anella to step into. Tilda carefully did up all the little hooks and eyes, then she tweaked and pulled the skirts so the dress stood out. Carefully on with the shoes – not the best, but they would hardly show – then the necklace and earrings and finally, the corsage. Tilda looked at Anella, admiring her hand-work, and beckoned her to take a look in the full-length looking glass

"Oh Tilda, I never looked like this on my wedding day!" She twisted and turned and yes, she looked just as good from the back as she did from the front.

"Madam," Tilda said, "you look very beautiful." She bobbed a curtsy. "Now, I think it's time to go down."

Anella nodded and made her way, no getting lost this time, down the stairs; from the hall, she could hear the rise and fall of conversation and occasional laughter. The Major came over to greet her as soon as she entered the room.

"Anella." He took her hand and covered it.

She looked lovely, the lustrous pearls against her creamy skin and the subtle glint in the fabric of her blue dress matched her eyes. The bun at the nape of her neck made her look particularly vulnerable. He seemed reluctant to take her to his other guests. In honesty, he'd much rather take her off to the library, where they usually met on a Friday, and chat to her there. He'd decided to ask Anella to marry him, but the difficulty was in choosing the right moment. He chewed his lip. What a dilemma; but now was not the right time, he saw that.

"Eade." She had a little laugh. He was still holding her hand, as if he'd forgotten to let her go.

"Mrs Hebb, I'd rather keep you to myself, but I must do my duty and you must mingle, I suppose." He took her arm and guided her towards the nearest group of guests. The Major's sister, spotting Anella, came over immediately.

"Anella, I love your dress, you look lovely. No wonder Eade won't let you go. Now, who don't you know?"

"Well, I don't know anyone, really. I've been introduced, but that's all. I know Miss Sorrell and Miss Garton and, oh, Mr Buchanen."

"Come and meet the girls, see what competition you're up against."

The two girls, Merissa and Daphne, were in light-hearted conversation with Mr Buchanen. She could hear their laughter. Merissa was looking devastatingly pretty. Her dress, slight and clinging to her slender figure, made her look as if she was wearing nothing at all. Her auburn hair was draped with ropes of beads and there was much fluttering of her fan. She looked very alluring, with her long cream gloves showing an inch of soft white skin. She was a young lady of great charm and she knew it.

Daphne was a much more solid girl, horsey, outdoorsy, but nevertheless, an attractive, fine-boned young woman, very sure of her place in society. She didn't know how to flirt but she could hold her own in an intelligent conversation, so probably had the edge over her rival this evening.

Anella was pleased to see Mr Buchanen mingling and talking to the guests. His moroseness seemed to have disappeared – maybe it was because of the whisky he was holding. *He has come on*, thought Anella, and she said so to Eliza.

"The thing is, Anella, is he married or not? That's what the ladies want to know. He's an attractive man; of few words, but the ladies like that sometimes. They always believe they can change a man, don't they? But there might be a wife somewhere up in the Highlands, maybe bairns? Who knows?" She shrugged her shoulders and handed Anella a small glass of Herez, just as a footman appeared, to announce the serving of dinner.

Sixteen sat for dinner and it was a lovely evening. There were many courses and between every other course, one half of the table had to move up a place and then the other side of the table had to move down. This caused a great deal of hilarity and lots of chatter, as you found yourself next to someone you didn't know. It wasn't boring.

The two young ladies flirted outrageously with the Major and then with Mr Buchanen. Neither of these two men seemed interested, but the young Edward Bussey was smitten. Anella did her fair share of flirting too, but when she sat next to Mr de Haas, he put his hand under the table and slid his hand up her leg. He gave Anella a sly glance and squeezed her thigh. She moved her leg pretty sharply away and imperceptibly shook her head with a very firm, mouthed "No."

After dinner, there was games and cards and someone played the piano and Daphne sang "How Beautiful are the Feet" from *The Messiah*. Anella sat by the fire, listening intently, and the Major came and joined her. There was silence between them.

"Do you play the piano, Anella?" he asked.

"No." She gave an embarrassed laugh. "Sometimes I sing. I have to be in the mood, tho', can't just warble to order."

The Major leant over to be nearer. "Would you sing if I played?"

"Goodness! I don't know. Yes, I suppose I would, if I knew something that you could play. Will you play tonight?"

He pursed his lips. "Might. Sometimes you have to, to help the evening along. Sometimes, things have a life of their own and the evening just sails along, know what I mean?"

She smiled sympathetically, and then the Major, Eade, did a surprising thing. He took hold of her hand and examined it. He rubbed his thumb and finger along each of her fingers, dwelling on her ring finger, and turning her hand palm upward, she grabbed his thumb and looked at him expectantly.

"Major?"

"Anella —" He stopped. There was a disturbing frisson between them.

As a woman, Anella knew instinctively what the Major had been about to say. She bit her lip, and took a deep breath before venturing a question.

"Major, what is it? I think I have an idea."

He looked at her, with a hint of laughter in his eyes. "I was going to ask whether you…"

"Want a sherry before retiring?"

"No, no. I was going to ask…"

"Whether I want breakfast in bed in the morning?" He laughed out loud at that.

"I don't think so! No, I was going to ask whether you would consider…"

"What?"

"Whether you would…"

"Be your wife?"

He looked at her in amazement. "Yes, how did you guess?"

"Major," she lowered her eyes, "call it woman's intuition."

"Well?"

"Well, Major, are you serious? Are you making fun of me?"

"What?" he was affronted. "No, of course not; Anella, will you marry me? Will you be my wife?"

She clasped his thumb even harder. "Major, this is very serious. I'm, I'm…"

"Not sure?"

"No."

"Don't want to?"

"No." She was stung then. "Yes, I mean. Sorry Eade, I'm flustered." She gave a little chuckle. She still had hold of his hand. She took a breath. "Major, Eade, I'm afraid to say yes."

"Why?" he whispered. "If you don't say yes, those two –" and he indicated with his head Daphne and Merrisa – "those two will eat me alive."

She really laughed then. Those two young ladies were very predatory.

"In that case then, Major," she was still, aggravatingly, biting her lip, "well, in that case, I'd better put you out of your misery and accept your offer – and save you from those two nubile young girls!"

He sighed with relief and looked at Anella keenly. "What a relief. We can celebrate now. Let's have a bottle of bubbly."

"Major, don't tell everybody yet, I haven't got used to the idea myself yet."

"No, no, only for us." He caught the footman's eye. "Thompson." He beckoned Thompson over. "A bottle of Champers, two glasses." He put his fingers to his lips in a gesture of secrecy. "Well," he turned to Anella, "I can't believe I've done it. You took your time saying yes." He chuckled. "I thought you were going to turn me down. Ah."

Thompson had arrived.

"I took the liberty of opening it downstairs, Sir. Don't want the cork popping to alert everyone." He gave the Major a secret wink. "Shall I pour?"

Eade nodded and then handed a glass to Anella.

"Let's drink to you, me and our future together. May we live long and be happy!"

"Yes." Anella's eyes were glowing with excitement. "And let's drink to the Major's new wife."

"Good idea," he agreed.

"Oh, and let's drink to the new husband."

"Good idea," he agreed.

"Well, can't have any more toasts," she looked dramatically forlorn.

"Why not?"

She held her glass upside down and giggled. The bubbly wine had gone straight to her head.

"You can only have another glass if you have a toast to make. I can think of many."

More lip biting from Anella. "Erm, well, what about a toast to our forthcoming nuptials?"

He filled her glass. She took a sip.

"Let's drink to us. We've sat here and just changed the course of our lives and no one over there –" he indicated to the four men playing cards – "has any idea." She nodded. "Anella, you've made me very happy. Are you happy?" She nodded. "I think tomorrow we'll have to start making plans, don't you?"

The guests were gradually drifting off to bed and Anella could sense the card playing was coming to an end.

"Oh Major, however am I going to sleep tonight? I won't be able to stop thinking." She leaned towards him. "I'm so excited. Are you?"

He laughed. "Of course I am," he agreed. Not about their wedding, but about getting Anella into bed. Now THAT excited him enormously!

"When you asked me, after the Harvest Festival, to come for Christmas, did you know then? Did you plan this?"

"Of course!" his eyes were wide with honesty. "Anella, from the first visit, I knew. I watched you walk down the drive, I just knew. I did think at one time, Buchanen was a rival. Evoking sympathy, bloody man. Not that he can hold a candle to me, of course" he laughed.

"You're right, Major. Mr Buchanen is a very nice man and his situation is very sad, but you do win." She shrugged her shoulders. "It's not your looks, though, and it's not personality." She shook her head. "It can only be your money." She got a fit of the giggles then and hoped she hadn't misjudged his sense of humour.

"Well, at least I've got something going for me. I might ask Mr Buchanen to be my aide on the day." He slapped his knee. "Anella, we have a lot to organise, a lot to talk about. We'll start tomorrow." He looked at Anella. "Exciting times, ay, lass?"

"Eade, I have to go up, that Champagne's gone straight to my head. I'll never sleep."

She stood up and Eade stood also. He noticed she was biting her lip again. Obviously, it was something she did in order to stop herself making improper suggestions to him. That made him smile.

"Anella." He took her hand and kissed it so softly, it made her shiver. Then he slipped his arms around her waist and pulled her close. How he wanted to kiss her properly and whisk her upstairs to bed, but hey-ho. He sighed. *Soon, Eade, soon,* he thought to himself. He had to release her then, before he forgot his manners. She didn't move away.

"I'm going up now," she said.

"Yes." He sighed.

"Well, goodnight then."

"Night, Nell."

"Nell?"

"Anella. Night, Anella."

"See you in the morning."

"Yes." He clasped her close, unable to let her get away.

They just stood there.

He gave a theatrical sigh. "Off you go then, sleep well." He pulled her even tighter, so close, she could feel him against her. She closed her eyes, he was making her breathless.

"You have to let me go, you know." She laughed.

"I know, I know, I'm just wondering what I can do to keep you down here for a few minutes longer!" He released her and she turned to go. Eade, with a giant step, was right in front of her again and again. His arms embraced her and he held her tightly.

"Anella," he reprimanded, "you must stop this." He swayed with her. "You really must leave me alone. I'll never sleep tonight." He kissed the top of her head.

She laughed. "Eade!" She pulled herself together "Major, I will say goodnight."

They could have carried on like this all night, but they were interrupted by the men who, having finished their card game, were retiring to bed. Only then did Eade release her.

"Goodnight, gentlemen," she said gravely, and slipped away before Eade could grasp her and embarrass her in front of his guests.

Good Tilda was waiting for her when she arrived upstairs. How lovely to have someone on call, to undo all those tiny hooks and eyes and hang her dresses up for her, to brush her hair patiently and pour her a port before sleep.

"Do you want any more on the fire, Ma'am, before I go?"

"Thank you, no. I shall be asleep within minutes, Tilda. You get off now. Thank you for everything, I'll see you in the morning."

And quickly, Anella was in her warm bed, candles extinguished, only the crackling glow of the fire keeping her awake; but not for long. Outside, the snow was gently and silently falling and, through the night, would create a whole new world for them all to discover in the morning.

CHAPTER NINE

Breakfast was a late and relaxed affair on Christmas Eve, lots of chatter and noise, servants replenishing chaffing dishes and making up the fires. There was a feast to be eaten: kedgeree, kidneys, kippers, eggs, scrambled and fried, fat bacon and mushrooms, hot rolls and toasted bread, tea and chocolate and coffee for Mr de Haas. Anella sat in quiet contemplation until Eliza arrived. She quickly helped herself to a cup of chocolate and joined Anella.

"Oh, the children! They are wild with excitement over the snow. I've left them with Nanny, she can take them out. Did you sleep well? It must have snowed all night, mustn't it? You're very quiet, are you alright?" she looked at Anella inquiringly.

"Tired, that's all. We don't keep late hours at home, on the farm. A bit of fresh air is what I need. That'll sort me out."

She smiled and wondered whether she should say anything and decided, no, it had to be a joint affair, with Eade and her sharing the good news with everybody.

"Don't look now, but Mr Bussey's on his way over," whispered Eliza and sure enough, he asked whether he could join the ladies.

"Of course. Good morning, Mr Bussey. What time did we all go up last night? You men were playing cards quite late." Anella smiled a greeting.

"Late, late", he said, tapping his nose in a secretive gesture. He put his breakfast plate on the table and Eliza looked quickly at Anella, astonished. For a thin, undernourished-looking old man, Mr Bussey obviously had a huge appetite. He caught the ladies' glance and gave a low chuckle. "Well, I rather fancied the eggs, but you can't have eggs without a nice bit of fat bacon and, well, you can't have a nice bit of fat bacon without a nice fat sausage to go with it and then I thought, I'd better have a mushroom or two and the rolls looked so tempting, still warm, so had to have a couple of those. Don't want Eade's cook to think she's wasting her time. And then, I saw the kidneys; well ladies, I was quite undone then; shame to let them waste. I'll just have my kipper first. Have you tried the chocolate mixed with the coffee? It's delicious, you must try it. It's good for you, gives you energy." He began eating.

"Well, Mr Bussey, you are a very fortunate man that you can eat such quantities of food and stay so slim." Eliza was slightly disapproving.

"As my mother would say, rather keep you for a week than a fortnight," Anella joked.

He laughed. "Yes, my son cannot eat as I do, but he has my build. He's on the skinny side; hopefully his appetite will increase as he gets older. He needs a wife, he does, to feed him up. Mrs Anella, can I speak with you in the library? After breakfast? About ten-thirty?" He glanced at the wall clock.

Somewhat surprised, Anella agreed and left the table then with Eliza to help kit the children with their outdoor clothes. They were impatient to get outside to the snow and were jumping around with excitement. A few guests were attempting to walk to church, some lounged by the fires, others went out with the children; the hardier ones were armed with fireside shovels and spades, in order to dig themselves out of drifts or help create snowmen with the children.

The boys were intent on digging out a tunnel. They soon

gave up when they realised the amount of work involved. Their nanny wisely gave them free rein to expend excess energy. The afternoon would be quieter and more relaxing for the adults if the children were tired.

Anella was prompt to the library and found Mr Bussey waiting for her.

"Ah, Mrs Anella, we'll just wait for Eade. I'm here to alter any wedding jewellery you may decide upon, in case you're wondering. He has a few items that might interest you – it depends. Ah, here he is."

Eade came in, in a dash of cold air and briskness.

"Anella, sorry, I've been caught up in estate business all morning. I was hoping to get back for breakfast with you, but I've only just got back."

He came across and kissed her! Really! Anella was astonished. They might be betrothed, but to kiss her in public, well, in front of Mr Bussey. Before she could feign indignation, Mr Bussey gave a polite cough and opened his little black bag and removed a jewellery roll.

"Now…" He adjusted his spectacles and looked at Eade. Eade nodded. "Well, we have a sapphire and diamond ring, the trio of diamonds, the ruby and diamond ring – lovely, that one; a ruby necklace and the ruby and diamond earrings, an eternity ring of diamonds, a cameo broach and a sapphire and diamond clasp. A few loose stones, tourmalines, yellow diamonds, pearls and opals. We can have them made up for you if you wish?" He looked at her inquiringly. "And of course, we have the string of pearls, the matching earrings and the little diamond and pearl broach."

Anella was bemused and she looked at Eade. He moved to be near her.

"I thought the diamond ring would be right for you as an engagement ring, then Mr Bussey can measure you for a wedding ring. Maybe have a diamond or two in that one also. What say you? Try it on."

She tried them all on and agreed with Eade. The trio of diamonds it was, and Mr Bussey measured her finger. He would be back in a few weeks with the wedding ring for her to try, he said, and Anella was alive with excitement. She felt humbled. Eade's love for her was apparent and moved her to tears. He noticed immediately.

"What's up? What is it? Why are you shaking your head? Why are you saying no?"

"Eade, I don't mean no. I'm just overcome; I'm so happy. I love the diamond ring." She wiped away a tear. "It's just…" She shrugged her shoulders. "I'm overcome."

She crossed to Eade and gave him a big hug and felt a shiver of excitement course through her body. She certainly had not expected events to move so fast. The Major was not one to let the grass grow under his feet.

"Will it be soon, then?" she asked.

"What?"

"Our wedding?"

"Anella, I would like it as soon as possible. In the new year? We don't have to wait, do we? I'm thinking March sometime? We can announce our betrothal at dinner tonight. Mr Bussey, thank you. Tell no one."

Bussey gave a wry smile. "Mum's the word," he said, rolling up the jewels. He patted his pockets. "I'll leave you now," and he diplomatically left them.

Anella cuddled into Eade's arms.

"I'm so excited. Just think, at breakfast, I knew nothing. Eliza and I had breakfast with Mr Bussey, he never said a word."

"I should think not. Now, stop trying to seduce me with your charms. We have a date to fix. Do you fancy a big do or a small affair? A day off for the school children? A shindig for the villagers? A ball for us? Fireworks?" He kissed her lightly on her head. "Of course, we'll have to visit my tailor."

"Me?"

"No, sorry, Buchanen and I. The dressmaker will come here for you. I'll get the tailor to come at the same time as you have your fittings. We'll have to talk to Mrs Harvey about food and staffing and Mr Gillamoor about flowers. Lots to do." He moved across to the library window. "I think we should go to Italy, Venice, do the grand tour, you know? Like everybody does now. You will need many new clothes. In fact, you'll need a whole new wardrobe. We'll have to get the dressmaker straight away."

"Do I look that bad, then?"

He laughed. "No, of course not, but you'll have a new station in life, and your clothes will have to reflect that." He smiled at Anella and felt a surge of excitement. What woman doesn't like new clothes?

Money was not a worry for Eade. His father had been an immensely wealthy man, accumulating his vast wealth from his sugar plantations in Barbados. He had been the proud owner of hundreds of slaves.

He was never an absentee owner, he wasn't going to allow any managers or merchants make free with his profits. Fortunately for Mr Jameson senior, he'd managed to remove most of his fortune before the slave rebellion in 1816. The rebellion only lasted a few days and his negro workers went back to making sugar and he resumed to making even more money. Eade was comfortable with his inheritance; he was used to living life as a wealthy landowner and the status that it afforded him. In earlier days, he did feel remorse at the enslavement of Africans. The one way he appeased his conscience was in his involvement with the villagers and their families; locally, he was known as a kind and benevolent man, never one to stand apart.

Lunchtime was amusing to Eade, as Merissa flirted outrageously with him. Anella felt pangs of jealousy. She'd never had these feelings before but was mollified by the thought of what a surprise it would be for Merissa tonight when they made their announcement. It would put paid to her antics once and for all.

Early afternoon, Anella retired to her room, thinking she was far too excited to sleep, but she was awoken by Tilda, announcing that her bath was ready. The little room was heavenly, so cosy, the towels warming in front of a blazing fire, candles everywhere.

Anella submerged herself in the warm water; it was fragrant and bubbly. She told herself that when she was married, she would have one of these baths every day, whether she needed it or not. Later, back in her bedroom, Tilda helped her dress. Tonight she was wearing a deep ruby red dress of wild silk, square-necked to reveal her lovely neck and creamy shoulders. She wore her little silver necklace and her Luckenbooth broach. Tilda cleverly brushed her hair up into a tight coil and dressed it with a dark red ribbon.

Anella twirled in front of the mirror. "Tilda, I don't know how you do it, but you make me look…"

"Lovely, Ma'am? Actually, it's easy with you. It's a pleasure." She began to tidy the room. "Do you want the fire kept in? There's more snow coming, according to Mr Gillamoor."

"Oooooh, yes please." What luxury, a fire virtually all night. She had a fleeting memory of her cold, unloved bedroom at the farm and hoped Mrs Bosworth was keeping her word and lighting a fire there and in some of the other bedrooms to try and keep the house warm.

One last look at her reflection. She was ready. Ready to socialise and enjoy her first evening with her husband-to-be.

Anella made her way downstairs. She could hear music, very gay, and as she entered the room, the Major immediately came forward to greet her. He looked at her admiringly for a few minutes, not saying a word. Finally he spoke, very quietly, as he put his arm around her waist and pulled her towards him. "Mrs Anella, you look very beautiful tonight. I think you need the ruby necklace to go with that dress, don't you?"

"Yes I do! I'm having to make do with my little silver chain. I'm soon to be a married woman, you know; I deserve rubies."

The Major held her even closer; she could feel his hot breath on her neck. "You're not going to be difficult are you? I might have to change my affections. There's a certain young lady who wants my attention." He kissed her below her ear, which made her laugh, and he took her arm and led her into dinner.

From the beginning, this was a light-hearted and jolly evening; the musicians played all through dinner. Before the gentleman retired to their port and cigars, Eade stood and tapped his glass with a knife.

"Friends, just a quick announcement. As many of you know, I have been a single man for many years now. I have seen many a companion succumb to matrimony and take on the yoke of a wife and then children and all the responsibilities that becoming a husband and father entails, and I've often thought, 'Not for Me'; but," and here he held his hands up, "but, love is a funny thing. It tames us all, and that is the reason I'm standing here tonight, to tell you, I'm to be married."

There was a collective gasp from all the guests. "Friends, raise your glasses, please. My wife to be is Anella Hebb."

At this, everyone stood and held their glasses aloft.

"Please," he held a hand out to Anella. "Join me," he

asked. She did, whilst the servants took round trays of Champagne.

There was much swapping of glasses then, as the only appropriate drink for such an occasion was a glass of bubbly. There was much noise then and offers of congratulation and Eade held his hands up in supplication.

"I know, I know, it's unbelievable that a lady of such quality has condescended to marry the likes of me, but there you are. Stranger things have happened, I think. The wedding will be on March, the 15th, Friday. Invitations will be sent so you'll know times and everything. Now gentlemen, let's go for the port, leave the ladies in peace. I'm sure they'll have lots to talk about."

Later there was dancing and everyone said they couldn't possibly dance, having eaten so much food, but they were reassured it would be only the most sedate dances tonight. No galloping or cavorting. They could waltz, tho'. There was a collective gasp at this. The waltz? Where you held your partner's body so close to your own? Yes, so Eade grasped Anella.

"Put your feet on mine," he ordered, "and I hold you like this."

Anella gasped and looked quickly around. This wasn't decent, was it? She could feel Eade's body pressing against her own. Surely, this type of dancing couldn't be tolerated, could it? Surely it was immoral? Immoral or not, Anella decided she liked it and they danced the rest of the evening together, ignoring everyone else. Eade was exciting and funny on the dance floor. If he didn't know the dance, he made it up and swung Anella around, holding her tightly, breaking all the rules of propriety. Much later, the musicians took a break so Harold played the piano and they sang Christmas carols and then sat around the fire, drinking hot chocolate with brandy. Eade sat with Anella by the glowing fire, talking softly, until she felt herself falling asleep.

"Bed for you, I think." Eade escorted her to the foot of the stairs and gravely thanked her for making the evening such a success. She couldn't quite recall what she had done, but she graciously accepted his thanks, said goodnight and went up to bed. Within minutes, with Tilda's help, she was snuggled up in bed drifting off to sleep with the fire crackling and glowing and the snow falling silently outside her window.

Christmas Day dawned to deep, deep snow. The children were wild with excitement. The servants had decorated the eating room in a fabulous manner, swathes of holly and ivy, and red roses, red ribbons everywhere. It looked very festive with the table candles already lit. Luncheon would be at one o'clock today, so breakfast was an insignificant affair. As it was impossible to get to church, they held their own impromptu service in the great hall, with the servants and children and Harold playing the piano and lots of joyful carolling. It didn't last too long; the servants had to get back to the kitchens and the children had to get outside, Florrie to see how her snowman was faring.

Eade took this opportunity to enlist Anella's help in placing gifts on the table, beautifully wrapped and intriguing – and there was one for her. She suppressed an urge to shake the little box as it was time to change for luncheon.

CHAPTER TEN

Everyone gathered in the reception room for Champagne and canapés, and they toasted Anella and Eade and talked about the wedding in March. The good thing with Champagne is it gets you in party mode straight away, so the atmosphere was loud and jovial as they entered the eating room. The fire was blazing merrily and the candles lit, and it wasn't long before they were tucking into a gargantuan meal of roast turkey, roast pheasant, a sirloin of beef and every vegetable under the sun, followed by a flaming Christmas pudding. It was Calenna de Haas who found the lucky coin and everyone cheered, for good fortune was assured her in the coming year.

The gentlemen did not retire but stayed with the ladies, as the presents were about to be opened. Anella felt huge guilt as Eade had bought these gifts for everyone, but didn't have one for himself. The ladies opened theirs – gold necklaces, pretty – and the gentlemen had cufflinks. Anella, however, had a fine twisted chain interspersed with tiny, sparkly diamonds.

"Eade! I love it." She draped it between her fingers. "Oh, it is so lovely." She handed it to him and turned her back. "Can you put it on?"

"Wife, only too happy to oblige." He kissed the back of her neck.

"Major!" Anella darted a look around the table but was relieved no one had noticed. She felt the gold cold against her skin. "Well?" she asked and without waiting for an answer, she joined the rest of the ladies in front of the hall mirror. She turned and moved her head and shoulders in order that the diamonds twinkled in the candlelight.

She bit her lip and deep down inside, she hoped Eade didn't lavish too much money on her; she was aware she was marrying above her station, but she didn't want to be thought of as a "gold-digger".

Back in the eating room, she sat closely to Eade and squeezed his hand. "Major, this is lovely," she touched the necklace, "but I have nothing for you."

He laughed and shook his head. "Don't worry, necklaces don't suit me." He carefully clasped her warm hand and stroked her wrist very gently.

No, she couldn't do this.

"Eade, no, don't do this," she whispered. Instead of stopping, he opened the palm of her hand and kissed it so softly, it sent shivers down her spine. "Eade, stop."

He was making her feel weak and hot.

The servants had bought in the cheeses and port, and in spite of everyone eating too much at luncheon, they were all up for a smidgen of ripe cheese and some walnuts and a glass or two of the Major's crusted port.

"What is a crusted port then?" asked Daphne. "I know I like it; well, only the odd glass at Christmas, you know."

She addressed her question to Mr Buchanen. Did he notice she liked him? Did she really care about the port?

Mr Buchanen pursed his lips. "Well, basically a crusted port is a quality ruby port bottled young. Years ago, it was customary to lay down a 'pipe of port' as your first son's inheritance. Not sure how much a pipe is, though. It's a fortified wine, shipped from Oporto in Portugal. It comes from the Douro Valley. That's about all I know..." and he stopped suddenly.

He was quietly amazed at himself. How did he know all this? Every day, information came back, but unfortunately, most of it wasn't any help in furthering his memory about his past.

"Hold on, a pipe of port is, mmm, I think, I think it's about 121 gallons." He did a quick calculation. "Nine hundred and sixty odd pints. I'd like to think the Major has that sort of amount in his cellar, but I doubt it."

He was quietly pleased. He wondered what else he knew. Maybe he was a wine importer? He knew a lot about wines. He certainly drank a lot of it. He smiled to himself and was grateful to Daphne for asking the question in the first place.

It was becoming dusk and they had sat at table most of the afternoon. The Major stood up.

"Anyone for a stroll before the light goes? I feel the need for some fresh air."

He looked round expectantly and raised an eyebrow. Was he hoping no one would take him up on his offer, so he could take Anella for a private stroll around the grounds? If so, he was to be disappointed. As a man, the whole table stood up and agreed, yes, they would like a breath of fresh air, and there was general noise and confusion as the ladies retrieved hats and gloves and mufflers and capes and coats. The men were ready quickly and impatiently waiting, and then the four children came downstairs and wanted to come also. The Major clasped Anella's arm and together they slipped out of the door and were away down the drive before anyone noticed.

"I love the snow, don't you?" asked Anella. "If I was home now, I'd be cursing this weather, it makes everything so difficult. I hope the boys are keeping the house nice and warm."

The Major grabbed her arm. "Come," he said and dashed over to the trees. He began furiously making snowballs. "Hurry up," he ordered, "make a pile." He never stopped. "When the young 'uns come, we'll pelt them – not too hard, don't want to make them cry, just for a bit of fun."

He was like a child, and she could feel the excitement in him. She obeyed and relished the thought of becoming chief snowball-maker until he shushed her.

She was indignant. "I'm not making any noise," she protested.

"Shush, they're coming." He looked at her. "Wait. Wait until you see the whites of their eyes, then let them have it."

It was then Anella got a fit of the giggles. She hoped Ellis and Adam had a sense of fun. They could see the group strolling down the drive, their voices echoing in the cold afternoon air and the children running ahead and kicking up great clouds of snow.

Eade whispered, "When you throw, throw in front of them, as a warning, sort of. Then, when they retaliate, let them have it."

"Yes, Major. Eade, here they come, don't throw too hard, don't hurt the girls."

She stopped to take aim, but it was Eade who threw the first ball. He let out a big cheer, deliberately letting the boys know where they were hiding, and it wasn't long before they succumbed to a hail of snowballs. Of course, the children had any number of adults on their side, Harold and Edward and Mr Buchanen being their main supporters, the ladies not deigning to wet their gloves or fingers. The boys wholeheartedly entered the battle and were not to be beaten by one old uncle and a GIRL!!

Anella, close to submitting under the deluge, stepped out of the shadows with her hands up. "No, you've won, we give –" She was roughly dragged backwards by Eade.

He was horrified. "Nooooo, woman, what are you doing? This is the enemy, you can't just give in." He waved his hands wildly at the boys. "No, take no notice, she's a renegade."

The boys jumped up and down with glee and proceeded

to pelt them with roughly made snowballs, made by members of their gang. Anella succumbed and fell to the ground, onto the soft snow, and the girls Florrie and Freda raced to her aid and ended up flinging themselves on top of her to "protect" her, they said. All three ended up laying in the snow, wet, dishevelled and giggling and quite unable to stand up without help.

She heard Eade sigh. "Guess that's it then, guess we've lost." He flung himself down in the snow and grabbed Freda. "Why didn't you come and help us? And you, Flower? How could you? I'm injured." He held his arm. "You girls are just too girlie. It won't do. Tomorrow you'll have to be trained. Don't tell your brothers," he said, knowing full well, they could hear every word.

Eade jumped up, covered in snow and helped Anella and the girls up. They were busy brushing themselves down.

"Home, I think," and all the adults agreed. The light was failing fast and they were becoming chilled. Anella and the girls raced back to the house. All she wanted to do now was to have a nice warm bath and put on dry clothes.

They all arrived in the hall, noisy, wet, with snow melting on the floor and went off to their various rooms to change.

CHAPTER ELEVEN

Later, refreshed, they all met again in the reception room. Harold was playing the piano and they all spontaneously began to sing. Anella joined the girls and asked them, what could they sing? Freda said, "'Leonidas is combing his hair' and 'Oh Whaley, Whaley'."

"I know those," said Anella. "Shall we sing them to everybody? Are you brave enough?"

Freda was scornful. "Of course. We sing 'Leonidas' as a roundelay. I start, then Florrie. You can come in last if you like."

Anella went across to speak to Harold. Yes, he loved to play for his daughters. So they grouped and the audience sat in expectant silence.

Freda began:

"Leonidas is combing his hair, his hair,
  King of Persia beware, beware,
  Leonidas is combing his hair."

When Freda finished the first line, Florrie piped up, and when she finished, Anella began. It actually sounded quite musical and the girls were very pleased with themselves when they finished. Everyone applauded enthusiastically.

Freda, very grown-up, then announced their next song and they began in unison.

"The water is wide, I cannot get o'er
  And neither have I wings to fly,
  Give me a boat that will carry two

And I will row my love and I."

Anella loved singing with the girls, and then Eade took over the piano.

"What do you want me to play?" he asked.

"'The Jackdaw of Rheims'?" asked Anella. Eade ran his fingers over the keys and hummed the tune to himself.

"Yep. Let's go, then." And they were off, Anella's voice sweet and pure and Eade supporting her with his playing. There was complete silence until the end and then everyone applauded enthusiastically.

"More, more," they called, so Anella sang "Scarborough Fair"; the wrong song for the time of year, but it was all she could think of.

"Someone else's turn now," she said, and Eliza volunteered with Harold, and the evening was off on a musical theme, which lasted best part of the night. Eade and Anella sat side by side, absorbed in each other, quietly laughing over the antics earlier in the snow.

"Anella?" Eade looked at her seriously. He was, as was the way with him, stroking the back of her hand.

Anella stiffened. As was the way with her, being a woman, she knew the unasked question in Eade's eyes.

"Eade, don't look at me like that. No, it's not possible." She looked around at the assembled company. "No," she mouthed.

He turned towards her. "Why can't I have my wicked way with you? After all, in three months, we'll be married. You'll be my wife. We really ought to get to know each other, hadn't we?"

Goodness, he was crafty! She gave a laugh. "Yes, that's what you say, but what if, after trying the goods, you change your mind? I'm branded a fallen woman."

"But I love a fallen woman," Eade pleaded through his laughter.

"Stop it! No more. I'm going up to my bed now."

She said no more to him and stood to say her good nights, pleading fatigue from too much snowball fighting. She literally raced upstairs and called for Tilda to draw her her second bath of the day. Twenty minutes later she was cleansed, dried and powdered and in a fresh muslin slip and bodice. She hastily put on her robe. Tilda had made up the fire and snuffed out most of the candles and wished her goodnight. Anella poured herself a glass of port and downed it in one. She sat there in silence, waiting, hairbrush in hand, knowing Eade would come and that if she asked him, he would brush out her thick, dark hair. After all, she reasoned, there had to be a little bit of love play to begin with, didn't there? She heard his quiet tap on the door and he was in, in a trice and turning the lock behind him.

"Eade."

Now she was afraid; afraid of being found wanting, of not being sophisticated, of not being worldly wise, of revealing her naivety. After all, Major Eade Jameson was a man of the world. She said nothing, neither did he. He came across the room and sat on the bed so Anella dropped the hairbrush and gently clasped his hand. Deliberately and slowly, she turned his hand over and very softly, kissed his wrist. He'd done this to her earlier and it sent shivers up her spine, and she knew from Eade's reaction, it had the same effect on him. It was time to be brave.

"Anella." He was gruff, and reached to untie the belt of her robe. No! She couldn't let him do this. Why, he would see her semi-naked. Too late. He never took his eyes off her, and she knew that if she moved forward, the strap of her slip would drop and reveal the curve of her breast, and in those few minutes of hesitation and doubt, she decided, and moved towards him, deliberately.

Eade was undone then and said, "I think I have to take these clothes off you, don't you agree?"

She did agree and laid back and closed her eyes, waiting and then, when things didn't happen, she opened her eyes to find Eade slipping into her bed.

She gave a nervous laugh. "I thought you meant take my things off, but not my necklace though." She held on to it as if it were a talisman.

"I know, I did. You looked so scared, though. I couldn't do it." He laughed then. "Get into bed, keep your stuff on. We'll take it all off under cover, bit by bit. I'll keep my eyes closed." And at this, he laughed out loud and nuzzled her neck, which made her giggle.

So she did, but Eade was not a man of his word, but a man of needs. He was naked and she could feel his need pressing against her thigh. Within minutes, he had divested her of all her garments and she lay there, revelling in being naked. She turned to him, to touch his bristly chin, knowing her breasts would press against his chest. He kissed her then, on her shoulders and nuzzled her neck and ran light kisses over her breast and nipples. Oh! The feeling was extraordinary. She raised her arm to grab the curls on Eade's neck and he suddenly kissed and licked her armpit. This was such a surprise, so unexpected, it made her laugh out loud and sent a great wave of sexual desire through her body. She pressed her hips against him then and cupped his buttocks in her hands, pulling him closer.

"Eade," she whispered, opening her legs. She caressed him gently and guided him in and tried to slow him down, but he was away then and so was she. His desire made her desire all the greater and she could feel need coursing through her body. She was moving her hips in unison with him.

"Eade." It was becoming unbearable. She couldn't say any more, he was knocking the breath out of her body

"Eade," she gasped. She felt him climax and come, warm and wet inside her. She lay there quiet, amazed and unbelieving and then felt his hand between her legs and he touched her in a secret place, a gentle, insistent rub and within seconds, her body convulsed, spasm after spasm. She gasped in surprise and wonder and held her hands over his hips, and Eade could feel her writhing underneath him. They stayed locked together.

"Anella." He crooned in her ear, his hot breath making her shiver. "I've been waiting for you, for this. I knew from the very first time I saw you." He lightly nibbled her ear.

"You knew? That first time we met? Surely not."

"Of course. That first time. I knew. You were lovely. Not intimidated. Every visit you made, I watched you walk down the drive. You annoyed me, really. Why was I so fascinated by you? And you didn't even know!"

He threw his arm around her body and squeezed her tightly. They lay there in companionable silence and Anella knew there wouldn't be much sleep for them tonight. Eade ran his fingers down her spine and caressed her bum.

She tightened her buttocks and was nervous of what he would do, but inevitably his fingers followed the cleft of her backside, exploring.

"Oh, Eade, no, don't do this," but he did, and quickly entered her from behind. A rictus sped through her body and she was spreading her thighs and pushing her hips into Eade and moving back and forth before she could tell herself no. Eade, further ahead than she, came spectacularly and tried to withdraw, but ended up pressed against her bum. His hand came round to her belly and softly over her mound of Venus and then, so, so, gently, between her thighs and into that most secret of places which caused her body to convulse and she came again and again, giving little yelps of ecstasy she just couldn't suppress.

"Eade." He never moved, leaving his hand inside her thigh. She was warm and wet and overcome with satiated desire, as Eade nuzzled her shoulder and nibbled her ear.

"Anella." He loved her and this is how they stayed, locked together, touching, feeling, caressing, exploring, nothing out of bounds and actually, nothing was as important as this. They didn't want the morning to come or the world to intrude. Anella only wanted to stay in this rumpled bed and have Eade make love to her again and again. Eade felt the same; he twirled her hair around his fingers and pressed his face against her body, smelling her, as if by knowing her smell, he could possess her. Anella ran her hands over his body: where she was soft, he was hard; where he was strong, she was weak. Oh to think, in just a few weeks, this man would be hers and excitingly, she would be his. She lay there still, in wonderment and gradually, drifted off to sleep.

In the morning, Eade called her softly awake and thoughtfully informed her she had to come down for breakfast, as today was the great snowball battle. Instead of laying in her warm, cosy bed, he insisted she got up and got dressed. Anella secretly smiled as in giving her these instructions, he constantly called her "Wife". No more Mrs Hebb, no more Anella, but "Wife".

He rolled onto the bed, fully clothed with his boots on, and landed a noisy kiss on her cheek. He quietened for a minute and kissed her softly on the mouth.

"Wife, no good you trying to seduce me into staying here; I have things to do, places to go, people to see, children to instruct in the art of snowball warfare. And you are in dereliction of your duty, so, wife, up, before I have to tip you out of your pit."

Anella was only too delighted to obey. She didn't ring for Tilda; instead, Eade helped her into her gown and patiently hooked every hook and eye.

"What a palaver," he complained. "If you ever needed proof of my affection, wife, there's not many a husband who would stand and do THIS!"

She laughed. "No, true, but you haven't put my boots on yet. Don't think you've finished. I have to have my face washed, my hair brushed, my stockings on. I don't think you should help with those, or we'll never get out."

He gave her a wolfish look, biting his lip, as if seriously contemplating a quick bit of naughtiness, but unfortunately, time was pressing. The children would be amassing for battle and neither of them had had breakfast.

"Anella, you do the rest. I'll brush your hair, tho'. Never done it before, but as it's probably part of my military training, I'll oblige."

Eventually the two of them made it down for breakfast. It was a meal to be enjoyed; relaxed, lots of noise and chatter. Some of the guests were going home today, Mr Bussey and his son, Edward and Lady Westcott and her daughter Daphne, which was fortuitous, as Edward had high hopes, quite above his station, about Daphne. There was no shortage of money on his side, so he was in with a chance, or so he thought.

A few hours later, they were wrapped up against the chill, waving farewell to the guests and readying themselves for battle. What the children didn't know was that Eade had been out earlier, stockpiling frozen missiles, but so had Mr Buchanen, acting under instruction from Eade. He did have a sense of fair play. So battle commenced, Anella and Eade and the two girls against Eliza, Harold and the two boys,

Ellis and Adam. Buchanen was go-between. The boys were underhand and attacked from the rear, so Eades' group were unprepared and at a disadvantage and were thoroughly pelted; quite unfairly, according to the girls later. It was fierce fighting, no quarter given. Mr Buchanen was called in and so was Mr de Haas and his daughter Merissa and from then on, it deteriorated into a free-for-all. The snowballs ran out and there was much falling about unnecessarily in the snow, and eventually, everyone trooped back to the house, dishevelled, noisy, full of laughter and chat. It was the same when they entered the eating room. It was a loud, disorganised lunch that the children were allowed to attend, in order to discuss their failed tactics.

Eventually, Eade and Nell (if he didn't call her "Wife", he now called her Nell) escaped to the library to make wedding plans undisturbed. The 15th March had already been agreed upon; now, plans for Nell's dress, Eade's suit and Mantel's outfit had to be made. Mrs Harvey was called up to talk about the wedding breakfast and that extra staff would have to be bought in. Next in was Mr Gillamoor, the head gardener. Anella didn't mind what flowers were used, but nothing too colourful and they had to be everywhere, in all the public rooms and in all the bedrooms. A wedding holiday had to be arranged, a feast for the villagers and a day free from school for the children. Messages were sent to Mrs Tichborne and her daughter, Helena, to attend on Nell as soon as possible to get her gown underway. She would need plenty of other gowns also and endless sets of underwear. New shoes and hats, Eade was adamant, she needed. She now had to be dressed as befitting her new station in life. All this took hours, but eventually all was done and they retired to the sitting room for a drink before dinner. They sat by the fire and Nell was saddened to see the snow rapidly melting. Eade was buoyant, tho'. Much had been organised.

It had been decided the tailor should attend Eade and Mr Buchanen at the same time Mrs Tichborne and her daughter would attend on Anella, so all was good.

"Are you excited?" he asked.

"Oh Eade, I can't tell you. I can't wait. It's going to be just wonderful; how can we organise it all, so much still to do?"

He grasped her then. "Of course we can." Then, gruffly, "Let's go upstairs and celebrate."

She laughed and pretended to be shocked "What? Before dinner? Never. Maybe later." She promised and excited by his enthusiasm, reached for the lapel of his jacket and leaned across to kiss his cheek. She could feel his stubbly chin and deep down, it excited her.

"Eade, we will be so happy."

"Of course we will, wife. You will have to learn to leave me alone," he laughed, "and I have to leave you alone or we'll never get any work done. Talking of work, I must meet with the farm manager quickly, so I'll leave you now and see you at dinner."

He kissed her gently on the cheek and left her, so she decided to explore the downstairs rooms, of which there were many. The orangery was her favourite room, warm and damp and smelling of exotica and full of jungle-type greenery. Anella sat on a windowsill and above the chatter of their guests, she could hear birdsong. They must be trapped in here, she thought. She slipped her shoes off and the floor was warm; there were hot pipes under the floor. Such luxury, and this for the plants! She discovered a servants' staircase behind a panel in the hall, which she pressed open. She could hear noise and clatter and general busyness and hastily retreated, back to the entrance hall where she found the Erskine family descending the staircase, noisily, with their nanny in tow.

"Are you off?" asked Anella in surprise. "Are you not staying for dinner? I thought you were going home in the morning."

"No, Anella, we're off now. We've seen Eade. He has business with the farm manager, so we've said our goodbyes." Eliza came across to give Anella a big hug. "Let us know your final plans."

Anella, overcome with emotion, gave Eliza a sisterly kiss. After all, it's not every day one acquires a new sister-in-law, especially one such as Eliza. Next it was a hug and a kiss for Harold, not something she would usually do and then the children. The boys were disgusted and wiped their mouths when they thought no one was looking, but the girls were much more affectionate. Anella was already feeling a great deal for them. It seemed to take forever to get their carriage loaded, and getting all four children in and the nanny was a squash.

Finally, they were away down the drive, with long waves and shouts from the children, the carriage wheels slushing in the melting snow. Anella felt forlorn at their leaving. She decided to retire to her bedroom and have Tilda draw her a bath, so she could relax before dinner.

A short while later, Anella was ensconced in the hip bath, the fire blazing merrily away, and she could see fresh snow falling outside. She sighed and relaxed back, the soft water enveloping her. This bathing was truly a wonderful idea and it was with a great deal of reluctance that she vacated her bathing room. Tilda helped her dry and get dressed and she was ready in plenty of time for dinner. Tilda brushed her hair and twirled it up in a bun and secured it at the back of her neck with the sparkling pin.

Anella was ready in good time and was down in the sitting room with a glass of Madeira engaged in polite conversation with the de Haases. Eade came in in a dash. He'd arrived back late and washed and changed in a hurry, eager to see the last of his guests and Anella. It had been a good few hours since he'd seen her and his face lit up. He came straight over to her and put his arm around her waist and pulled her towards him and whispered something obscene in her ear. She looked quickly over to the de Hasses to see if they had heard him, but they were engrossed in conversation, so all was well, although his language sent a frisson of excitement through her.

Mr Buchanen arrived just as the footman announced dinner and they all went in together and as there was so few of them, they had a cosy, warm evening, chatting and laughing. Eade played the piano afterwards while Mr Buchanen sat with him and tried to remember if he had ever played the piano too. Merissa was very attentive, offering to turn the music; maybe she could sit with Mr Buchanen to assist in his memory recovery? Such a kind girl.

The de Haases were leaving in the morning, so Anella thought she should go also. She did have to get back to the farm and check with the twins how they were managing. She would inform Eade later, she thought.

Anella went up to her room, secretly hoping Eade would come to her and while Tilda was still brushing her hair, he arrived. Anella was mortified with embarrassment. She was sure the servants were aware of all the indiscretions of house guests, but she didn't want to be thought of as "one of those", even though, actually, she was.

Tilda bobbed a curtsy and left them immediately, so Eade crossed the room to sit on the dressing table stool with her and picked up the brush to continue brushing her hair. He also kissed the back of her neck.

"Mrs Jameson," he slipped his arm around her waist and held her. She was stiff with nerves and Eade could sense it, so he stood and poured a port for her and a brandy for him.

As was his way, he held her hand and examined it intently, turning it over, before saying a word.

"You haven't much to say for yourself tonight, wife. Are you afraid?" She nodded. "Drink this," and he offered her the glass of port which she drank down in one gulp. Eade looked at her in amazement. "'Grief woman, I hope you won't always knock the port back in that manner."

She shook her head, "No, of course I won't. It's your fault. You make me a bit afraid; you make me nervous."

"I think you had better take my boots off for me, then, if you wouldn't mind; and when you've done that, the socks need to come off, left one first."

Anella, realising his ploy to distract her, dutifully knelt at his feet and did as she was instructed. Next, his shirt had to come off, after she had removed the links and undone every pearl button carefully. It was a beautifully fine, soft fabric; Anella wouldn't have minded it for herself. A bit breathless now, she knew she had to undo his breeches and she did this, heart in mouth, with Eade watching her every move. And that was it! There he was, before her, ready for action. She was a little surprised: no underwear. When she thought of the layers and layers that women had to wear... but she had no time to dwell before Eade had carefully clasped her and led her to the bed.

"Nell, nowt to worry," he whispered, and he slipped the bodice strap over her shoulder and kissed her so softly, little butterfly kisses then, across the rise of her breast, then up to her neck and ears. He stopped and ran his thumb along her bottom lip and kissed her there, very softly, very gently so she could feel his warm breath on her face, which made her shiver. He drew her face with his fingers, outlining her eyes and eyebrows, carefully down her nose and, teasingly, around her ears. He nibbled her ear lobes and snuggled into her neck. He circled her cheeks and traced her lips with a finger and then ran his tongue over. These tiny little movements tickled; they were so loving that she felt an overwhelming desire for him. He didn't want Anella to do anything; she just had to lay there while he paid homage to her body. He ran his fingers up and down her arms, kissed her wrists and played "ring-a-roses" on the palms of her hands and, tantalisingly, kissed her armpits, which was so ticklish, it set Anella off in giggles. She so wanted to kiss him, but he wouldn't have it; it was her legs and thighs he turned his attention to next, massaging her toes and then, her instep and ankles. Carefully, he made his way up her calves to her thighs, and this is where matters became even more exciting for Anella. She could feel her body loosening and an urgency mounting within her.

"Eade." He was kissing her breasts and she knew, no matter what her needs were now, his were paramount and – Oh! – Anella laid back and let sensation after sensation wash over her. She clasped the curly hair at the back of his neck.

"Eade." She just needed to kiss him and whisper sweet nothings to him and hold him like a mother would a baby.

"Eade." She was amazed. He was quickly and urgently coming, she couldn't delay him; his head on her breast, his legs entwined with hers, and there he stayed and there she stayed, neither of them moving or speaking, just revelling in being together, sated with love. Anella kissed the top of his head and whispered, "I love you, Eade" and he stirred and kissed her chin.

"Wife, I love you too." She could tell, without seeing his face, that he was smiling. He raised himself up, his hair tousled and a sheen of sweat on his chest. "You'll have to exercise a little self-restraint, you know; can't have you having your wicked way with me ALL the time." He ran his hand over the swell of her breast and fell back on the bed and laughed and drew her with him.

She sighed. "I must return home tomorrow, so need to be up early to pack. Will you take me?"

He held her tightly. "Of course I'll take you home, but you don't need to take anything with you, do you? Leave it all here. You'll be living here permanently soon, so it doesn't matter. Tilda will look after everything for you. You have to come back here for your dress fittings."

He shrugged his shoulders. There was no problem that he could see.

They lay together, Anella's head on his chest, but neither of them could sleep; and it wasn't long before Eade was crooning in her ear and blowing on her neck and cupping a breast in his hand and tickling a nipple and complaining that she was insatiable; and so it began over again and it was almost dawn before they fell asleep.

CHAPTER TWELVE

Bowling along in the gig the following morning, discussing matters, Anella decided she would offer the farm to rent to the twins. They could have their mother and siblings to live there, and Anella's bedroom had to be kept aired and warm and made up for her whenever she wanted to visit or stay. Mr Graves' rental agreement would still stand. It would give Anella a pitiful amount of money, but it would be her own. She felt she couldn't ask Eade for money, although he would give it to her willingly.

As the Major's wife, all work would have to cease. Good works she could undertake, but that would be all, so plans for expanding her goat herd would have to cease, unless the boys wanted to take over her ideas for expansion. And her bees? She felt she must instruct the boys more fully into the way of beekeeping practices. Anella knew herself to be an extraordinarily efficient beekeeper and she wanted the boys to be the same. She loved her bees; they had never stung her and she held them in high regard. Maybe there would be a way she could still work with her bees. After all, who would know?

Coming up the driveway, she could see great improvements, everything clean and tidy, the gravel raked and swept. Both the barns looked in good order. The farmhouse looked quaintly shabby, but it was welcoming, and the melting snow made it look picturesque. Anella felt quite proud arriving with the Major. The boys were working hard and it showed.

They made their way to the kitchen, and it was warm and

welcoming. The stove was glowing and a casserole, gently stewing on the back burner, made the room smell appetising. The first thing Anella did was check the oven as, so often, she had been distracted by events outside and forgotten she had bread and a cake baking away. As she thought, there was a loaf just about to catch, so she saved it and placed it on the table. The boys came in shortly for their tea break and were surprised to see Anella. They sat around the kitchen table with Eade discussing the future of the farm and their role in its developments. It didn't take long, really. Eade was a businessman, whereas Anella was a housewife. Eade was direct and to the point and the twins could see all the advantages of working the farm for a rent. It wasn't long before Anella was upstairs packing a few bags with the last of her clothes and shoes. She left many items behind; they held too many memories of Neft and her past life and marriage, which was sometimes far from happy. It was her fault, though, as Neft had told her. She was barren and so all his sadness stemmed from her. The fact that *that* side of their marriage was dire was due to innocence on Anella's part and ignorance on Neft's.

She sat upstairs in her chill bedroom, overcome with a sense of forlornness. Neft's parents thought she was a bit flighty; not with other men, but sometimes, she would sing or hum as she worked, sometimes she would laugh and Neft would laugh with her. He would forget his disapproving parents, but not for long; and as the years wore on, Neft became more obtuse and Anella's high spirits slowly ebbed away. To carry the expectations of all three of them on her shoulders was an unbearable burden and she became sadder and sadder and overcome with guilt. It was too much to bear. Neft's parents succumbed to old age, one following the other in the space of nine months; such a sad time for Neft. She did think that, once he overcame his initial grief, they could re-vitalise their marriage; but it was too late. Neft was too set in his ways, and Anella resigned herself to a sad and lonely life as wife of an impoverished farmer. There was never any sign of a baby, not even a missed menses, nor even a miscarriage, and for this, Neft could never forgive her; and then, he died. Poor, poor Neft. Some disease, illness he had picked up and he lingered for weeks, the doctor shaking his head and telling Anella it was just a question of time and so it was, one morning, he gave up the battle and slipped away quietly and uneventfully. She cried and cried, not really for Neft but for herself. What would she do? How would she manage?

Now, Anella, sitting on her bedroom floor, was enveloped in sadness. She felt such guilt. Neft was gone, and she was abandoning herself to a man she hadn't even met until a few months ago. She shook herself out of her reverie as she heard Eade call for her. He came along the corridor and found her, still sitting on the floor, a picture of abject misery. He sat down with her, not saying a word, just holding her hand and realising she was suffering a tumult of feelings. She cried then, and he held her close and kissed her gently.

"Nell, that life is over. Your new life is with me at Chilworth. Don't be sad, be excited. We are going to be good together. It's time we got going, leave the boys to it. Come."

He stood up and held out his hand.

CHAPTER THIRTEEN

Friday was an important day for Anella. Mrs Tichborne would be arriving with her daughter, Helena, to measure Anella and discuss wedding gowns, nightwear, evening wear, day wear and everything else that went with all these outfits.

Of course, Eade took charge. "I thought you could use the second reception room, it's warm in there and private and the light's good. I've been told I can't have anything to do with this dress. Is that right?"

"I'm afraid it is, Eade. The bridal gown has to remain a secret, that's the tradition."

He stuffed his hands in his pockets. "Well, good job I've got my tailor arriving, then. Mantel and I will be in the library from eleven. Remember, you will need your trousseau, a going-away outfit, holiday clothes; don't stint. Whatever you choose, double it. You're kitting yourself out for a new way of life." He came over to her and kissed her and he growled in her ear. "But we could go upstairs and take your clothes off now." He pressed her to him in a tight embrace, so she could feel the hardness of his body.

"Eade." He always made her laugh and she shifted her head, so he could nuzzle her neck. "You're naughty, and you will just have to wait."

She kissed him on his stubbly cheek and pulled the hair on the back of his neck. He was almost undone then and Anella, for two pins, would have dashed upstairs with him; but fate would inevitably intervene, so common sense, unfortunately, prevailed. She didn't want to let him go, but a footman knocked to say the dressmaker had arrived and was in the reception room waiting for Anella.

"See you for lunch, Nell." He let her go.

It didn't take long to get down to business with Mrs Tichborne and her daughter, Helena.

Boxes of beautiful fabrics: laces, ribbons, silver light, floaty fabrics for undergarments, heavy-duty tweeds for walking and riding and then, gossamer fine, shimmering films for evening wear – there were fabrics draped everywhere. Many day and evening gowns were chosen and ordered, gloves, shoes and little bags, set after set of underwear and nightwear, all very pretty and virginal, just perfect for Anella's trousseau and finally, the most important dress of all, the wedding gown. Miss Tichborne draped her in a deep ruby fabric, knubbly and darkly shining and drew Anella to the full-length glass arranged there by the house staff for her use this day.

"Oh!" Anella gasped. "This is so lovely."

She twirled and turned and nodded to say yes, this is the one; but Helena wasn't having it. Her mother produced a floaty green and gold lightweight roll and draped it over Anella's shoulder. This would make a delicious evening dress for her holiday, but not as a wedding outfit; but it was ordered anyway – another distraction! Helena then unrolled a length of smoky-blue, opalescent silk. As it caught the light, it changed colour from dark to light blue, from sky to turquoise. Mrs Tichborne held it to Anella's throat, and it made the blue of her eyes even bluer. It was perfect; no other fabric need be considered. So now it was down to style. The groom and Mr Buchanen, his attendant, would have no idea of the discussions, differences and plans that went into the styling and making up of this most important of gowns. It was to be slim-fitting, with a little bolero jacket with a mandarin collar and a poke of guipure lace at the V of the neck. So it was to be; and then, shoes to be made to match and two switches of this same fabric to be made into cravats for the gentlemen.

Later, Tilda arrived for her fitting. As Anella's attendant on the day, she needed to be appropriately attired in a suitably important outfit – and so it was chosen, in a complementary colour, and all the ladies expressed themselves pleased. Eventually, Mrs Tichborne and daughter departed, having arranged a first fitting the following week. Much clearing up needed doing and Tilda finally resumed her normal duties.

It was a late lunch that day, only the three of them, all house guests finally having left. Mr Buchanen and Eade were deep in conversation when Anella entered the small dining room.

Eade broke off. "Well, how did it go?"

"Oh, exhausting, but so exciting." She clasped her hands together and managed a sedate twirl around the floor. "So many. Gowns, frocks, dresses, outfits, suits, hats, shoes, gloves – dozens. All colours. I know you said I needed it all, so I've ordered it all." She finally turned to look at Eade mischievously. He looked surprised, shocked even.

"Careful, Eade," growled Mr Buchanen. "Whatever she says, double it and that'll be nearer the true amount."

She laughed and then became serious.

"You did say."

Eade held his hand up. "I know. I did. No matter. Mantel's just a troublemaker. Come on, let's eat. Ordering clothes and spending money is guaranteed to give one an appetite."

They had such a pleasant luncheon that day and most of the talk was about the wedding; more plans put into place. Every day, little things were fitting into the jigsaw and the great day was taking shape nicely.

CHAPTER FOURTEEN

The following weeks fell into a regular pattern, with Anella returning to her farm every week. Mrs Bosworth would be moving in with the rest of her brood and the house had to be arranged accordingly. Anella was pleased. At last, all the empty rooms would have a use. There would be noise, clutter and a busyness about the place which it hadn't had for many years. More excitingly, Ella, one of the farm dogs, had had a litter of pups, and Anella had arranged with Clance that she should have the pick of the litter as soon as they were old enough. She wanted two, one as a gift for Eade and the other as a companion for Mr Buchanen. He always struck Anella as a lonely man. A dog would be a good friend for him. It was arranged that the puppies would be collected the following week.

It became a ritual that Clem would accompany Anella when she attended her bees on her farm visits; not every week, but if the weather was right, it was important to instruct Clem on his duties. He must approach them clean, with no aromas, in light-coloured clothing, never anything heavy or dark. He must never be noisy or clumsy, but calm, quiet and gentle and talk to them in a low voice. Anella was aware that to be married in March, just as the bees' year was beginning, was very bad planning on her part, so she introduced Clem to the hive. He proved himself to be a quick and eager learner. He took great pride in his embryonic skills as a beekeeper. Anella was pleased: she was an apiarist of some renown, and she wished Clem to follow in her footsteps.

Back at Chilworth, her meetings with Mrs Tichborne

were carrying on apace. Quite a few gowns were finished and her trousseau was coming along nicely. The wedding dress was almost finished, the shoes completed and Anella wasted many minutes trying them on and walking up and down the bedroom and admiring them in the mirror.

The wedding holiday was planned. They would visit Italy, Venice being their first port of call. Eade reassured her she would love it. This was the place to buy leather handbags and shoes and Italian gifts, then they would visit the Murano glass factory, maybe purchase a chandelier or two. She was full of excitement over this trip but a little worried about the language difficulty. She had learned French with her governess, but never had the opportunity to practice, but Italian – how would they ever make themselves understood?! She hoped they might even have a trip on a gondola.

At eight weeks, the puppies were ready. Anella had watched them develop and had chosen a brave little male for Eade; he was feisty and unafraid and came to you, tail wagging and yapping incessantly. He wanted to interact with humans and when you stroked him, his little body writhed and wriggled with excitement. He would clamp his tiny, sharp teeth around your fingers and wouldn't let go. He was just the right dog for Eade. And for Mr Buchanen, the little female. Anella was concerned he would regard such a little dog as an insult to his manhood. She wasn't as brave as her brother, but, oh, she was just adorable, sweet-natured and a little bit shy, but she would become brave under Mr Buchanen's tutorage, Anella was sure. She had collected them from the boys earlier in the day and now they were curled together in a dog basket, hidden in the second reception room. Anella wanted the men to have their pups after lunch, so they had time to get used to their new surroundings. Coming from a line of working dogs, they would be hardy and accepting of a life lived outside, but that was a choice to be made by the men.

Anella heard the two arrive, in conversation with the factor. Eade and Mr Buchanen were keen to start up a dairy herd and once the wedding was over, those plans would begin.

"Gentlemen," Anella interrupted them. "Sorry to intrude, but I've got a surprise for you both."

Eade gave a nod of dismissal to the factor and he discreetly left them, the two men wondering what the secrecy could be.

"Will you both go to the library? I'll meet you there in a few minutes." Mr Buchanen glanced at Eade: not more wedding stuff, surely? With a barely contained sigh, he did as he was told and Eade, sensing his impatience, commented, "It's only once Mantel. It'll soon all be over, and we can get back to normal."

So they waited and within a few minutes, Anella was back, struggling with the large wicker basket.

Eade was leaning up against his desk, arms folded, one foot crossed over the other and Mantel had his back to them, looking out of the library window. Anella sensed they thought she was wasting their time.

She gave an important cough. "Gentlemen, look what I have for you," and she gently extricated the two lively puppies. "Eade, this one's for you, and Mr Buchanen, this littly is for you."

Oh my goodness, the atmosphere in the room changed immediately. Both the men were enchanted. Eade held his puppy up gently by its scruff. "Anella, what's his name? Hey, he's a brave little chap, look, he's not a bit afraid."

Mantel was quietly shaking his head. "Well, I've never seen anything so small. What sort have I got here?" He held her up. "A little lady. Well, I think her and I will get along just fine together."

He whipped off his tie and undid the top two buttons of his shirt and popped his little dog inside. There she would stay, comforted by the warmth of Mr Buchanen's body, and by his movements and his smells, she would get to know him and not miss her doggy family quite so much.

"What's her name, then?" he asked Anella.

"Neither are named. I thought I would leave that to you both. Are you pleased?" Anella's eyes were bright with excitement.

Unbelievably, Mr Buchanen came across the room and gave Anella a respectful kiss on her cheek and said gravely:

"You've made my day. I shall make sure she's a good, hard-working dog." He thought for a minute. "I'll call her Jess. Yep, that's it. She's to be Jess." And he fished her tenderly out of her cosy darkness. "I name you Jess Buchanen O'Kyan," and he planted a smacking kiss on her nose, which made her sneeze and everyone else laugh.

"Well, Eade? Any ideas for your little man?"

"Wife, he's going to be Ruff, because that's exactly what he is. Look, look at him, he's so rough and tumble." Eade was trying to remove the puppy's sharp little teeth from the cuff of his jacket. "Get off, you little devil!" he said and laughed. "This will mean a change of routine now in the mornings, Mantel, just for a while."

Mantel laughed in agreement. It certainly would.

CHAPTER FIFTEEN

As the weeks progressed, Anella's new wardrobe came on apace. Most outfits were finished and ready, the wedding gown being the last.

"Why do you leave the most important dress until the very last?" Anella asked Mrs Tichborne, who was kneeling at her feet, pulling gently at the hem of her dress.

Helena, her daughter, replied.

"Most brides lose a little weight leading up to the day. Nerves come into play, you know, so we leave it until the last possible moment. We want the best possible fit. After all, this is the dress of a lifetime. It has to be right and you have lost weight, you know. Look." She looked at Anella in the mirror and pulled the bodice to the side. "This will have to be taken in. Please try not to lose any more weight."

Mrs Tichborne, still on the floor, with a mouthful of pins, grunted in agreement.

"Well, one more fitting should see us done and then it'll be the big day. We will need a couple of your manservants to come and collect everything. It all has to be hung."

Helena began to gather everything up while her mother helped Anella out of her gown.

Anella thanked them cordially for all their hard work and looked forward to seeing them next week and left them in order to find the men. As was usual nowadays, they were both outside with the puppies. Mr Buchanen's Jess, if not ensconced inside his shirt, was often seen draped on the saddle of his heavy horse with a restraining hand to keep her safe. She was coming on apace and growing in confidence daily. She was becoming a devoted little dog and could not bear her master out of her sight. Where he went, she went, and it was lovely to see.

Eade, in order to align Ruff to him, had tied a pair of smelly socks around his neck for the first few days and then left them in his bedding. It was amusing to see the little dog bringing a sock to Eade as a gift. He was in no doubt as to who was his master and now, wherever Eade went, Ruff was there with him. Anella found it very satisfying to see how the men had bonded with their respective dogs.

The deep cold and bleakness of winter began to recede ; the snow melted to reveal the snowdrops, the village dew pond melted and February, usually the worst month of the year, became benign. Frequently, there were days of weak sunshine and springlike breezes. The nights were still early and long and exceedingly chill, but animals and humans could sense that spring was in the air.

As the wedding day drew nearer, arrangements had to be made for Anella to stay at Chilworth house, without Eade or any of the guests being aware that she was there and of course, she mustn't be seen by anyone. They had obeyed local custom and had not attended church to hear the banns being read, as it was considered bad luck. It was unthinkable that she should spend her last night at the farm; it was too cold and bleak, and Tilda could not stay there. Anella needed the bathing room also as part of her wedding preparations.

For a few days before the wedding, Anella and Eade hadn't met up; servants and friends had conspired to keep them apart. One chill, March, springtime morning, Anella slipped into the house by way of the servants' entrance, much to the surprise of the kitchen staff. By pre-arrangement, she was taken to a small, little-used room that had been Eade's mother's study. Since she passed away, the room was never used, but the domestic staff had been in and cleaned it and freshened the furnishings, flung open the windows and polished everything. Flowers were everywhere, as befitting a bride-to-be. It was a lovely room, and Anella was quite happy to spend the day there; the staff bringing in lunch and then afternoon tea and finally, when Eade and the guests assembled for dinner in the evening, she was sneaked upstairs to her rooms. Anella was truly shocked when she saw the amount of clothes she'd had made by the Tilbornes. Centre stage of course, was THE dress and it made Anella gasp. It was truly breathtaking. At first, she was almost over-whelmed and felt quite panicked, but Tilda's calm deliber-ations and common sense approach, soothed Anella. Tilda bought up a light meal and wine and, later, Anella bathed and was back ensconced in her room without any guest knowing she was there. She could hear them downstairs; they played games and Eade, as the groom, was subject to much ribaldry and risqué innuendo. Being Eade, he took it all in good heart and, of course, in spite of the subter-fuge, he was well aware that Anella was in his house. He had secretly arranged it with Tilda.

Anella sat quietly by the bedroom window; it was slightly open to let in a breath of air.

It was a moment of quiet reflection. If she had taken the solicitor's advice, she'd have sold up and never met Eade and wouldn't be sitting here in excitement about the morrow. In the evening darkness, she could hear birdsong. She caught her breath: how wonderful. A nightingale. It was entrancing, and Anella realised she would always remember this moment and that she was on the brink of a new life and all it had to offer. The song of the nightingale would stay with her for ever.

CHAPTER SIXTEEN

Excitement and anticipation had Anella awake early the following morning. A quick glance outside proved it would be a dry, fresh day. Not much wind by the look of it.

Superb, and a shiver coursed through Anella. This was going to be the most perfect of days, and from today, she would be Mrs Jameson, Mrs Eade Jameson, wife of one of the most respected and powerful men in the county. What a wonderful, wonderful life they were going to have together, and that life would start today. So when Tilda arrived discreetly with a breakfast tray, she was surprised to see Anella up and re-organising her wedding underwear and shoes and moving things unnecessarily on her dressing table.

"Here, Ma'am, your breakfast. Soft-boiled eggs and warm rolls from Mrs Harvey and a nice pot of tea. There's a few down for breakfast, not many, but the Major's told them he wants to leave by 10.15."

"Goodness, that early?"

"I think he's done it for you, Ma'am."

"Me?"

"Yes, Ma'am, so's you can use all your rooms without worry. No one here to see you, so you can relax a bit. I mean, I know you won't, but we don't have to keep hidden, do we?"

"Oh Tilda, he thinks of everything, doesn't he?"

While Anella breakfasted, the room was busy; two maids arrived to strip the bed and put fresh linen on for the bridal couple; a footman arrived with Champagne and glasses and even Mr Gillamoor arrived, very apologetic, doffing his cap and requesting that Tilda show the bouquet to "Her Ladyship" to confirm it was just what she wanted. It was and Anella stood and marvelled at the heady aroma and the exquisite beauty of the blooms.

CHAPTER SEVENTEEN

After downstairs breakfast, the passageway outside Anella's bedroom was busy: much coming and going, laughter and chatting. She could feel the guests' excitement, but this was an anxious time for Anella. It seemed an age before they all gathered downstairs to leave for the church. She watched them go and then rushed to bathe in her little private room, assisted by a young undermaid; not Tilda's job today. After all, she also had to get herself ready.

Mrs Tichborne and her daughter arrived, just as Anella flew to the window to secretly watch Eade and Mr Buchanen gather outside. If Anella was the swooning type then this was certainly the time for a full-blown swoon. Oh, both of them looked impossibly handsome: Mr Buchanen, only a little taller than Eade, but much broader and solid – if that's what eating porridge did for you, Scotland must be full of giants – but her Eade, tall and dark; she could see he was freshly shaved in an exceptional, impeccable dark suit. Both of them wearing the cravats to match her dress.

Anella couldn't wait, then, to get ready and no time was lost. Gown on, shoes on, and Mrs Tichborne pulling at the hem and her daughter Helena assiduously doing up every tiny hook and tweaking the fabric as she went. Then the little bolero jacket carefully on and the poke of Guipure lace at the neck adjusted. Anella could tell by the ladies' admiring glances that she looked beautiful. Tilda had brushed her hair and secured flowers there that matched those in her bouquet. Just as they were ready to leave, Tilda disappeared for a few minutes only to return with a small box, which she handed to Anella.

"The Major instructed me to give you this just before we leave," she said.

Oh! Anella knew this little gift was something precious and sure enough, nestled inside, was a gold necklace interspersed with the bluest of sapphires.

"Oh, Eade." She was almost in tears. A little note on vellum simply said, "For my wife, from her husband."

"Ma'am, let me put it on for you. Don't want to be late, do we?"

Very carefully, Tilda placed this most beautiful necklace around Anella's throat and stepped back for Anella to view herself in the full-length mirror. All the ladies gasped. "How can I look like this?" she thought to herself.

"Ladies, thank you so much. I NEVER in my life believed I could look, could…"

"Could look so beautiful." Mrs Tichborne's daughter finished for her.

"Shall we go?" ventured Tilda. They must get going before emotion overcame them all! She handed Mr Gillamoor's flowers to Anella and they were off, carefully down the wide staircase and even more carefully into the waiting carriage.

It was a chill day, and the slight breeze whipped colour into Anella's cheeks. They waved to the last few servants waiting in the cold to cheer her on her way, and she was overcome with trepidation and emotion.

Tilda, ever watchful today, whipped out of her bag a little bottle. "Ma'am, put a few drops of this under your tongue." Anella hesitated.

"Do it," Tilda insisted, "It will calm you. There's nothing harmful in it. It will make you beautifully calm. More rather than less."

Anella did as she was told. Although the day was cold, nerves were making her hot, but she was beginning to feel less anxious as they approached the church. The pealing bells suddenly stopped as their carriage drew up. As Anella cautiously alighted, she could hear the choir burst into song. This was to announce her arrival to the congregation. The three ladies busied themselves like moths to a flame, gently tweaking her dress and generally making sure she looked perfect. Suddenly, all was calm and she was ready. Quietly they entered the church to a fanfare of "The Arrival of the Queen of Sheba".

Mrs Tichborne and her daughter immediately took the back pew allocated for them, and Tilda followed Nell at a discreet and respectful distance, watching her carefully.

Anella was composed now and she focused on the upright figure of her husband-to-be.

My goodness! she thought; even from the back, the two men looked overwhelmingly masculine and dashing. She walked slowly, Tilda behind her. It seemed an agonizingly long walk, but suddenly, Eade, unable to contain himself any longer, turned and faced her full on. He spread his hands in wonderment at the sight of her and gave her such a smile. "Hurry up!" he mouthed at her and made a gesture of impatience, which caused a few giggles in the congregation. He then came halfway down the aisle to meet her and slipped his arm through hers. She needed that support. She was so grateful. Trust Eade, nothing intimidated him.

By this time, Mr Buchanen had turned also and was looking at her in wonderment. They approached the vicar, but Eade was still taking in Anella's appearance. For the first time, he saw THAT dress that matched his cravat. To say he was taken aback was an understatement. He noticed the necklace gently sparkling on her skin, the flowers in her softly folded hair. He was lost: that this woman condescended to be his wife…

And so the sacred ceremony began. Firstly words of

welcome and then, the importance of marriage and its place in the civilised world. Beautiful hymns were sung and then another, shorter sermon and finally their wedding vows, said with quiet resolution by them both. Mr Buchanen stepped forward with the ring and placed it on a velvet cushion; Eade then slipped it on Anella's finger with a quiet sense of relief. He'd had this constant worry that it wouldn't fit.

Eade never once took his eyes off his new bride and Anella was almost overcome by the significance of their marriage vows. It was akin to a religious awakening.

Then more hymns and a final blessing, and suddenly it was over and they were being sung out of the church, the bells peeling. Hand in hand, they hastened to the waiting carriage, which was festooned with garlands and flowers – and so were the horses.. Four footman held a balachin aloft to protect them from the elements and to announce to the world what an important couple they were.

They were first away, bowling along, the coloured plumes on the horses' heads rippling in the breeze; an air of excite-ment between them, the new Mr and Mrs Jameson. The servants had dashed home ahead of them in order to prepare for their arrival; and it was as they drew up, the servants had the glasses of Champagne and canapes ready. Major Jameson and his wife stood in the grand entrance hall to greet their guests and there was such noise and happiness, much handshaking and good wishing and much Champagne drunk before the Master of Ceremonies thumped his staff on the wooden floor to announce the wedding breakfast was served and would the guests please make their way. He held his hand up to Eade and Anella to indicate they were to stay where they were. When everyone was settled, he collected his bridal couple and stood in the doorway to announce: "Would everyone be upstanding for Mr and Mrs Jameson?"

On entering the eating room, there was a wave of clapping

and cheering. Anella was amazed and clutched Eade's arm; as his wife, she could do this openly now. The day passed as in a dream, the food was endless and delicious; the speeches made by Mr Buchanen and then brother-in-law Harold were hilarious and many secrets of Eade's revealed that he'd rather have kept secret. Cake cutting next, more funny speeches, more Champagne drunk. Such happiness. Only after all of this did Eade and Anella find time for a few minutes alone together. Guests were everywhere and the children ran amok outside, free at last from the constraints of dining. They slipped into Eade's study and held each other in a close embrace, and before they could even have a kiss, a footman knocked on the door.

"Pardon me, Sir, but the dancing can't begin without you." He looked at them both.

"We'd better go then." Eade smiled and took his wife's hand to lead the way. Once again, as they entered the room, there was a great noise and much foot stamping and demands that they attend the dance floor. So Eade, good husband that he was, swept his beautiful bride off her feet and whisked her dangerously fast around the room. Anella was convulsed with giggles and her husband, not one to be bound by convention, ordered Anella to place her feet on his, as this was the only way she would be able to keep up the frantic pace. Everyone was quick to join in the fun, and it wasn't long before the room was filled with adults and children, dancing merrily.

Later in the evening, everyone congregated outside to watch the firework display.

It was a still, cloudy evening, no visible moon, so it was very dark and the guests, wrapped up warmly now in shawls and capes, sipped cups of hot chocolate and brandy.

There was lots of excited chatter, when suddenly, a huge rocket exploded in the sky, surprising everyone. They were hypnotised and it was at this moment Eade put his finger to his lips and signalled to Anella to be quiet. He grabbed her hand and stealthily stole back into the house. Quickly, they sneaked through the servants' secret doorway and made haste upstairs to Anella's room.

Oh, her room was wonderful: flowers everywhere. There was an ice bucket of Champagne, a little tray of Mrs Harvey's chocolates and the decanters of port and brandy. The fire was gently crackling in the grate and the bed was turned back invitingly. Anella's bridal nightgown was full-length and floaty, the lace gossamer fine and delicate and very, very pretty. Tilda had laid it out for her with a matching robe.

Eade closed the door firmly and, without saying a word, grabbed Nell and nuzzled her neck passionately. She could feel his hot breath and his intensity made her shiver.

"Eade, undo my dress," Nell gasped, urgent now. She turned her back to him. "Be careful," she chided, as Eade, in his haste, was not as careful as he should be. To Nell, this wedding dress was very precious. He lovingly slipped it from her shoulders and Nell stepped out of it as it fell to the floor. She stood there in her chemise, nervous, but full of anticipation.

She lifted the hem of the flimsy garment to deliberately entice Eade. "Look at my wedding stockings. Aren't they lovely?" He didn't reply, just looked. "Well?" She looked at him, biting her lip nervously.

He closed his eyes. "Nell, sit," he managed to say and guided her to the bed and knelt before her. Her legs were encased in gossamer-fine silk with lacy garters, above which was a tantalising glimpse of plump white flesh. Eade was mesmerised and ran his hand up her thigh and, slipping a finger between her leg and the fabric, gently, oh so gently, pulled the stocking down over her knee and calf, then carefully over her ankle and foot. He crumpled the stocking up tightly and shoved it deep into a pocket of his trousers, before running his hands over her leg and caressing her foot and pulling on her toes. He touched the fine skin at the back of her knee and then, on up to her thigh, squeezing her soft flesh. Oh! Nell was quivering in anticipation, but Eade was not for rushing. He kissed the top of her thigh, a light little butterfly kiss which made Nell's stomach contract, and then he repeated his ritual on her other leg. She lay back on the downy pillows, feeling his hands on her body. She wanted to get his clothes off, to feel him hard against her, to get him ready for action with no delays. Together, they quickly removed all his wedding finery; Nell was beside herself with desire, and she was writhing in anticipation as Eade kissed her thighs up to her mound of Venus. She grabbed his shoulders, wanting desperately for him to enter her, but no. He ran his stubbly face over her belly, whispering her name again and again and then, buried his face in her navel, his hands kneading her full bum. Eade knew this was bringing her to the point of no return; her body was shivering. She ran her fingers through his hair, not wanting him to stop, aching for him to do more. She guided his face to her breasts; she knew, if he touched her there, kissed her there, suckled her there, she would come and feel that welcome muscular tightening and then, loosening, again and again and she would spasm out of control.

"Eade, please," she begged. She arched her back in exquisite pleasure as Eade finally latched onto a nipple. She couldn't wait any longer. She grasped his manhood and pushed herself onto him. She put her legs up around his buttocks. She couldn't speak, only gasp, and there was no stopping either of them now. They were moving to a rhythm and Eade was knocking the breath from her body. Nell, head thrown back, was tipping over the edge when Eade came in a powerful ejaculation. "Fuck!" he gasped and Nell sailed away then, her body bucking out of control. She was in exquisite agony, almost to the point of losing consciousness.

"Oh, Oh, Oh!" she shouted, and she clung to Eade as if she was falling back to reality.

Eade was stilled. He lay on top of her, waiting. She grabbed his shoulders and repeated his name over and over in wonderment. She could feel his hot breath on her neck and ear and his hands on her body. She could smell him and she kissed him gently and nuzzled into his neck. She tightened her vaginal muscles to stop him slipping away and it worked. He stayed put and she loved him so much for that. Eade was perfectly content to let Nell do with him as she wished, and this afterplay was very desirous to her. There was a quietness, a gentleness, an even closer intimacy; their whole world was here, in them, in their bodies. They kissed; stroked and touched; explored and caressed without sexual desire for a few minutes. And then Eade grabbed a fistful of hair and pulled it roughly so she had to raise her head to him and he kissed and kissed her face and shoulders, a thousand tiny pin-pricks of his stubble on her skin. He pulled on her ear lobes and pressed his soft lips on hers, his tongue tickling her mouth. They were waiting and it was exciting, the waiting. They knew they would come together soon.

Sure enough, second time around, Eade's arousal was quicker, more violent and demanding, and Nell met him all the way. There were no preliminaries, no foreplay; they were ready in minutes. This sex was greedy, dirty; painful and animalistic. Sexual lust overtook them both. Nell was astride Eade, her hips grinding onto his hips; she came, loudly, and that was all Eade needed to power up into her. He was left gasping and growling under his breath. He bit down hard on her shoulder.

"Fucking hell!" he laughed.

He grabbed Nell's bum and gently slid her onto the bed beside him and held her close. She was still trembling from sexual excess.

They lay together for a few minutes beyond words. There would be very little sleep, if any, this night as, already, Eade was whispering dirty words in her ear and exploring her with his fingers.

"Oh Eade," she groaned, opening herself up for him.

By morning, they were exhausted and jubilant.

Tilda knocked and came in with an early breakfast, which Eade fed to Nell and ate the remainder himself quickly, as they had to get dressed in their wedding outfits. Eade was ready within a few minutes, not quite so immaculate as yesterday, but he still managed to look incredibly handsome, albeit, a little tired…

It took Nell a little longer, but Tilda managed to pin her hair up with a ribbon of wedding dress fabric. She looked just as lovely this morning as she did yesterday, albeit a little tired…

Nell had no idea what was happening; she was just doing what Eade instructed. They were away down the stairs and out the back to a waiting carriage and were off at speed.

"Eade?" she questioned. "Where are we going?"

"Church. We're going to do it all over again, just you and me. No one else there, only the vicar." He kissed her ring hand

"Oh Eade!" She was overjoyed.

CHAPTER EIGHTEEN

The church was cold and the vicar wasted no time in repeating their marriage vows. For Nell, it was truly magical. Eade never took his eyes from her face. Oh, how she loved him.

After they were pronounced man and wife, Eade gave her a chaste kiss and asked the vicar if he would come back for breakfast. It would be a noisy, happy meal, just like yesterday, Eade knew. The vicar accepted with alacrity, so they would see him back at the house.

They set off at a spanking pace and it was exhilarating, the wind whipping colour into their cheeks. Nell was high on excitement, and within a short space of time, they were back at Chilworth House creeping in the back entrance, to the surprise of the servants, and up the servants staircase to their room. The maids had been in already and the bed was freshly made and the fire crackling away. Eade, man of action that he was, lost no time in divesting himself and Nell of their clothes and laying with her on their bed.

"Nell, what are we going to do?" he asked – meaning, how could he stop this sexual roundabout they were on? After all, one day, however unwelcome, they would have to face real life and get out of bed in the mornings and ignore each other.

"Eade." She touched his face and pulled the curls at the back of his neck. "I know what I'm going to do."

She turned to him and pressed her body to his and took his hand, pulling each of his fingers before placing it on her bum. Eade, obliging, squeezed and kneaded her soft flesh and gave in, burying his face in her neck. She was touching him, gently pulling on his manhood, insistent and demanding. He felt that now familiar spark ignite within him and he roughly turned her over, making her kneel, so he could clasp and part her bum in order to enter her from behind.

"Eade," Nell gasped. He was rough, and this excited her beyond measure. He was in, hard, quick and fast and urgent, his skin smacking against hers, her breasts swinging to the rhythm of their coupling. She was coming, oh God, her thighs cramping, the muscles in her stomach convulsing.

"Eade." He couldn't help her, being lost in his own climax.

"Nell" he shot inside her and collapsed on her back. She couldn't sustain his weight and fell, helplessly onto the bed, giggling with the sheets and pillows all around her. Eade fell with her and they lay in a tangle of limbs, not caring. As was the way with them, they crooned, softly, his lips on hers, biting softly and rubbing his face on her face. Nell cuddled him like a baby and pulled on the hair at the back of his neck, eventually drifting off to sleep – for how long, she had no idea. She was woken by Eade biting her neck.

"Are you hungry?" he asked, turning his mouth to her collarbone.

"Silly! Of course, I'm starving." She grabbed his face and nibbled his mouth; her tongue licked his lips.

"Nell, no." He tried to move his face, not trying very hard. "Nell, leave me woman," he laughed. She was irresistible and insatiable, and he loved her beyond measure.

"Nell." He looked her in the eye while slipping his hand down her belly and tickling her belly button.

"Eade, do you know – for a minute, I thought you were going to disappoint me. I should have known better; you are such a good boy!"

She lay on her back and welcomed him in and another hour was spent lost in each other Nell touching and tickling him, licking her fingers and manipulating him and Eade, far gone, lay back and watched her in wonderment. She saddled him then, her eyes dark with lust, her hands on his chest, pulling at him and thrusting her hips relentlessly up and down. He could feel her coming, if he could only hold on! No! He was there, his body unstoppable. He grabbed onto Nell as she orgasmed.

She made him feel week and helpless, but she fell on him then, laughing at him and, pulling his ears, kissed his face.

"Eade, do you think we ought to get up? We've been here nearly all morning."

"Is that all? We're celebrating, aren't we? What have we to go downstairs for? Are you hungry for food this time? We'll get Tilda to bring lunch up. I could feed you." He rolled her off him and looked at her. "Nell, you are so lovely. I could eat you." He gazed at her lovingly.

She raised her head, exposing her neck. "Start here, please," she grinned at him.

"Nell, I don't want to go downstairs. Shit, it's our honeymoon." He pulled the cord. "We'll have lunch here and Tilda can draw a bath." He shrugged on his robe and he threw Nell's at her, so she could make herself decent in front of the servants.

And because Eade was the boss, they had a long, lazy lunch, Eade feeding Nell the tastiest morsels. It was very sexual. Nell felt Eade would have chewed the food for her if he could. They drank far too much wine, Champagne, and then, afterwards, brandies. Eade kissed her with a mouthful and nearly choked her, which set off a fit of giggles between the two of them.

They bathed together, the little room candlelit and warm, Eade's muscular body wrapped around Nell, one long leg over hers. He soaped her, then rinsed her, then bit her neck and then her shoulders. He carefully rubbed behind her ears and raised her arms to wash her armpits, which aroused him immensely. He had a thing about armpits. He cupped each breast and was very particular and gentle in cleansing her there and then made her kneel up with her back to him, so he could soap her bum. He was tickling her and because she was slippery and wet, she was easy to enter. Eade thought she was like a woman who hadn't had a man in years. She was moving in tune with him as waves of water cascaded onto the floor.

"Eade, more," she demanded, and Eade, ever one to oblige, pulled her even closer so she could have all of him. It didn't take long. Nell could feel Eade's body along her back and felt him convulse just as she climaxed. She could only gasp, being beyond words, and Eade could only hold on tight. He closed his eyes in ecstasy.

It was with great reluctance they agreed they really should go down for dinner. With a houseful of guests, they had to make an appearance. Nell, with Eade's help, dressed very carefully. Her husband's attentions meant her neck and shoulders needed to be covered, so a dress had to be chosen accordingly. Even dressing had its hazards for Nell. Eade couldn't keep his hands to himself; he was touching her, tickling her, squeezing her in rude places. He had no reservations. She was his wife and if he wanted her, he would take her; sod everyone else, he thought, until Nell reasoned with him and made all sorts of wild promises for later, if only he would leave her alone long enough to get through dinner, but he insisted on helping her dress.

Eade tutted with impatience.

"God, you women wear so many clothes. What do you need all these layers for?" He was struggling to lace Nell's bodice.

"Eade, leave it, you're not a patch on Tilda. I'll give this

a miss tonight, but if you could unlace me, I'll take it off."
She stood with her back to him. Oh dear!

Apart from being unable to help with Nell's dressing, he was completely unable to resist Nell's womanly curves. He pulled her towards him and gently kissed her back, running his lips up and down and softly kissing her shoulder.

"Eade, no!"

"Nell, yes!" he growled and turned her to face him. He pulled her close, so she could feel his body.

"Eade," she whispered, "we have to go downstairs."

"Yes, we do," he agreed, burying his head on her breast, pulling her underwear down her body. She knew she could not stop him, but no point giving in too easily.

She attempted to push him away. "No, Eade," she said firmly. "No."

She was grabbing her underwear, trying to cover herself up. He laughed and enveloped her in a bear hug and swung her round.

"Nell." His voice was husky with desire. "Shame to waste this fire." He pulled her down and was roughly dragging her clothes off her.

"Naked, Nell," he ordered and she gave in then and slipped what remained of her underwear away and lay back on the rug.

She looked at him disapprovingly and coyly, crossed her arms to cover her breasts.

"Nell, you're playing with me." He was glowering at her. "Don't do it."

She gave him a "come hither" smile then and uncrossed her arms and Eade, like a man possessed, delightedly took his wife in front of a brightly glowing fire.

They finally managed to get downstairs for dinner, and there was much cheering and clapping as they entered the eating room. The men stamped their feet on the floor, making a great noise and Eade, without embarrassment, acknowledged their approval of his and his wife's non-appearance for the whole day. Nell was mortified and kept her head down, but Eade squeezed her hand and looked at her quizzically. Why this silly shyness? Everyone in this room envied them. He was proud of his wife and himself. He thought he was a bit of a stud…

Nevertheless, the evening was wonderful; so much chat about their forthcoming trip to Italy. Eliza, especially, craved to travel and Italy was one country she would especially like to visit.

Nell noticed Merissa de Haas was making great play for Mr Buchanen, and he seemed to be responding. It was good to see him coming out of his reclusiveness. He was a man of seriousness and gravitas, but Nell didn't really believe he was such. His memory loss made him so. Underneath was an enlightened, entertaining man just needing to get out. Was Merissa the right female for him? She was flighty and Nell thought her a bit shallow, but inwardly – she shrugged her shoulders – who knew?

Nell also noticed Lady Helen's daughter, Daphne, was making great progress in her pursuit of Edward Bussey. The pair were preoccupied with each other and Lady Helen was not too pleased over this state of affairs, but the Busseys were a very wealthy family and at the end of the day, money counted. Daphne would be much happier if she were married with no concerns over finances. Lady Helen was a firm believer you could not be hard up and happy. Ridiculous! So she was coming round, gradually.

Such was the cordial atmosphere around the table that evening, the gentlemen didn't leave the ladies for their port and cigars. They sat helping themselves to the Stilton and other cheeses and drinking the port. The men pretended to be alarmed at the ladies liking for Eade's port.

"Better double your order next time from Berry Brothers." Harold winked at Eade, which made him laugh, thinking of Nell's ability to knock back a glass in one.

"Well, if Nell has a son for me, I'll lay down a pipe for him – I'll keep it at Berry's, not here, but I will increase my cellar; but can you see it, Harold, the ladies sneaking down to my cellars at night, not for a love tryst but for my bloody port?' There was much laughter around the table at this.

"Eade, you know, we're off tomorrow. Just want to say, old man, this has been lovely. Best wedding, thoroughly enjoyed it. My pack get on so well with Nell, it's nice to see, and I think Eliza and your wife are becoming firm friends. It's just what Eliza needs; I think she ought to mix more, but there we are." He paused reflectively.

"Harold, you know, you're always welcome. It's nice to have this place full of life, the children make it so. Nell loves them and besides, what's the point of all this –" he waved his arms expansively – "if it's not used? Anyway, you know, we're setting up a dairy herd and you're the expert, so I expect to see a lot of you, if only to give us good advice." He looked round the table. "Do you ladies mind if we smoke?" He beckoned to a waiting footman. "Helena," he called down the table where there was deep conversation with the Busseys. "We're smoking."

The footman returned with the humidor and then the brandy appeared and some of the gentlemen agreed to play cards. Eade refused, holding his hands up in refusal.

"Gentlemen, sorry, my wife says I'm looking a bit peaky, not getting enough sleep, you know how it is."

There were roars of laughter at this and so they left him alone. The ladies soon retired to their rooms. The Busseys and the de Hasses would be leaving in the morning, so there would be much to do. Of course, once the eating room emptied, Eade lost no time in getting Nell upstairs, leaving the card players to it.

Sitting in front of their bedroom fire with brandies, Eade remarked: "Tomorrow will be a strange day, won't it? The house will seem strange. What will we do with ourselves all day?" he looked at Nell shyly.

She laughed, "Take up a new hobby, I suppose, I could dry flowers. You could collect butterflies."

He looked at her and patted his knee. "Come, Nell. I know what my new hobby will be."

She put down her brandy and came and sat on Eade's lap. He shifted slightly. "Bloody hell, woman, you're heavy."

Nell was stung. "Eade, that's not very gentlemanly! I can't help it if I weigh a ton. I've just eaten a four-course meal and drunk a lot of liquid and we all know, liquids weigh heavy. It's your fault, I blame you, you're not giving me enough exercise." She snuggled into him. "Maybe I should go on a reducing regime. We could do it together, you know, boiled fish, no wine, just water, oh and boiled greens. You'd love it, Eade." She placed a hand on his cheek.

Eade was horrified. "Lose weight? I forbid you. No living skeletons in this house, thank you. No wine? Can you imagine! Not do-able." He buried his head on her chest. "Let's go to bed, wife, and get some exercise." He sniffed her. "You smell good," he said and with that, he managed to lift his wife and stand up and carry her to their bed and there divest her of her clothes, much to his delight, and Nell's.

Over and over, they made love that night; Eade just couldn't leave her alone. He touched her, caressed her. He felt her, squeezed her, kissed her, rubbed her, put his fingers in all those intimate places that he knew would excite Nell and make her weak with want. He nuzzled her belly, sucked her breasts, licked her armpits while Nell curled up with laughter and pretended to fend him off. Even after loving, they lay in sated silence, Nell stroking Eade's body, unable to leave him alone and Eade, regaining his libido, waited, for he knew, given time, he would be ready to service Nell again and she would love it and welcome him in. How would he ever sleep? Nell was everything. Never had he expected their married life to be like this. He lay on his side, head propped on his hand, looking at Nell. She wasn't asleep, just laying still, knowing Eade was admiring her body. She was tender and well used, and instead of making her tired, it spiked her up. The more Eade wanted her, the more she needed him. They didn't sleep until day was dawning, an exhausted tumble of limbs.

The house gradually emptied over the next few days and the servants settled back into their usual routine.

Eade spent one morning in the library with his solicitor, then Mr Buchanen was called in, then the factor, then the land agent and the farm manager. They were together all morning, not appearing until lunchtime. When they finally emerged, Eade went in search of Nell to inform her they were having an informal lunch; did she want to join them or eat in her study?

"I don't think it would be seemly, would it?" she asked. "All you men and just me?"

"Nell, they would love you. You'd change the subject for us. We've talked nothing but dairy herds all morning, Oh, and my will."

"Your will? Why?"

"Well, I'm married now, things have changed. I have to make provision for you, should anything happen to me. All standard stuff, nothing to worry about." He smiled and placed his hand in the small of her back to guide her to the eating room.

CHAPTER NINETEEN

That afternoon, Nell met Eade in the library.

"I thought I'd go to the farm tomorrow. You'll be on your own, will you mind?"

"Nell, we're picking up the heifers tomorrow. Me, Buchanen, the stockman, the factor maybe, maybe not. We weren't going 'til next week, but it all falls into place quite nicely, if we go tomorrow. You can spend all day there if you want to, we won't be home 'til late. It's strange, isn't it, the house empty?"

"Oh Eade, I'm missing the children already."

"Yep, I know. It's nice to have them, nice to see them go, always nice to have them back. I like the house busy, you know what I mean?"

"Yes, I know what you mean."

Eade looked meaningfully at Nell. "The house is empty."

"Yes, Eade, I know."

"Well," he came close; she could feel the warmth of his body.

"Nell." He touched her, then placed his hands on her shoulders and drew her close. "Nell." He pulled her even closer, so he could feel her. He bent to kiss her neck. "Nell." He was nuzzling her now and embracing her tightly. "Nell," a whisper, "we could go upstairs and celebrate!"

She laughed. "Are we still on our wedding holiday, then?"

He looked at her amazed. "OF COURSE WE ARE." He took her hand. "Nell, let's go upstairs, otherwise I will have to take you on the library desk and that will be messy."

He kissed her passionately and lifted her up. He would not be denied and Nell, secretly, was as needy as he. If he wanted her, then she wanted him and her insides melted at the thought of him needing her.

So, in haste, they made their way upstairs to their bedroom and Eade was quick to disrobe. Nell watched him delightedly, but needed Eade to unhook her gown. She liked him to do this. It was a voyage of discovery. Her dress would slip to the floor, she would stand there, in a state of semi-undress, more or less inviting Eade to touch her, and of course, he did. He buried his head in her breasts and kissed her there tenderly, whilst running his hands under her petticoat and squeezing her thigh.

"Eade," she sighed, taking his bottom lip in her mouth and biting him ever so gently. If she bit him, then he bit her, her neck, her shoulders, her breasts and then, down to her hips, biting all the way. She writhed underneath him.

"Eade, please," she whispered and because she couldn't wait any longer, she grabbed him and moved his skin up and down ever so gently. She was opening herself up to him and desperately desired him to come into her. She was having these feelings, rising and rising inside her; her back arching, her legs trembling, she needed to orgasm. Eade's back received the brunt of her frustrations; she scratched him, beat him, bit hard down on his shoulder and, oh, she could feel him come inside her, which sparked her into a seismic convulsion, again and again.

Oh, how she loved this. Eade knew now what she needed and once they had achieved it once, then Nell demanded it again and again.

They lay, naked, entwined, still needy, Eade waiting, knowing it was only a matter of time, and Nell, unable to keep her hands from him, stroked him softly, nuzzling his belly, teasing him as to what she would do to him when he was ready. He pulled her on top of him, so her breasts were on his chest and her belly pressing on his belly and her womanhood laying on his manhood.

The following morning, the men were up and out early. There was much noise and confusion, the dogs running around and barking. The two puppies, Ruff and Jess, were being left behind with Nell, it was far too far for them to walk, but oh my goodness, the crying and whining when they realised they were not going. Nell could only pop them into an improvised pen, with Eade's socks as a comfort.

Nell made all haste then. She wanted back to her farm, not only to see the twins and the work they had done – they were always improving something – but also to go through the house with Mrs Bosworth, to see if she agreed with Nell as to what needed to be done to many of the rooms. So she left Chilworth House not long after the men, off in the gig at a spanking pace, the wind whipping colour into her cheeks and blowing her hair awry. Although they were heading into spring, the weather had become much colder. Nell was grateful she had wrapped up warmly. She hoped Mrs Bosworth was keeping the house warm, as Nell had asked.

Sure enough, the kitchen was welcoming, the range gently glowing in the alcove and the smell of baking bread wafting through the boot room as Nell was divesting herself of her heavy, outdoor clothes. Mrs Bosworth immediately put the heavy kettle on to boil; the boys would be in shortly for their break and she whipped out of the oven, two loaves of bread and a seeded cake. Of course, the twins came in, in a great rush of cold air and noise. My goodness, they had come on, thought Nell; they must have grown a good inch and filled out. Their voices had deepened considerably. Nell was proud of them; goodness knows what their mother thought.

It was lovely for Nell to sit in her old kitchen. It was all shabby and familiar and cosy, and she felt so much more comfortable sitting at her battered table of all work, than she did at Chilworth. She felt a sadness; how she would love to live here with Eade. She sighed. It was not to be: as Haswell Farm was loved by her, Chilworth was cherished by Eade. Morning break over, Mrs Bosworth and Nell toured the bedrooms and Nell had to admit, they looked very shabby. Threadbare rugs, sun-bleached curtains, the old furniture looking very dull indeed. Every room needed decorating and maybe the window frames needed attention. They were oak, though, thought Nell. She would like one of the smaller rooms to be a dedicated room for bathing, just like at Chilworth. *Maybe on the main staircase; we could have carpet.* The back stairs didn't matter, only the servants used those in the old days. Yes. Much needed to be done. She would have a lot to tell Eade when he was back.

She left much later than she intended; the light was failing, so she made haste and got back just before the rain. She scooped up the puppies and took them into the house and spent a pleasant twenty minutes playing with them in front of the fire in the drawing room.

She could hear noise outside and rushed out to see a posse on horseback, all the men and the shuffle and that transference of heat that you get from a group of animals. *Oh, my goodness,* thought Nell, *so many.* The dogs were working tirelessly and yapping and instructions were being given to waiting farm workers. This was an exciting moment for Eade. This was the start of their dairy herd.

The farm workers had been hedging and ditching for days and repairing and replacing fencing in order to contain the cattle; the posse had had a long, hard day in the saddle. Nell dashed into the kitchen and arranged for the men's food to be served up in one of "back" rooms. Within a short space of time, a buffet table had been set up and laid with

food bowls, cutlery, baskets of bread, great mounds of potatoes and casseroles of beef and vegetables. Nell went back
outside and shushed the talking men in for food. Such a
smell in that room! They smelt of animals, of outdoors, of
fresh air. Nell retreated and left them to it and asked for her
meal to be served in the small eating room. She ate alone
and couldn't wait for Eade and Buchanen to come and tell
her everything.

CHAPTER TWENTY

"So what have we got?" Nell asked.

"Heifers," said Mr Buchanen shortly.

"Man! Take no notice of him, Nell. We've got dairy shorthorns, some white, some roan, thirty five and two Red Polls." Eade shrugged his shoulders and laughed. "They were there, so why not?"

"So what happens now?"

"We'll let them settle down for a while now, then we'll get the bull man to service the heifers."

Nell laughed out loud at this. "Really?"

"Well, we'll get Mr Graves across with his British White. We've spoken to him already." Eade had to smile. "I have to say, they're much bigger than I expected. If they're in calf within the next month, how long will it take, roughly?"

Mantel rubbed his chin. "Mmmm, do you know, I'm not sure, no, hold on," he pursed his lips, "maybe nine months, two hundred odd days, maybe?" He looked at Eade questioningly. "Another useless fact remembered."

Eade had to laugh. "Mantel, why is it you can he relied on to remember all the rubbish, but not anything of any use to you?"

"God knows." Mr Buchanen shook his head in frustration. "Never mind. I just hope it comes back one day."

"Eade, did I tell you, Mr Graves rents land from me? Fifty odd acres."

Eade was surprised "Really? He pays you? Do you have any other sources of income you're not telling me about? Maybe you have more money than me?"

"Well, the twins pay me a peppercorn rent for the farm.

When they actually start to make money, then the rent will increase. You won't make money out of me, I'm afraid."

"Listen, let the factor deal with this sort of thing. It's not for you to deal with matters like that. Mantel, I'd like the heifers sorted before we go away, so it's all done and dusted. I'll just concentrate on our holiday and nothing else."

Nell was indignant. "But it was my matter!"

"Yes, but not now," Eade said impatiently. "It's unbecoming. Don't worry, the money will still be yours. I won't take it, although it would come in handy!" he joked, looking at Mr Buchanen.

"You men are infuriating, really. I had to cope with everything when I was on my own. Now I'm married, I'm apparently helpless." Nell shrugged her shoulders with impatience.

Mr Buchanen stood up, he turned to Eade and nodded. "I'll say Goodnight, let you two get on with your arguing. I'll speak to Mr Graves tomorrow." He touched his forelock and left.

Eade came to Nell then. "Sorry, Nell, I don't want you occupied with money matters. You deal with how you want your farm run and leave the money side to me." He held her close and kissed her head. *So be it,* thought Nell.

Their days fell into a regular pattern. Mr Buchanen announced Mr Graves would be arriving the following week, so Eade suggested, diplomatically, that maybe Nell would like to spend the day at her farm. Naturally, Eade and Nell were still very ardent in bed, but that didn't mean Eade wanted her to witness the bull with the heifers!

After evening dinner, sitting before the fire with Mr Buchanen, brandies for the men and a port for Nell, Eade was talking enthusiastically about their forthcoming wedding holiday.

"Nell, you will love Venice, the square, the canals, the whole atmosphere, lots of stuff to buy."

Nell was indignant. "Stuff? Stuff! I never buy stuff! No, I don't want souvenirs. I want the more cultural side of thing: you know, museums, art galleries, sailing on a gondola."

At this, Eade almost choked with laughter. Even Mr Buchanen was chuckling.

"Ah, of course, Nell, sailing. Is it. a particular pastime of yours?"

Nell had to laugh, realising somewhere in her statement she'd made a bloomer "Is a gondola not a boat, then?" she guessed.

Mr Buchanen said, "Don't be misled by your husband, Mrs Jameson; a gondola is a rare type of bird, not often seen." He lowered his face into his brandy balloon, studying his drink.

"Why is it," Nell asked, I get the feeling, you two are having me on?"

"Nell, never," Eade replied, mock surprise on his face.

"WELL, TELL ME. A gondola, is it a boat? Or a bird?" she turned to Mr Buchanen and looked at him hard. "Mr Buchanen, I wouldn't like to think you are making fun of my ignorance. Or you, Mr Jameson." She turned to look at Eade.

Mr Buchanen dissolved into laughter. "Mrs Jameson, I'm sorry."

Eade jumped in then. "Mantel, how could you?" he asked in mock outrage. "Nell, take it from me, a gondola is a type of glass-blower; skilled man, expert in glass, honestly." Nell could tell by his over eager expression that he was deceiving her.

She had to laugh. "You men." She shook her head. "Neither of you are telling me the truth, so, I'm off to bed – and I hope in the morning, one of you will tell me the truth.

Goodnight, gentlemen." She smiled at them both, to take the sting out of her words.

Upstairs, she knew, those two would sit and sup their brandies and joke over her mistake. Eade would not be up for a long time.

And so it was.

Nell, snuggly asleep, was woken by a selfish, needy husband, who thought nothing of disturbing her slumber. He spooned his body around hers and nuzzled her neck. He smelled of brandy and cigars.

"Nell," he whispered.

Nothing. She feigned sleep.

"Nell," more urgently.

No.

"Nell, it's not like you to sulk. Just trying to apologise, that's all." He laughed and blew hot breath on her shoulder.

She turned. "Mr Jameson, just because I'm ignorant! I've a good mind to withhold your privileges."

He was quiet for a minute. "Nell, you'd never do such a thing, would you, really?" He squeezed her tighter. "You'd never be that cruel." He ran his hand over her hip and gently kneaded her bum. "Ah, Nell, that's you, being provocative." He ran his fingers over her belly and pubic mound and watched her reaction.

"Eade," she whispered, taking him into her hands. "Stop teasing. You haven't even given me a kiss yet."

She parted her lip and showed him the tip of her tongue. He was quick then and nipped it with his teeth, not hurting her, but not letting go. He was laughing and so was she. He let her go and turned his attention to her nipples.

"Oh Eade," she clutched his hair and pushed him onto her. She was moving under him; he well knew she wanted him to enter her, but he was teasing this night.

"Oh no, Nell, not yet," he growled low

"What? You come in here, wake me up and now, keep me waiting? Oh no, Mister."

She attacked him then, biting his ear, taking his lower lip in her mouth, love-biting his neck and pulling on his pubic hair and enfolding him in her soft hands. He surrendered to her completely and whatever she demanded, he did. Afterwards, as was usual with them now, they lay and talked silly love talk, and touched and stroked, their mouths so close, they were breathing each other's breath. Not a lot of sleep, but a lot of fun for them both. Nell knew, greedy as they were, once was never enough, so there was a busy night ahead. Eade held her close and gave a satisfied sigh. "Nell," he whispered, "I like sailing your boat."

The following week, Nell made ready early to visit her farm. She knew Mr Graves would be arriving soon to leave his bull, a British White, according to Eade. The heifers were bulling, so the sooner Nell was out of the way, the better.

It was a clear, still day, weak spring sunshine; today would be a good day for a spring inspection of her hives and make sure the boys were keeping up her standards of beekeeping. She was looking forward to her visit, she wanted to have a good look round outside, so it was with a sense of excitement and anticipation that she pulled up outside the boot room door. Mrs Bosworth was straight out to greet her.

"Good morning Ma'am. What a morning, ay? The boys will be in shortly. Shall you have tea first before you start?"

"Good idea," agreed Nell. The boys could bring her up to date with their ideas and plans. "I'll ask one of the boys to unhitch my horse and put him in a stall. I'll be here a few hours."

She followed Mrs Bosworth into the kitchen and as always, Nell felt that sense of coming home. How she loved that shabby kitchen and the battered old kitchen table. It was centuries old and the man who had made it carved his initials, C. W. H. 1722, on one of the legs. How many generations had sat at this table, eating, drinking, kicking the table legs with dirty boots? How many children had banged their spoons impatiently for food? The wood was scarred, burned, dented, marked and ringed with wet mug bottoms and even graffitied by some naughty family member. She ran her hands over the tabletop – and still in daily use, she thought.

As Mrs Bosworth was getting a lardy cake out of the oven, the boys were in, noisy, smelly, untidy, seeming to take up such a lot of kitchen room. They greeted Nell enthusiastically, but carried on splashing and washing at the sink before sitting down at the table. Great mugs of tea were poured and great slabs of cake were cut. The boys ate with gusto.

"Mrs Jameson, do you want to see everything today?"

Nell nodded. "Yes. Can we see the bees first?"

"Yep. Just have to go and get changed." Clem announced and he dashed away upstairs. A few minutes later, he was back, in light-coloured clothing.

"Right, shall we go?"

"Mrs Bosworth, I'll see you later then." Nell nodded and followed Clem out.

"Now, Clem, we must be quite quick, don't want to risk chilling the new brood. Ah, good, not much debris on the floor. Better, Clem, if we approach the hive from the side, not straight on. Have they water?"

Clem pointed to a shallow container filled with moss and stones. "Always keep it topped up Ma'am," he said. "I mixed their water with a little honey at first, just so they knew. The hazel is what tempts them out, I think they're making cleansing flights, look." He pointed to little streaks of yellow on the wooden frame. "Look," he said, sweeping debris away from the floor of the hive. "They have warmth," he waved his hand at the early sun, "water, pollen and honey, so all's good. Do you agree?"

"Yes." Nell had to agree. Clem was, as she was, completely fearless when it came to the bees. His manner was calm, confident and unafraid. He seemed to know instinctively how to deal with them. He had all the qualities of a good beekeeper and she was secretly proud of him.

Then down to see the pigs. Two sows in two sties, countless piglets running around. The pigs always made Nell laugh, their squealing and grunting, their sheer greediness was breathtaking. They were all good and would be let out to lower field later that week. Then it was up to see the goats. Clance was there, cleaning out their pen. *My goodness,* thought Nell, they looked fine; he was just taking them and the dogs down to the chicken field.

Then she inspected the barns. There was a tremendous amount of wood stacked for cutting; there was no mess, everything was tidy and swept. The boys were still living in the bothy, preferring to live apart from their mother and siblings. The courtyard had an air of orderliness about it. Nell was so pleased. When the work on the house was finished (it wasn't even started yet), it would be a place of some significance. She couldn't wait to get back to Chilworth to let Eade know work could start whenever he agreed.

She stayed for lunch, Mrs Bosworth had made a rabbit pie and they all sat at the table, the twins, the two littlies, Nell and Mrs Bosworth; the daughters, being in work, were away.

CHAPTER TWENTY-ONE

It was much later than she planned before she finally got away and made haste to get back before losing the light. She was interested to find out how the day had gone for the men. She pulled up in the stable yard and noticed a stable boy swishing water and scrubbing down the cobbles with a broom. She expected him to stop and come over to her, but he studiously ignored her.

She sat in the gig, becoming slightly annoyed.

"Boy," she called.

He looked up and stopped working.

"Yes, Ma'am?" he asked nervously.

"You must take my horse," she said. "You know what needs to be done. You need to be quicker about it. Understand?"

He nodded, but kept his eyes down. He didn't want to look at her. How odd he was, thought Nell. She would have to have a word with Eade about him.

She came into the house the back way and could hear servants' chatter which abruptly stopped when they saw Nell. They looked at her. She walked through, sensing something was wrong; the atmosphere was strange and heavy. As she walked into the hall, Mr Buchanen was coming down the stairs.

"Mrs Jameson," he called, raising his hand. "Mrs Jameson, come into the library."

Nell followed him in, waiting expectantly.

"I think you should have a brandy," he said, pouring

one for himself as well. His hands were shaking. He looked dreadful, Nell thought. His face was ashen.

"Mr Buchanen, what is it? What's wrong? Has something happened?" She was looking at him closely.

He took a breath. His voice shook.

"It's Eade."

"Eade? What? What has happened? Mr Buchanen, what? What is it?" She was fighting down a terrible panic.

He cleared his throat. "Eade, the bull hefted. Must weigh over a ton. Eade slipped on the cobbles. The stockman fell…" He couldn't continue.

"Mr Buchanen, what are you saying? You're not making any sense. What's happened?" A dreadful fear was beginning to overwhelm her.

"Mrs Jameson." Mr Buchanen closed his eyes, he really didn't want to say this. "Eade and the stockman were knocked over by the bull. Eade banged his head on the cobbles. The doctor's with him now. He was unconscious for a while. The herdsman's damaged his shoulder."

"And Eade?" she felt Mr Buchanen was holding back. "Mr Buchanen!" A great wave of faintness almost overcame her. "You're not being honest with me. Where is Eade now? Don't prevaricate, just tell me."

Mr Buchanen shook his head, he couldn't continue.

Nell took fright then and dashed out of the room and made for the stairs; she raced up and along the passageway and into their bedroom. She stopped short. The curtains were drawn, the doctor was leaning over the bed. He straightened at Nell's entrance.

"Mrs Jameson, I'm Doctor Murray," he said gravely, looking at her over his glasses. She came straight to the bed and gasped in shock and horror at the sight of Eade's head and face. The right side was battered and bloody. He was almost unrecognisable. There was huge bruising down his neck and shoulder. She felt a violent, powerful shudder riot through her body. She felt shock, disbelief and a huge, uncontrollable anger.

"I don't understand." She turned to Mr Buchanen who had followed her up. "How has this happened? How is it possible?" She shook her head in disbelief. She was shaking with rage. "How can you have allowed this to happen? I hope the bull's been shot." She turned to look at Eade and gave a strange howl of grief. "When I left this morning..."

"Mr Buchanen, get the lady a chair," The doctor pulled the bell cord. "Mrs Jameson, try to be calm. We have confidence Mr Jameson will come round, he will recover. It will take time. The only way the body can overcome trauma is through sleep. His injuries are bad, but he is strong and healthy."

Tilda arrived then, looked at Nell and pulled from her pocket the smelling salts.

"Ma'am, here, please, this will calm you. Breathe deeply."

Tilda was afraid. Afraid for the Major, but also, afraid for her mistress. Nell had collapsed into the chair and was incapable of speech. Tilda left her then, in order to light the candles. The daylight was fading. Thank goodness she was sitting on Eade's left side, so she couldn't see his terrible, crushed face. She let out a heart-rending sob. She was so, so angry at Mr Buchanen. Eade saved him when they were out in Bussaco, then saved him again when injured by a falling tree here at Chilworth; and what had he done for Eade? Nothing, just allowed his friend and blood-brother to be seriously injured by an out-of-control bull. She felt utter contempt for Mr Buchanen: what a useless, bloody stupid man. *He will have to go,* she thought. Tilda came to her with a brandy; she hadn't drunk the one downstairs. She felt the liquid course through her body and felt calmer. She looked at Eade.

"Eade," she whispered, "Eade, can you hear me?" She picked up his hand and gently squeezed it and ran a finger over his knuckles. *Oh God,* she pleaded, *let him be alright, please.* She longed to gently push his hair off his forehead, but she didn't dare to touch him. Again she felt a terrible anger well up. That Mr Graves, that bloody stupid bull, this useless doctor and that odious Buchanen man. She couldn't bear it. "Eade!" His name came out in a howl.

Mr Buchanen looked at the doctor in alarm. "Is there anything we can give her, doctor?" he asked.

"Be quiet," she demanded. "I don't need anything." She grasped Eade's hand and kissed it gently. "Eade, you need to get well, love. You have your new dairy herd. We can't manage without you. You have to concentrate on getting better." She rubbed his arm and touched the good side of his face. There was no response whatsoever. Hot tears spilled then and she didn't bother to wipe them away.

A footman knocked and entered then to inform the men that food was ready for them in the small eating room. Nell was secretly outraged. How could they? How could they eat, when Eade was mortally injured? They could sit and eat – it was beyond belief. How dare they?

They went down for their food, leaving Nell with Eade. *Please,* she begged God, please, *let him be alright. I will NEVER ask for anything, ever again. I will go to church every Sunday without fail,* she promised. Could one make a deal with God, she wondered?

The men came back up.

"Nell," Mr Buchanen spoke, "do you want to go down for something to eat? I'll stay. Doctor Murray will be here all night. We will not leave him."

She shook her head, unable to speak.

Mr Buchanen sighed and turned away from Nell. He walked over to the window, looking at the doctor and shaking his head. He stood, silent, glancing out at the world but without seeing. His guilt and misery were fathomless. Already, he had gone over and over and over in his mind what had happened this afternoon in the courtyard. How had it happened? It was so fast. Why couldn't he have done something? He chewed on a finger and sent up a silent prayer.

Let him live, let him come through this. He shook his head. He knew deep inside, Eade would not survive. When they heard the terrible crack of his skull on the cobbles, there was a collective silence of shock. Eade was breathing, so he was alive. While he lived, there was hope. Wasn't there? No. There was no hope. All they could do was watch and wait, but they dare not tell Nell that.

Much later, Nell nodded off in the chair for a few minutes and awoke with a start, dazed and confused. Immediately, she checked Eade.

"Eade," she whispered, "I love you, darling. There's so much to do." She rubbed his arm tenderly and squeezed his hand. On and on she spoke to him, continuously, only stopping when Tilda bought her a pot of chocolate. She really needed a drink, so she asked Mr Buchanen to take over and talk to him.

So the long, lonely day dragged on and much to Nell's sadness, Eade did not respond to her entreaties.

Doctor Murray tried to get her to take a break and eat something, even have a little nap, but she refused. She would not leave his side. All through the long night, she sat and held his hand and spoke softly to him. There was no response from Eade. If anything, his breathing had become even more shallow. Nell was nearing exhaustion, but she would not listen to the doctor or Mr Buchanen. She dozed little and often through the night and finally gave in in the early dawn and staggered to bed for a few hours.

Nell, once in her room, cried and cried and could not stop. She kicked her shoes off, but couldn't unhook her dress, so she had an uncomfortable night, restlessly tossing and turning and getting very little sleep. She was awake far too early, thick-headed and muzzy, so she splashed water over her face and combed her hair back anyhow and crept down the corridor to Eade. Entering the room, it was obvious nothing had changed, so Nell decided she was going to talk to him constantly today, to try to get through to him; he had to come round, he had to wake up. She expected the room to be warm and in semi-darkness, but she was surprised to find the drapes pulled back and the windows slightly open. The fire was low and two maids were bustling around, silent but busy. Nell looked at the doctor in surprise. Mr Buchanen was staring out of the window, his hand over his mouth. He knew what Nell did not know.

Doctor Murray had realised overnight, there would be no coming back for Eade. His duty now was to Nell and get her to a place of acceptance. This occupied him greatly and it was with great reluctance he requested the maids clean down the room.

"Doctor, I'll go down now for breakfast, if that's alright with you?" Mr Buchanen looked at the doctor cautiously and waited. The doctor gave him the nod. It was safer not to say anything at the moment.

"Mrs Jameson, would you go down for food? You've had nothing since the day before."

He knew she would shake her head.

"Please. Let us finish the room. I will come and get you if there is any change." He looked at her sternly. She wavered; she had such a queasy feeling in her stomach. A little food might help. She nodded and left the room and went down-stairs to the lonely eating room. Mr Buchanen was there, pouring himself a cup of tea. He offered it to Nell and she accepted it gratefully. She was subdued, silent, her anger from the day before dissipated. She felt lost. Deep within herself, she had a dreadful feeling. She had this awful feeling Eade was going to leave her.

She couldn't eat. There was a churning and sickness in her body. She had to get back to him. She rushed back upstairs and took her place at the bedside.

"Eade." She took his hand and rubbed it gently. Hot tears coursed down her face. "Eade, don't leave me. We have lots of packing to do, Mr Buchanen needs your help with the heifers. Eade, just give me a sign, please." She clung to his hand. No response.

And so another day passed and Doctor Murray conferred with Mr Buchanen and they agreed, Nell must be told, so that she could gradually come to that place of acceptance.

"Mrs Jameson." The doctor was hesitant and spoke low. "Your husband…" He faltered and tried again. "Mrs Jameson, your husband."

She looked at him. "Yes?"

The doctor looked discomforted, Mrs Jameson had to be told. "Mrs Jameson, your husband's injuries are, are such that he will not recover from them."

"No!" Nell shouted.

She stood up immediately, her person rigid with outrage and an almost uncontrollable anger. "How dare you? How dare you? You said yourself, the only way a body recovers from trauma, is by sleeping. He will recover, he will get better, you're not giving him enough time." She was wringing her handkerchief in her hands. She had bitten her lip so hard, it was bleeding. "No." She began pacing up and down the room. "No. Eade. Is. Not. Going. To. Die. He is not!" she shouted at the doctor. "And what about you, Buchanen? You're keeping very quiet, you, who allowed this accident to happen! You coward, skulking in the corner over there

– what have you got to say, hey? You fucking, despicable man. Call yourself a friend?"

Tears coursed down her cheeks and Buchanen looked at the doctor in alarm. He didn't want to say anything that would ignite her fury even more.

The doctor raised his hands in supplication and imperceptibly shook his head.

"Mrs Jameson, for your husband's final few hours, you must control yourself." Without taking his eyes off Nell, he asked Buchanen to ring for the maid. He went to take her hand and she shook him away.

Tilda arrived then and the doctor gave her a phial of liquid. He knew Nell, in her present state of mind, would refuse anything the doctor offered her.

"Ma'am." Tilda came to her,. "Ma'am, calm, for your husband's sake. You have to contain yourself. Here, take this, I've made it up for you. Come and sit. Take it all," and Tilda watched her carefully to make sure she drank it all.

"Mrs Jameson," the doctor spoke very softly now, "your husband needs your permission to go. You have to release him. He needs your permission. He feels he cannot leave you. While you talk of things, your holiday, farming matters, the estate, you are tying him to you. Only you can free him. There is no hope of recovery now. You have to tell him he can go." He laid his hand on her arm as hot tears coursed down her face. "He is suffering, but he will not go. Only when you tell him it's alright, will he leave."

There was a long silence, interspersed with Nell's sobs. The doctor said no more, but did not release his hold on Nell.

Buchanen had his back to them, looking out of the window. He was also silent, but his shoulders shook with grief. His friend, his stalwart through thick and thin, Eade had saved his life once, in war, in desperate circumstances, no food, no water, their horses shot from underneath them, surrounded by the dead and dying and the stench and brutality of war – and yet they had survived. They'd looked out for each other – and now, there was this, in comfortable, middle-class England, Eade was meeting his end. He shook his head in disbelief. How did this happen? They'd been strong for each other once; now he must be strong again, not only for himself, but for Eade's new wife, whose hatred of him was palpable.

Nell gradually calmed and looked blankly ahead.

"What must I do?"

The doctor spoke very gently. "Hold his hand, tell him he can go. Don't mention anything else. Of course, tell him you love him, say your goodbyes. Brave now, Mrs Jameson. Time to let him go."

Nell was aware Eade's breathing had changed. It was heavy and laboured. She gently took his hand and squeezed it in the forlorn hope he would respond.

"Eade." She swallowed hard. How could she do this? She was gasping for air.

"Eade." She kissed his hand, "Eade, it's time to go. Don't worry, everything will be alright, you can leave now. We'll look after everything for you. It will be fine, I love you very much; we all love you."

She kissed the back of his hand and watched. She felt a loosening in the muscles of his hand and she pulled back, to look at his face. No, nothing outwardly had changed, but something had happened. His breathing had quietened and his breathing was shallower, his chest barely rising. She held onto his hand and softly, oh so softly, ran her fingers up his arm.

"Goodbye, my love," she whispered and she lowered her head onto his arm.

The doctor stood silently. Buchanen stood silently. Tilda

stood by the door, silently. They were waiting; the end was very near. The silence was deafening and then it happened. Eade stopped. He stopped breathing. He stopped living. An aura of peace descended upon him.

"No." Nell stood up so abruptly, she knocked over the chair. "No, Eade, no, please, no." She turned to the doctor and Buchanen in despair. She was beyond coherent speech. No, the unbelievable, the unthinkable had happened. Her Eade, husband of weeks, gone. She howled with grief. She couldn't catch her breath, she couldn't speak. No! The doctor and Mantel caught her before she hit the floor and propped her in a chair.

How could this be? How could it have happened that she went to her farm and all was well and she came back to disaster? How had this happened? She looked at Eade. He was peaceful; his face looked the same, but strangely different. What was it? Her eyes were devouring him. She looked at his hair, the way it curled around his ears, his broad shoulders, the stubble on his chin. Why? How could she live without him? She felt a terrible heaving of her stomach and covered her mouth. She couldn't be ill, here at his bedside, it was unthinkable. She swallowed the bile and gasped.

"Wave this under her nose." The doctor shook a bottle of salts at Buchanen. "I have duties now concerning my patient."

Mantel, aware of the. rituals of death, knew he had to get Mrs Jameson out of the room, in order that the doctor could begin the laying-out process. Normally, this work would be done by a village woman, but the good doctor, aware of the importance of the deceased, felt it incumbent upon himself to fulfil his duty to this man. Mantel very carefully lifted Anella out of the chair and took her along the passageway to a guest bedroom. He laid her gently on the bed, hoping she would not come out of her swoon too soon. He pulled the bell cord, and within minutes, Tilda had appeared.

"We need a fire lit, we need brandy, we need a tray of hot sweet tea and quickly." He approached Tilda and said in a whisper, "Your master has passed. The house will be in mourning now. Let the other staff know."

He nodded his dismissal and she was gone in a flash, but almost immediately, another little maid was in, setting a fire.

Anella was rousing. He went straight over to her. "Mrs Jameson." She made to get up and he put a restraining hand on her arm. "No. The doctor has things to do. We cannot go in. He will let us know."

"Mantel, what am I going to do? Why, why? I can't live without Eade." She was sobbing and heaving for breath. "What am I going to do? I can't, I can't live. We must let the family know. How am I going to tell them?" Tears poured down her face. "You must help me." A look of panic, then: "We'll have to arrange a funeral. No, I can't, I can't. I can't do it."

"Mrs Jameson," he spoke oh so quietly, "arrangements are already underway. The doctor and I spoke last night. We knew. Word has been sent to Harold and Eliza. They are probably on their way." He was sitting by the bed, with a look of such sadness, Anella felt a sweeping loneliness over-power her.

"Mantel, how am I going to get through this? Why do we have to have a funeral? Why can't we keep him here, on the estate? I can't bear the thought of all these people. I cannot, cannot go through with this." Fresh hot tears coursed down her face. She was in danger of becoming hysterical.

"You can cope and you will cope, and you will cope for the love of Eade. He deserves a proper send-off, and you will give it him. You are not alone. I'm here; I love Eade as much as you, he's a brother." He couldn't talk about Eade in the past tense. He was still here, the house was full of his presence, he was here in spirit, he hadn't left yet. Mantel cleared his throat. "I will speak to the doctor in the morning before he leaves. Then you must tell me what you want for Eade." He gripped her arm, as he could sense the rising panic. "Take a breath, slowly, in, out, slow, that's it. I'm going to send down for a light supper for you." He held his hand up to stop her protest. "You must eat; if not for your sake, then for Eade's. Whatever, you have to keep yourself together. You must not let him down. You have to be strong. He was a grand man, now you have to be the widow of a grand man."

He went over and tugged at the cord. Within minutes, a little maid appeared and Mantel ordered food for her and requested Tilda come.

He explained he called for Tilda as he expected she, Anella, would like to have a bath and maybe wash her hair and Tilda could help her. He was going downstairs now, but if she needed him, send Tilda. The doctor would leave a sleeping draught for her and a tincture for her nerves, he would send it up when she was back in her room.

He gave a little, formal bow. "Goodnight Ma'am."

He turned and left, his mind full of thoughts. He'd sustained a massive head injury and survived; he'd lost his memory, but he'd survived. Eade, in completely different circumstances, had also sustained a massive head injury – and died. He shook his head in disbelief. For this to happen, on home ground, was an incident of epic proportions. He kept shaking his head as if he found it difficult to comprehend. Had he been negligent? Could he have done anything? Going over the accident in his mind, was the speed with which it happened. One minute they were gathered round the massive beast, Mr Graves slapping his hindquarters and running his hand down a flank and praising its abilities as a sire, when, suddenly, the bull shifted, shook his great head and hefted left, knocking the herdsman off his feet; he fell against Eade, who then fell against the bull, who moved his great bulk so fast as if flicking a fly. Eade went down before they were aware of what had happened and smacked his head on the cobblestones. They all knew, from the sound, that this was an injury of magnitude. And then all hell was let loose. Copious amount of blood, the bull barely containable, aware of the panic around it and the smell of blood. Mr Graves and a couple of farm workers managed to get him in a stable. Mr Buchanen was shouting orders; someone had already been sent to get the doctor. They had to stem the blood, get him upstairs, assess the damage to his person, get the blood and mess cleaned away. God Almighty, how had this happened with them all there? And now Eade was dead. Dead. What sort of a brother-in-arms was he to have let this happen? He had no doubt in his mind, at the time, that Eade would not recover from this freak accident. Mantel's one thought was to get to his room and it was only there that he could rest his head in his hands and let the tears flow. He felt an enormous weight of guilt. And now, of course, he had the responsibility of Mrs Jameson. It had crossed his mind that he ought to offer his resignation and he'd decided he would, but after the funeral; and then he would go, whenever she dictated. Memories were flooding into his mind now, unbidden, memories of unspeakable, unbearable hardships of war, of the loyalties of their men, of the sea journey home and fearing they would be shipwrecked and drowned and finally reaching safe harbour: and now this! He needed sleep badly, but knew it would be impossible, what with all these new memories swamping his brain and knowing there would be much to organize in the following days.

CHAPTER TWENTY-TWO

The following morning, the doctor left, only to return later with the coffin maker and, dreadfully, Harold and Eliza arrived. The children had been left at home with nanny. Eliza had packed suitable mourning clothes, but she, too, was in a state of turmoil. So many questions needed answering. Inside, she was angry, as Anella had been angry. She was determined to find out what actually happened. With servants, there was always blame, but finding out who to blame was the difficulty. Without preamble, she threw her coat to a footman and dashed upstairs as Tilda was leaving Anella's room.

"Well?"

Tilda bobbed. "Madam is resting, Ma'am."

"Is she sleeping?"

"Not yet. The doctors left a draft for her. She's not sleeping nights, but wandering around. I thought to give her a spoonful later after supper."

"Good." Eliza quickly opened the bedroom door.

"Ma'am…" Tilda objected, only to have the door closed firmly in her face.

"Anella."

Eliza walked quickly across to the bed. She was taken aback at the sight of her sister-in-law. Huge dark black shadows under her eyes, her face full of grief, her hair a tangled, unbrushed mess. Her mouth turned down as if any minute, she would be overcome by crying.

"Eliza," she gasped, and then the tears came, spilling down her face and soaking her gown. "Eliza, I can't believe it, he's gone, my Eade, he's gone." She was beyond reason. Eliza stood and watched, tears welling up inside her. Oh God, she thought, it was alright to come with all these high-minded ideas of right and wrong and somebody must be to blame, but the reality… to see Anella, so broken, so stricken in grief. She knelt by her bedside, clasped her arm and gave way to huge noisy tears. Poor, poor Anella. She, Eliza, had lost her brother, but she still had her husband, her children, her family. She knew things must change now regarding Eade's estate, but that could not be thought about now.

Over the next few days, Eliza and Harold, Anella and Mantel arranged a funeral of magnitude in memory of Eade. Mr Gillamoor, the head gardener, was instructed as to the flowers necessary, Mrs Harvey as to the refreshments and Thompson as to the wines that should be served. Black-edged mourning invitations were sent out, the curtains pulled halfway, so the house was in a state of semi-darkness. A plain black dress from her previous life as Mrs Hebb was pressed and re-fitted by Tilda, but Anella turned her face to the wall. She didn't want to know of any of this: she didn't care. Let them get on with it. She had lost a lot of weight, not wanting to eat, and having a constantly upset stomach made things worse. She knew it was stress, sadness, worry; life would never be right for her again. Mr Buchanen would have to take over the running of everything. After all, it was his fault, and that Mr Graves. She hated the pair of them.

Come the day, Anella was in a state of collapse. Tilda had to get her dressed, Madam was incapable of doing anything. Tilda brushed her hair, brought out her mourning jewel-lery, even putting her earrings on for her. A footman and Mr Buchanen almost carried her to the carriage and both had to assist her out, once they had arrived at the church. She'd had a calmative from the doctor and Tilda was by her side with smelling salts, so she managed to sit in her pew almost upright. She was vaguely aware that there were hundreds of people present and that the church flowers smelled beautiful and that the choir sang and sang the most wondrous, heavenly music. And the eulogy was beautiful. How well the vicar knew Eade, his kindness, his generosity, his benevolence, his forward-thinking ideas regarding the village children in his care – oh, it went on and on and Anella felt she just couldn't cry any more.

Eventually, the service was over and the vicar was pleased that probably the biggest funeral of the year was completed without a hitch.

It was a long, slow procession back to the house and there was much to do. Extra servants, having been hired by Mr Buchanen, were in attendance everywhere; it wasn't long before people were eating and drinking and passing on their condolences to Eade's widow, but Anella was above it all. She just wanted all the people to go. She sat by the fire, waiting and watching, and willing them to leave; and eventually they did, and she sat on and watched the staff clearing down, all the hard work they did behind the scenes, and then Tilda came and tried to persuade her to move, change rooms, maybe eat a little something, but no, she didn't want to change rooms. She wanted to stay here; so she did. Mantel tried to move her, but Anella was adamant, she didn't want to go anywhere. She turned her head away.

So they left her there and she cried softly all night, and this is where Tilda found her the following morning.

"Oh, Madam!" she exclaimed in exasperation.

Mr Buchanen came in then and stopped short. He looked queryingly at Tilda.

"Mrs Jameson didn't feel able to go upstairs last night, she wanted to stay here."

Tilda was looking at Mr Buchanen, giving him a warning look. He approached with caution.

"Anella." He didn't want to call her Mrs Jameson and draw attention to her widowhood. He knelt in front of her. "Anella, Eade would like you to go upstairs. He doesn't want you to stay here like this." He looked at her.

"What?"

"Eade wants you to go upstairs."

She looked uncertain for a moment. "Upstairs?"

"Yes," Mantel nodded. He said in an aside, "Tilda, I'll send the doctor up before he leaves." He guided Anella, his hand in the small of her back. When they had gone, he rushed to the eating room and found the doctor eating in solitary splendour.

"Doctor, thank you for being in attendance yesterday."

The doctor nodded graciously.

"Before you go, will you please attend on Mrs Jameson? She's not herself, I know, but I'm beginning to wonder if something else is wrong."

"Oh?" The doctor stopped eating,

"She's acting strangely." He shrugged his shoulders. "It's worrying, that's all."

"Of course I will, Mr Buchanen; straight after breakfast, I will see to her. Now, will you join me?"

Mantel sat and helped himself; in the last few days food had been erratic. Not that Mrs Harvey hadn't cooked anything, she had; they had been in such disarray. His thoughts were interrupted by Harold and Eliza. There were "Good mornings" all around, albeit very subdued. They helped themselves, not talking, and Mantel indicated to the doctor that perhaps they should go upstairs.

Tilda met them in the corridor. "Madam is very tired."

"Yes, I won't keep her, I just want to make sure she is coping with things."

The doctor entered the bedroom and Mantel followed. The doctor paused.

"Mr Mantel, would you send the maid in please and could you wait outside? I'd be most grateful."

Mantel, realizing he had overstepped the mark, exited quickly and beckoned Tilda to return to the room.

"Now, Mrs Jameson…" The doctor looked at her searchingly and removed from his case a small ear trumpet. She looked exhausted and deathly pale and wasn't in any mood to communicate. "I'm going to listen to your heart first. Just breathe normally." He concentrated and listened. "And in yourself? Your courses? Are they regular? Normally, do you eat well? Do you manage to get out in the fresh air? Now, I'm going to have a listen to your tummy." He asked Tilda to lift the skirt of Anella's nightgown, so that he only had the thin fabric of her shift to listen through. His concentration was intense." Mrs Jameson, when did you last have your menses?" He looked at her maid. "Can you remember?" She must have noticed something when she changed the sheets, surely? He listened again. There it was, a second heartbeat, faster. He looked intently into her eyes and examined her fingernails. "How do you feel in the mornings? Bit queasy? Unsettled?" He beckoned Tilda. "In the mornings, before Mrs Jameson gets out of bed, she needs black tea and two ginger biscuits; only ginger, no other will do. Is that clear?"

She bobbed. "Yes, Sir, and there's been no show as far back as I can remember."

The doctor gently took Anella's hand. "Mrs Jameson, you really must take better care of yourself. I want you to eat regularly, no more missing mealtimes. I'm going to leave you something to help you sleep. And try to walk, just a short stroll, ten minutes for the fresh air, every day, it will do you good." Still no response from Anella. "Mrs Jameson, do you know you're pregnant?"

"What?" She sat bolt upright, her mouth open. She was

shocked beyond words. "But I can't be." Her mind was racing back to Neft. She couldn't conceive, he'd told her. It wasn't his fault, it was hers. She looked at the doctor and shook her head. "No, it's not possible."

"Mrs Jameson, you had normal relations with your husband?"

She nodded.

"Well, usually the inevitable happens, that's what marriage is for. I can near two heartbeats, yours and the baby's. Now, did you take in everything I've said? Ginger biscuits, regular meals, exercise? You should progress well, but if you wish, I can come in and see you regularly."

"Yes. Yes please, doctor, I would like that." She was vague, genuinely shocked.

He looked at her piercingly. "So from now on, a new regime. Regular baths, regular food, regular exercise, regular sleep." He looked at his fob watch. "I must go." He gave a slight bow. "I'll see you in four weeks. Good day to you, Mrs Jameson. Keep yourself well, for your husband's sake; this will be his heir."

He left to speak with Mr Buchanen, who was waiting outside in the corridor.

"Mr Buchanen, Mrs Jameson is *enceinte*. Her mental condition is precarious. I've arranged to visit in four weeks. She must be kept calm and quiet; no unnecessary panics or excitements. I've instructed her maid: regular meals, exercise, hours. Oh, and ginger before she gets out of bed in the mornings. I'll bid you good day. I will send my bill on."

Mantel, in some shock himself, bade the good doctor farewell and shook his head in disbelief. So, Eade, the old devil, had been playing husband to Anella's wife for some time before the wedding. Good on him, randy bugger. Mantel laughed. Well, out of this God-awful mess, there would be a child, hopefully a son and heir. This might save Anella from her terrible grief. In years to come, this baby would be the future. *Thank God,* he thought and then was overcome with sadness. To think. They both had come through so much together and survived; now Eade was gone. Mantel stood alone in the corridor and made a silent pledge to Eade. He would care for his wife and child to the best of his ability and keep the house and estate up to the standards expected and, hopefully, maintain Eade's kindness and goodness. He had to give up his idea of resignation. Mantel mentally squared his shoulders. He knocked on Anella's bedroom door. Tilda opened the door to him.

"Tilda, you are aware of the doctor's diagnosis. I think it best if as few people as possible know about this. After all, it's a bit early."

Tilda nodded. She, more than anyone else, knew of Eade's and Anella's coming together, but as a good maid, she kept quiet. She and the mistress had a bond of trust. Tilda would never break it, but she would have to tell cook about the ginger biscuits.

"Tell her Mrs Jameson is anaemic and there's iron in the ginger – I don't know. I'll leave it to you," Mantel nodded.

He crossed the room to Anella's bedside. At one time, he would be shocked at doing this, but mindful of his new responsibilities made to himself in the corridor, he now had a duty of care and that duty would start today.

He sat by the bedside. "Anella," he said quietly, "the doctor has spoken with me. How do you feel?"

She looked at him with heavy eyes. "He says I'm pregnant. Stupid man. Of course I'm not."

Mantel stroked his chin. He had to tread carefully here. "He is the doctor, he knows. It would be nice to think you will have an heir for Eade. Imagine how happy Eade would be." He was watching her reaction closely. He took her hand. "The doctor has ordered a new regime, we can follow that. Do it for Eade, Anella, whether there's a baby or not. Let's do it for Eade."

She looked at him then and smiled, her eyes so tired and listless. "Can we do it?" she wondered.

"Of course, and Tilda's always here to help you. You won't have to do anything on your own."

He left her then and went out on farm business, knowing Harold and Eliza would be wishing to see her sometime during the day. They would be staying until the solicitor had been and then, of course, there was the trip to sort out.

Later that evening, in the eating room, Anella was present, looking very frail, but composed. She was talking rationally to Eliza and Harold. She beckoned Mantel over.

"Mr Buchanen, I'm trying to persuade them to take over our trip."

Mantel shook his head, slightly confused "Sorry?"

"I want Harold and Eliza to go to Italy; take over our trip. Of course, I cannot go. I have no wish to go; but they could. Would it be possible? Can it be done?"

"Hold on," interrupted Harold. "It's too soon and anyway, there's the children. What would people think if they knew we would be gadding off to the continent not two weeks after my brother-in-law passed?"

He looked to Eliza. She was hesitant. "I agree, Harold, but we could say we are going on this trip in memory of Eade. It would be a shame to think all his planning was going to waste; it's not a bad thing to enjoy what he wanted. In years to come, we will talk about this trip and how it was organized by Eade."

"The children you could leave with me," Anella butted in. "In fact, I would love to have the children. It would give me a focus, something to occupy me. We could go out every day, I could teach them."

There was a silence amongst the three other adults. For

the first time. Anella had sparked up and it was the thought of the children that had triggered it.

Cautiously, Mantel agreed it probably would be possible to change the holiday from the Jamesons to the Erskines, and as long as Harold was agreeable, then yes, why not? All in memory of Eade – and Anella would surely improve, having the children. It was agreed then and Eliza, in spite of her sadness, looked forward with excitement to a trip abroad.

CHAPTER TWENTY-THREE

Later in the week, the solicitor arrived, a serious-looking man, with an underdog, a young, pimply faced young man who was obviously learning the ropes. They all assembled in the drawing room, but not before Mantel had drawn Harold and Eliza aside and cautioned them of Amelia's condition. Eliza, at first, in her naivety, disclaimed the news as ridiculous, but as Harold quietly mentioned, a couple due to marry often sampled the goods first. It wasn't unknown, after all; he looked secretly at Eliza.

"But this changes things as regards the estate, doesn't it?" she asked. They all were aware that the estate, farms and house would eventually come down to their son, Ellis, as the next male heir in line with Eade having no son of his own. There was as much possibility of Anella having a girl as a boy.

At two o'clock, they assembled in the with-drawing room; not a room much used, probably because it was on the north side of the house and was rather dismal in its outlook, but for Anella. it was fine. She didn't want, in the future, an association of bad news with any other room in the house. It might as well be this one.

The solicitor had requested that Miss Sorrel, the schoolmistress, be present, and Tilda the maid and Thompson the footman, besides Harold and Eliza, Mantel and herself, and they sat in a semi-circle in front of him. Anella felt her heart fluttering and the now usual feelings of hopelessness and despair. She didn't want to be here, she didn't want to hear about Eade's estate. She would go back to her own farm. Live there, an ordinary life… Her mind wandered as the last will and testament of Eade William Jameson, being of sound mind, was read out. After much legal preamble, it came about that £200 was to be given to the school annually to be used for improvements generally, subject to agreement by the school committee. As the school building belonged to Eade and was on his land, there was no school board to consider. Tilda, for her care and loyalty to her mistress, was left £175. Tilda was so overcome by this that she stood up, hands covering her mouth; why, she had only known Anella really for a few months. Next was Thompson: £190 for being a good and faithful servant. There was a trust to be set up for village children to further their education if they were considered bright enough, money for a new library and reading room in the village and a parcel of land given so that every dwelling would have an acre to grow produce or keep pigs or whatever, and lastly, a community orchard to be established within walking distance of the school, as one condition was that the children should be responsible for the good heart of the trees, after their initial planting. Distribution of the fruit would take place within the school grounds, but other than that, the fruit grown could be picked by anyone in the village as long as it was not for commercial gain. Monies were to be made available for every servant to receive a bonus of £5 a year. This bought gasps of amazement from everybody. Anella felt the tears welling up. Eade was such a good man; surely, there was no one in the world as kind as him. There was a halt in the proceedings then, as the staff were allowed to leave. Anella looked out of the window. Now came the serious business; and it was as they all thought, surprisingly straightforward, that Ellis Erskine, twelve years of age, would become the next incumbent of Chilworth House, subject to there being no issue of the Major's. Well, there would be issue, even though Anella was in denial and it could be a girl, in which case, nothing would change. Then there was money distributed, jewellery to the ladies, a fob watch to Harold, Eade's horse to Mantel and saddle, etc. Money was left for Anella, so much annually and she could live in the house for as long as she lived or until she re-married. The same conditions were applied to Mantel, who would have to move out of the dower house and into the main house, as it would be his responsibility, from now on, to take charge of the estate and its affairs. What Harold and Eliza made of Eade's will did not surface at the time, but they might have fostered a hope that Anella's baby would be a girl.

And so all was done. The servants bought in afternoon tea and there was polite conversation which Anella forbore to take part in. She sat, in silent misery, near the fire, barely able to contain her grief. The solicitor came over to say farewell and to inform her that as soon as the "issue" was born, she or Mr Buchanen would have to let him know because of the implications of the will. With that he took his leave.

So began a new and sad chapter in Anella's life. Her loneliness was abject. She never made any effort to overcome her grief. Every morning Mr Buchanen would escort her on a ten-minute walk around the gardens. He couldn't persuade her to any longer. She took no interest in the coming flowers, no interest in the plants in the orangery, no interest in her own farm or bees; nothing held her interest.

Eliza and Harold went on their trip and Anella, as promised, had the children. They occupied her in their way; their interest in everything was always surprising, but the spark was gone. Some days, she just wanted to be rid of them, so she could be sad and think of Eade. One thing interested her, though, and it secretly excited her very much. One particularly fine morning, walking the lawns, not listening to Mr Buchanen's talking, she felt the most peculiar flutter-ing sensation in her belly. She stopped suddenly.

Mr Buchanen looked at her in some alarm. "Ma'am?"

"No, no, carry on," she said, but inside, her feelings soared. *Doctor Murray might be right after all,* she thought. She couldn't wait to get back to the house. She wanted to examine her body, see it there was change, that she, in her grief and denial, had overlooked, in which case, baby things would be needed. She had to sort out a crib, a cot; so much to do. Suddenly, she was filled with excitement.

Mantel noticed a change in her over the next tew days. She was still uninterested in the garden, but she talked more, was more aware, more alive. He shook his head; maybe she was coming out of her deep depression. They hadn't discussed Eade's will, it was too raw a subject, but she would bring him up in conversation.

As the year wore on, summer led to autumn and Anel-la's baby bump became more noticeable; she wasn't modest about it. Doctor Murray came every four weeks as promised and had become a good friend of Mr Buchanen. It was their names. The Murray clan, the doctor was quick to point out, was the Murrays of Tullibardine and his cousin, the 7th Duke of Atholl, was rebuilding Blair Castle as they spoke. This prompted Mantel to boast their clan society was the oldest of all the Highland societies and still had possession of the island of Clarinch. Buchanen clansmen used "Clar-inch" as their battle cry.

More amazingly, they announced the surname "Erskine" was also of Scottish origin and even managed to get Harold interested, so much so, that all three men sent away to the kilt makers in Edinburgh for the full sett. They agreed to wear them at a Christmas function together.

The doctor kept a close watch on Anella and was pleased that, at last, she had finally accepted her pregnancy and was actively making plans for the baby's arrival. He told her he thought the baby was due late December or early January: what better present for the New Year, he said, than a new baby?

Anella, inwardly, was very excited. She and Tilda had spent many hours over the summer, making tiny baby outfits, preparing a layette, finding an old baby bath and chair and cleaning them up.

Come the time of Christmas, they were all busy. There was the annual children's Christmas party, then the staff had a "do" and Mrs Bosworth and the twins came. Anella was so pleased to see them and there was so much gossip, Anella perhaps breaking out of her shell of sadness at last. There was the carol service at the church and it began to snow as they were leaving. There was great excitement and expectation in the air as Doctor Murray, Mantel, Harold, Eliza and herself trotted home in the icy blackness, muffled in blankets and shawls. It was lovely to arrive home to the warm welcome of the house, decorated in traditional style with great swags of ivy and holly, plenty of berries and red ribbons and roses from Mr Gillamoor's hot houses. Hundreds of candles lit, and the group had to hurry upstairs to their rooms to prepare for a grand dinner and dance this evening. All Eade's friends were coming: the Busseys, the de Haases, Lady Helen and her daughter. Daphne, friends of Harold and Eliza, associates of Mr Buchanen; oh so many, the schoolteachers, the vicar and his little wife. Anella wasn't sure such a gathering was meet in view of Eade's passing only nine months previous, but there it was. Tilda helped her into an adapted gown that didn't show her bump too much; she looked at her reflection in the mirror and shrugged. It would do. She went down early, knowing that if she left it later, she would lose her nerve and not come down at all.

As guests began arriving, Harold and Eliza appeared, Harold wearing for the first time the Erskine tartan of red and black; a new tartan, in fact, originating in 1842. Eliza was obviously very proud of her husband's new-found ancestry, and Anella had to agree with her that a man in a kilt was a very handsome fellow indeed. Guests arrived in a steady flow and then Doctor Murray came down in his tartan of red and green – the Tullibardine. *My goodness*, thought Anella, these men in their kilts were as vain as the ladies. Still, she had to admit, they looked very handsome. She was looking forward to seeing Mr Buchanen. He finally arrived in his clan tartan, an asymmetrical design of yellow and red. Oh my goodness. Anella's heart skipped a beat. He looked very handsome, every bit the Scottish laird. Naturally, the ladies flocked around the gentlemen in their kilts and Harold loved it. Never had he been so popular.

They all eventually went in for dinner, and it was a lovely evening, Mrs Harvey excelling herself (it must be the thought of her bonus, Anella said to herself unkindly). About ten o'clock, they departed the eating room and followed the sound of music. The great hall had been emptied and a quartet were playing general music until given the signal for dancing. Anella was a little put-out that Mr Buchanen had not approached her during the course of the evening so far; he appeared to be too busy with his coterie of lady admirers. Doctor Murray came to her, ever on alert, and asked her how she was feeling. She smiled at him and said she was feeling fine, but actually, all day, she'd had a nagging backache. Probably her own fault, as she had insisted she and Tilda get everything out for the baby and double-check the nursery. Never mind; once this evening was over, she could sink into bed and relax.

Finally, Mr Mantel managed to attend to her. She was aloof. "Well, Mr Buchanen, how does it feel to be so popular? The ladies certainly love a man in a kilt, don't they?" She smiled her most patronizing smile.

"Ma'am," he gave a little bow, "if I give the nod, we can start the dancing. Is that alright with you?"

"Oh! Yes, of course; sorry, I didn't realise."

He stood there waiting. "Well, we can start the dancing." He held out his hand.

"Mr Buchanen, I didn't know you meant me. It's unseemly in my condition. I can't."

With that, he gripped her tightly around the waist and proceeded the waltz, that most unseemly and decadent of dances; although he couldn't hold her too close because of her bump. One circuit of the floor was enough for her and Mantel released her and helped her to a chair. After bringing her a drink, he was off to dance the night away with a bevy of ladies. Anella sat and watched. She wasn't jealous. She did think that Mr Buchanen, Mantel, looked exceedingly handsome and dashing in his kilt and it was whilst watching him, she was overcome with a great wave of sadness. This time last year, she would have been on the dance floor with Eade and later in her room, he would have made love to her again and again. She swallowed hard; a wave of pain shot through her which made her gasp. *Mustn't think of Eade*, she said to herself, *not good for the baby*.

The rest of the evening she sat there, guests coming to her, talking, chatting, exchanging pleasantries, bringing her refreshments and all the time, she knew, something was happening. That niggly back pain, the spasms of pain crossing her stomach, gentle at first, but steadily becoming stronger as she sat there. They weren't going away. She was outwardly calm. Inwardly, a little panicky. Still, the doctor was here, thank goodness, in case of trouble. And so the evening came to its end. *My goodness*, thought Anella, *why does it take people so long to say goodbye?* She gritted her teeth and was very polite to everyone, even those brazen ladies after Mantel. Eventually, all had gone and the servants came in to start clearing down. Still Anella sat there; she wasn't sure, now, whether she could move or not. Eventually, Mr Buchanen arrived. He looked concerned. He came straight over to Anella and leant over her and took her hand.

"Anella?" He observed her closely. "Tell me." He waited.

"Well, I'm not sure. No, actually, I'm fine. Everything's fine. I've got a bit of backache, that's all. Overdid it today, that's all." She managed a smile. Actually, she did feel alright. Those nagging pains had gone. "Mr Buchanen, if you could just give me a help up the stairs, I would be grateful."

And so, very gentlemanly, he took her arm and escorted her to her bedroom, not leaving until Tilda appeared.

"Tilda, Mrs Jameson is feeling a little unwell, keep an eye on her tonight. Can you call a couple of maids to get the blue room ready for me?" He nodded to a room just down the passageway. "I think I might be needed to call the doctor later." He smiled and nodded.

Tilda was not best pleased to have to find a couple of maids at this late hour to light a fire and make a bed up. Still, it had to be done.

So it came to pass that night, one of the little maids slipped on the back stairs in her haste to prepare the blue room. Pressed, Doctor Murray was called to attend. Tilda was with her; the poor girl was in such a lot of pain, she'd dropped a water glass and broken it and had cut her hand badly. The blood frightened her. She sustained a twisted ankle and that also had to be strapped up, and the doctor and Tilda and a host of other servants crowded round to try and help. While this was happening, Anella, sleeping fitfully, was awoken by a searing pain across her back, like someone had branded her with a red-hot poker. She could feel sweat beading on her brow. *Oh, God, here it is again.* It shot through her, sending her back into a spasm. She was gasping for breath now. *Tilda. Where's Tilda?* Here it was again, this time so extreme she passed out.

She came round a few seconds later. "Help. Help me, please," she shouted. It wasn't very loud, she didn't have the energy. Where was Doctor Murray? Where was Tilda? "Oh Christ," she blasphemed, "someone help me, please." Another bolt spasmed her body. "Oh! Help, help." The last pain had made her bladder go. Anella didn't know her waters had broken.

Mantel, retiring, thought he heard a call and stopped what he was doing. Yes, there it was again. He was down the corridor in seconds and, not bothering to knock, found Anella in acute distress.

"Where's Tilda?" he demanded. Anella couldn't speak, she just shook her head. "Anella. I'll just go and get the doctor."

Again, she shook her head. "No, don't leave me". Another pain was searing across her back and stomach. She grabbed his hand; Mantel in only a slight panic now.

"Oh, God in heaven, please," she pleaded; she was soaked in perspiration now. "I can't do this." She turned to Mantel. "I can't do this anymore. Please, where's the doctor? Help me, please help me." She was crying now, but feeling an urge to push and push. Mantel was thoroughly alarmed and just didn't know what to do. He gripped her hand tightly.

"Anella, you must have this baby. I don't know where Doctor Murray is, but I'm here. Keep calm, breathe deeply. Don't be afraid. This baby will be born, no matter what. Now, breathe, count to ten, breathe out, count to ten, breathe in –" And then he knew another spike of pain had come. He saw her body arch and again, for a few seconds, she fainted.

"Jesus." He grabbed a towel and wiped her forehead and watched her carefully until she came round.

"Mr Buchanen, I'm sorry, I'm so sorry – Ooooooh. Please help me, please." Mantel could have cried for her then; this was not right. Where was the doctor? He couldn't leave her like this to go and find him.

She appeared to have fainted again, when he heard a commotion in the corridor outside. The doctor and Tilda both appeared. Tilda looked flustered.

"Sir, the maid fell. We heard Madam in the passageway, so sorry."

The doctor was straight to examining Mrs Jameson closely; Mantel felt compelled to move away for decency's sake.

"Mrs Jameson, no more noise from you. Don't waste your energy on yelling; concentrate on the work you've got to do. No one's going to have this baby but you, there's no magic wand. Now, when I say push, I want you to push down as hard as you can. When I say stop, you MUST stop immediately. And hold your breath until I say." He gently pushed and pressed her belly. "Well, you've done very well so far, with Mr Buchanen's help. Now, do as I say, another contraction is coming." Suddenly, with the doctor there, the panic subsided and Anella got on with the lonely job of child-bearing, hating Eade for what he was putting her through.

Mantel sat by the fire; they had forgotten he was there. *Is this what all women went through?* he thought. It was a wonder there were any babies born at all.

"Right, Mrs Jameson, baby's head has crowned, stop breathing."

Anella was exhausted now. "One more push, gently, gently, there we are…"

The baby cried and the doctor oh so gently guided him out and placed him on Anella's belly.

She looked down and saw her little son for the first time. He was face-down, his little red naked back and mass of dark, curly hair the two things she noticed first. Hot tears of joy raced down her cheeks.

The doctor picked him up and turned him over and examined him. "He's perfect, mother, you've done an excellent job. Now, you'll feel another urge to push. Let it come, then we're done."

Anella was aware of Mantel hovering in the background.

"Come and see," she said, holding the baby close. She couldn't take her eyes from him. What a wonder. She was aware of Tilda fussing around with hot water and towels. Mantel had to leave the room. The baby was washed and swaddled. Anella was washed and helped out of bed so that sheets could be changed. She was made comfortable and given back her baby, and Mantel was allowed back into the room.

She gave him a beautiful smile. "Mantel, I'm sorry to have put you through that. I don't think I could have done it without your help. Come and see." She patted the bed.

He came and sat and looked. "Why, he's bloody tiny," he said in amazement. "You made all that fuss, woman, and he's the size of a pea." He saw her react. "A very beautiful pea, I have to say, just like his mother."

Anella ignored him then. Her baby was all. She couldn't stop looking at him. Each tiny finger was examined, each tiny toe and minute fingernail. She traced his little face, his shell-like ears, the little nose, the downy lashes – Oh God in Heaven, was there ever a baby such as this? She was so excited. Doctor Murray approached her then with a hot drink, made by Tilda.

"Mrs Jameson, drink this, it will help you sleep." She

shook her head. "You will need your sleep. Baby will sleep now for a while. He's had a tiring journey. You have to learn, when baby sleeps, so do you – and so do we tonight." He took the swaddled baby from her arms and laid him in the crib. "Now," he looked around the room, "I suggest, Mr Buchanen, you get some rest, and Tilda, you too. I'll stay, keep an eye. Off you go." And they did and left the good doctor sitting at the bedside, watching Anella take her drink to ensure a good night's rest. Eade's son was born on the 15th December, while the snow fell gently and the house settled into warm, comfortable silence after a momentous day.

CHAPTER TWENTY-FOUR

Christmas and the New Year meant nothing to Anella. so engrossed was she with her new baby. She called him Duff, because when she put him on her shoulder for winding, he made little burping noises, *duff, duff,* which she found highly amusing. She loved him, adored him; everywhere she went in the house, he went too. She fed him herself, disregarding the wet nurse. The female staff thought this was quietly outrageous, but Anella took no notice. At last, she was happy, never as gloriously as when with Eade, but his new son banished some of her terrible grief. They had a christening, not long after Christmas, as it was convenient, with the family and guests already there. James Edward Eade Jameson, son and heir. Anella believed that, every day, he looked more and more like his handsome father.

The month of March was an unhappy time for them all. The first anniversary of Eade's passing. Harold and Eliza and the children came to stay, out of respect, and Eliza and the girls Florrie and Freda adored the baby, which offset their sadness somewhat, but nevertheless… The house was a sad and empty place without Eade's vibrant personality.

But something happened that March.

So many times, Nell sat in her bedroom with baby Duff, feeding him, bathing him crooning to him and rocking him in her arms. Oh, he was so, so lovely. The image of his father. She would kiss him and stroke his downy head and look long into his impossibly dark eyes. She felt Eade was in this room somehow. She wasn't afraid; she would often call his name. Of course, he never replied. She would shrug her shoulders and tell herself not to be so silly. She had never got round to removing his clothes. They were still all there, all his possessions in cupboards and drawers, she couldn't face up to the task of clearing it all out. The thought of doing it panicked her and left her gasping for breath. To do that would be finally admitting that Eade really was dead. No! Unthinkable. There was always hope in her heart; somehow a mistake had been made and he would come breezing in, always in a dash, apologising for being late, always an excuse at the ready, always a hand slipped round her waist as he pulled her close and suggested in her ear that "They go upstairs and celebrate," and she would feel that bolt of desire shoot through her body. Oh how the tears flowed then. How lonely she was, and how alone she felt some days. Tilda? Mrs Bosworth and the twins? Eliza and Harold? There was no one. No one close, a helpmeet, a friend, a confidant. No one. Grief overwhelmed her. How she cried. Thank goodness for baby Duff. His needs were paramount. When he cried, her body sprang into action, her breasts would start tingling and she would have to feed him. It was quite a relief…

This particular day, Nell was very low and didn't want to leave her room. It wasn't a good day outside, rain battering the windows; it was grey, heavy clouds, not the weather to take a baby out in, so she didn't feel too much guilt.

Thank God for Mr Buchanen, Mantel, she thought. He could deal with all the business; that was his job. She had no liking for him at all, after what he let happen to Eade. He can deal with farming matters; she was slightly contemptuous of him. Actually, deep down, she knew she was being very unfair. In the early days, when she used to walk up to see the Major, Mr Buchanen, Mantel, was always around; he always engaged her in conversation, usually about his memory. She gave a little laugh. He always had that bit of string tied around his wrist. He always looked a bit dirty and unkempt. She supposed that was one thing in his favour, he had tidied himself up considerably.

Tilda bought up her lunch and tried to persuade her just to have a wonder around the house and Nell, surprisingly, agreed. Carrying Duff and with Tilda trailing behind her, she crossed to the other wing of the house. These bedrooms were mainly for the men, full of dark, heavy furniture and everything on a bigger scale. She came across two house-maids, chatting whilst cleaning and they were aghast that Nell had come across them working.

"Please," she held up her hand, "I'm sorry to disturb you. I'm just finding my way round. Is there a back staircase?"

"Yes, Ma'am," said the braver of the two. "There's two, actually. One off the main hall and then, if you carry on down this corridor and turn left, there's a portrait of Lady Jameson. If you push the panel inwards, it will click open."

"Does it go straight to the kitchens?"

"No Ma'am, the servants' hall. Some will be taking their break now."

"Thats alright, I have no wish to disturb them. I'll just go and look at her Ladyship's portrait, then we're done. Thank you."

She smiled and left them to carry on. And slowly, this interminably slow and sad day came to its inevitable end and Nell was glad to sink into bed, consumed by tears and dark thoughts. She didn't sleep for long. Something woke her and she shook her head disbelievingly.

That night, Eade came to her. Nell was overjoyed to see him and welcomed him eagerly.

He held his hand up to stop her coming too near. "Nell."
She hesitated and looked at him.
He shook his head. "No."
"Why?" she asked.

"Nell, I haven't got time to beat about the bush. I want you to marry Buchanen."

"What? Why? You know I don't like the man. He let you die, after all you'd done for him." Tears welled and threatened to overflow. She wiped them away.

Eade was exasperated "He didn't, Nell. There was nothing anyone could have done. It was a freak accident, it wasn't his fault. He's a good man and he loves you and the baby. I know he will take care of you both. We know he'll marry you for the right reasons; he's not a fortune hunter, is he?"

"He's a very poor comparison to you, Eade," she said sadly. "Why do you want this?"

"We're blood-brothers, Nell; we shared everything in the past, in bad times, he was there for me..."

"You were there for him," Nell interrupted hotly.

"Yes, I was, but now, he needs help. He's lost, Nell. Why shouldn't we share you?"

Nell was mortified. "Eade, how could you? What a thing to suggest!"

He shrugged his shoulders. "Nell, I loved you like I've never loved before. You made me very happy, and baby Duff is the result. He's my son and heir. Mantel loves him, you can see that; he will do his best for him. Don't hate him, Nell. I don't think he will ever get his memory back, it's gone. He'll never know all the facts. Be kind, Nell. Think, in years to come, what sort of person will baby Duff become with Mantel as his example and guide? And you as his mother? What child could need more? Think on, Nell..." His voice faded.

"Eade!" she shouted. "Don't go, wait, please, stay just a minute longer..."

He was shaking his head. "No, Nell, have to go..."

"No!" How could he leave her in the middle of such

an important discussion? Eade! She was so frustrated and confused. How could he suggest he shared her with Mr Buchanen, Mantel?

She did quite enjoy their daily walks every mornings. Was that a reason to marry someone? I don't think so, she told herself. Did she enjoy his company? Mmmmm, sometimes; actually, sometimes he was very entertaining and funny. Merissa de Haas certainly thought so. He was kind. She hadn't noticed any annoying habits in him. He had money – well, Eades' money, but then, so did she. It would be a consolidation of assets rather than a marriage. She would have to sleep with him. Oh God, she couldn't do that. Maybe they could come to an agreement, a business arrangement somehow. A marriage but without THAT! Somehow, she didn't think that would work.

From now on, she would observe Mr Buchanen, Mantel, a little more closely, just to see if he could be husband material. She bit her lip, something she always did when worried or unsure. Eade! What a position to put her in. He was good with the baby, though. It made her heart melt to see. He was such a big man, Duff was such a tiny baby. There was no doubt, baby Duff adored Mantel. His face lit up when he saw him. Was that any reason to marry someone? More lip-biting. Maybe. Did she have the right to deny her son? No. She could never deny Duff. Sometimes Mr Buchanen, Mantel, did things that touched her. He was kind, as Eade was kind. Was he as joyous? No. Was he as much fun? No. Oh Eade, she felt she was going to disappoint him. Give yourself time, she told herself. No rush. From now on, she would watch. Deep inside, Nell had the feeling that if she married Mr Buchanen, Eade would go. He would consider his job was done. She didn't want that, but was it fair? Eade was in limbo. She had to do the decent thing and free him. Sad tears came then. *Oh Eade, how could you leave me?* There would be no more sleep this night, and the morning found her heavy-eyed and very sad.

And so it began, her quiet observations of Mr Buchanen, Mantel. He was as astute in business as Eade was. He got on well with everybody, although his outside work for other farms stopped. He just didn't have the time anymore, but he was well known in the surrounding area and held in high regard. All points in his favour, thought Nell.

It was at this time, when Mr Buchanen, Mantel, was up at the folly, a shallow warm sun, the feeling of spring and renewal in the air, that he had a vision. Eade came to him. Quite frankly, he was astounded and at first, speechless. He stared at him, long and hard.

"Eade?" he asked disbelievingly.

"Ah, Mantel, glad you can see me."

Mr Buchanen, Mantel, shook his head. "Am I going mad?"

"No, Mantel. Look, I haven't got much time, so I'll come to the point. Mantel, I need you to marry Nell."

A snort of laughter from Mr Buchanen.

"Oh, really?"

"You have some feelings for her, don't you? She needs looking after. I worry she'll fall prey to some fortune hunter, some charming chap who'll talk his way into her affections and then squander her money. Mantel, we can't allow that to happen. You love baby Duff, don't you? I mean, you were there when he was born. This estate is his. My worry is Nell. She's vulnerable, she needs support. Sometimes she thinks she can't do this alone. You have to help her, Buchanen. If there was anyone I would want Nell to marry, it would be you. After all, we've shared everything in the past, haven't we? She'll be good for you Mantel."

"Eade, I don't think Nell holds me in high regard. There's too much dislike on her side…"

"Mr Buchanen, Mantel, don't let me down…" And then he faded away and Mantel was left standing there, astonished. He covered his mouth with his hand, something he always did when perplexed or worried.

CHAPTER TWENTY-FIVE

Mantel had always had feelings for Nell, always. He'd felt there was a bit of a spark there, until Eade jumped the gun and Mantel quickly realised Eade was going to win the race. Now? He didn't know where to start. Maybe baby Duff was the way in? Right, Eade, he would try. That's all he could do. He would start by resuming the morning's perambulations, so without more ado, he went back to the house.

Walking through the rooms, he came across Nell sitting on the floor in the sitting room, with baby Duff.

"Mr Buchanen, come." She waved him over. "Come and see." He came across. "Look." Nell patted the carpet. "Sit," she ordered. He knelt and waited. She was holding a wriggling Duff. "Watch, Mantel, look what he does."

She laid her baby on the floor on his back and for a few minutes, he waved his arms around excitedly and pumped his legs; there was copious amounts of dribble; he was using up a lot of energy, when suddenly, raising his head and twisting his little body, he managed to turn over. He looked in surprise at Mantel and gave him a wave, before breaking into a gummy, delighted grin.

Nell clapped her hands in delight.

"Well, Mr Buchanen, Mantel, what do you think of THAT? Isn't he amazing? He's a genius, isn't he?" She looked at him for confirmation. "That's the third time he's done that." The joy on her face was plain to see.

Mantel could only laugh. Of all the things that were happening on the farm and estate today, here he was, pretending to be impressed by baby Duff.

And then he felt a wave of shame. This was Eade's wife and son. He'd just spoken to Eade, hadn't he? Strike while the iron is hot, he thought.

"Nell, it's a nice day. Remember what Doctor Murray ordered? Ten minutes exercise every day. We have to resume your fitness regime. Sun's shining, it'll be lovely to get this boy out in the fresh air. I think we ought to do it, don't you?"

Before she could object, he swooped down and picked the baby up and even began to walk out of the room.

"Mr Buchanen, Mantel, wait, he has to have a shawl, wait, I have to get my things."

"Right, woman, don't hang about, the sun's shining, let's get out there." He didn't stop or make allowances for her fussing. She rushed after him with a baby bonnet, a shawl flung around her shoulders and another for Duff.

"Mr Buchanen, Mantel, stop. It's too chilly for him. Give him to me. I can wrap him up."

She took him and made a hash of it, while Mantel stood, waiting patiently. "Here, give him to me." It was as if he'd made an obscene suggestion. "Let me have him; he won't be as heavy for me as he is for you." Nell looked at him disapprovingly. "For God's sake, woman." He took an excited Duff and held him facing outwards, so he could see where he was going. This brought forth shrieks of excitement.

There was a lot of movement then, legs and arms wriggling. It was certainly good exercise for the baby, if not for Nell. Nevertheless, it was so enjoyable; the gardens and woods just opening up, the first primroses and pussy-willow. The bluebells just starting to make an appearance in the shady woodlands. Maybe because they were in a valley, everything seemed to start just that little bit earlier than anywhere else.

They were walking up to the folly where they could sit and admire the commanding views. Mr Buchanen, Mantel, walked all the way round it.. Was he showing it to baby Duff? Or was he looking for Eade secretly? Of course, there was no Eade, so he came and sat next to Nell with a big sigh and they sat in silence for a few, companionable minutes.

He bounced baby Duff a few times. then, carefully removed his bonnet.

"There, little man," he said softly, "now you can see properly. What do you think, eh? Everything you can see from here is yours – all yours – and we are looking after it for you."

Quietly, Nell began humming. This situation reminded her of a forgotten lullaby,

> "Oh hush thee, My baby.
>   Thy sire was a knight.
>   The woods and the fields
>   And the valleys you see,
>   They all, dear baby
>   Are belonging to thee."

She sang softly and baby Duff stilled, hearing his mother's voice.

"That's true," she said in wonderment. "I hadn't realised it before. All we can see from here?"

Mr Buchanen, Mantel nodded, "Yep, it's all Duff's. We have a great responsibility to him, Nell. Did you know there is a sugar plantation in Barbados? Or is it Mauritius? Can't remember now. Somewhere out there."

"What?" Nell was astonished.

"Nell, it was attributed in the will. I think you were too poorly to take note. But yes, it was Eade's father's. He was a great figure in the sugar industry and in the amassing of slaves. Barbados sugar is very fine; it used to sell for £25 to £50 a hogshead, don't know what it is now, but you see, a lot of Eade's income is still from sugar. We'll have to travel out there one day, Nell. Every now and again, a delegation arrive here, factor, merchant, shippers. They're here for weeks. Our weather usually sends them home. There's quite a mulatto population over there, thanks to Eades' father." Mr Buchanen, Mantel, smirked.

CHAPTER TWENTY-SIX

And so it began. Eade's visit to Mr Buchanen triggered in him a feeling of renewed responsibility. He didn't ever believe he could marry Nell – her feelings were ambivalent – but that didn't mean they couldn't get on. They could still work together, and they should work together, for the good of the estate and for the good of baby Duff.

Eade's visit to Nell had a profound effect on her. For days afterwards, she felt a terrible resentment. Why did he return, only to tell her she had to marry Mr Buchanen, Mantel? Even more hurtful, he said they shared everything; he didn't see anything wrong in sharing her. She could be a force for good as far as Buchanen was concerned. Eade could not leave until things were sorted, didn't Nell realise that?

During the later weeks of March, a slight thawing of relations occurred between Buchanen and Nell. She really did try to be nicer to him. She consulted him, asked him about the farm, the heifers; was the new barn nearly finished? She made a point of going out with him in the mornings for her ten minutes of fresh air, but sometimes, she bought baby Duff and they went in the carriage for a tour of the estate. Soon they would have the mammoth task of assessing the cottages and dwellings; the village school and buildings. Of course, this was a job for the factor and Buchanen, but Nell had made up her mind, she was going to be part of this too. New routines were set up daily for a few weeks and, as was the norm now, they met in the eating room for food and to discuss the day's events. Needless to say, baby Duff was always present, a not always silent observer, but he created the bond between both of them.

Buchanen was crafty. He knew he would get a good response if he praised the baby and compared him to Eade. This melted Nell's heart, as he knew it would.

One evening, Buchanen came into the eating room carrying Eade's dog, Ruff. He'd trodden on a flint and cut his pad. It had been quickly bandaged and Buchanen placed him gently in a roughly made dog bed and Nell flew to him.

"Oh Ruff, Ruff, what have you done?" She was full of concern. "He will be alright, won't he? She looked at Buchanen and felt her eyes welling up. She remembered giving the dogs to the men. "We can't let anything happen to him. He's all we've got left of Eade" and to her embarrassment, she began to cry. Baby Duff, alarmed by the change in his mother, then began to cry also.

Buchanen sighed with barely concealed impatience and observing the snotty tears of the baby – and Nell's – whipped out a handkerchief (clean, he was pleased to note) and handed it over. Still the two of them carried on, so Buchanen insisted on taking baby Duff. He walked him up and down the room, talking to him gently, non-stop, pointing out things in the room to him. The child quietened and gradually, his cries turned to coos, as he began to communicate.

"That's better, young man. No more of that silly noise from you. Leave that to your mother." He went and sat at the dining table, so Duff could bang his hands on its shiny surface.

He ignored Nell until she stopped her snivelling and had composed herself. He crossed the room to her, holding a now happy baby Duff.

"Nell, don't get so upset. Ruff will be fine. It's just a cut on his pad, that's all." He put his hand under her elbow.

"Come and sit here." He led her to the sofa. "Listen, when you get upset, Duff gets upset too. It's not fair on him. You have to keep reasonable." He was looking at her intently.

She gave a wry smile. "You're right, I know. It's because it's Eade. Anything to do with Eade, I can't cope." She grabbed the sleeve of his coat and wiped her tears on the rough fabric.

"Strewth, woman, where's the hankie I've just given you?"

They sat there together, Buchanen bouncing baby Duff on his knees, knowing there was a bond forming between them.

In May, they were married. Early morning at the village church. No fanfare, only Mr Buchanen and Nell and two witnesses: the grave digger, and an old woman they found outside, tending a grave. The church was cold, empty and bleak and not at all joyful as it had been with Eade. Buchanen paid them a guinea each and they were delighted. There was no celebration when they arrived back at the house; Tilda was the only person who knew what was going on, as she had care of baby Duff.

Nell couldn't speak when they arrived back; she went straight upstairs to her room and sank onto the rug in front of the fire and cried and within minutes, Eade was there.

"Nell."

She stopped and looked at him and went to grab his arm. He drew back and shook his head.

"Nell, no. Listen, I've told you before, be kind. You need to move out of this room, too many memories. Buchanen is a good man, a kind man, don't make it hard for him. He does love you, Nell – and you know well what he feels for Duff."

"No, Eade, I've made a dreadful mistake, this will never work. All I do is compare him to you."

"Nell, trust in yourself. I must go, Nell, my time is up. Give him your trust, it won't take too long Nell..."

He was gone and as she sat there, adrift and sorrowful, Buchanen entered the room and found Nell on the floor in misery.

He came straight over and knelt beside her and took her arm gently.

"Nell," he whispered, "what is it?"

"Buchanen, we've made a mistake. I can't do this. I'm afraid." Hot tears coursed down her cheeks. "I don't want to be married to you. I don't know what I was thinking of."

She was expecting him to deny they had made a mistake, to reassure her everything would be alright, but he didn't. He sat there, next to her and said nothing. Strangely, this calmed her down. She looked at him and still he said nothing.

Eventually: "Nell, first things first, we have to move to a different room, this one will not do. Then, we just have to be patient, Rome wasn't built in a day," he said and wondered where he was going with this conversation.

He didn't want to touch her, for it to be misconstrued. He could see, she was in a fragile state of mind.

"I think we need a brandy and then we must choose a new room." He slipped his hand into hers and squeezed it reassuringly. "Come on Nell, we can do this. It's not the end of the world."

He gave her a little smile, while she dabbed her nose on her sleeve. Buchanen whipped out of his pocket his wedding hankie, fine lawn, and waved it to Nell.

"Don't you ever have a handkerchief, woman?"

Her tears stopped and she even managed a tremulous smile. "I don't need one, I've always got yours." She wiped her face inelegantly and sniffed loudly. "Will you help me up?"

He did and insisted they look at the other empty rooms on this floor. Buchanen was determined they were not going to sleep in the old bedroom where memories of Eade were so prevalent. They came to the blue room where he was supposed to sleep that night baby Duff was born. He didn't mind it. What about Nell?

"What do you think of this room, Nell? There's the bathing room that side," he nodded, "and the dressing room this side. What do you reckon?"

Nell looked out of the window. The view was of the walled kitchen garden. She could see the gardeners working away there now. It would be interesting. She didn't want to enthuse too much, as it bought about ideas of sleeping here and sleeping with her new husband. She reluctantly nodded, so Buchanen did no more than pull the bell cord.

"Let's get the maids in here then, get the fire lit and the bed turned."

Tilda appeared then and was given instructions and she rushed off to get two other maids and a boy of all works to help with the heavy stuff while Nell went back to the original bedroom to check on baby Duff.

Buchanen was well aware of Nell's resistance to him. He wasn't too sure how he would stand up to Eade's perceived perfection. He shrugged his shoulders. This marriage was of convenience, of keeping Duff's inheritance safe; over time, maybe, there would be a thaw. Who knew?

Nell came back up later to see the room readied and she had to admit, it was charming. She crossed the room to show baby Duff the view from the window; when Buchanen, Mantel, walked in. He looked around, and stood behind Nell.

"I like this room, don't you? So we're in here from tonight?" The question was loaded.

Nell bit her lip and moved to the side. "Yes, I think so." Her voice was full of doubt.

He was well aware of her reluctance. He sighed and, ignoring baby Duff, left the room. Poor Duff. He was very disappointed. He always expected, when he waved, Buchanen would take him and much to his sadness, that didn't happen this evening. He let out a huge howl of anguish. *Not fair! Where are you?* Nell paced him up and down to no avail. He cried all the way along the corridor and down to the half landing, when Buchanen, hearing the baby's distress, came up the stairs to take him from Nell.

He looked at her inquiringly. "What's up?"

She shrugged her shoulders. "I think he was expecting you to take him."

Ignoring Nell, he took the baby and carried him downstairs, talking to him constantly, and the boy soon shut up and was crooning excitedly by the time they entered the eating room.

CHAPTER TWENTY-SEVEN

Theirs wasn't a loveless marriage; there was love, but not of the kind usually found between a man and wife. There was lots of love from both of them for baby Duff, but there remained this unbridgeable gulf between them. Nell wished Buchanen would sleep in a room of his own, but he wouldn't and she felt resentment about that.

Late back one morning, from visiting the new barn – it was a building of beauty: Flemish brickwork, oak beams – lunch was waiting in the eating room and Duff was demanding to be fed. Nell sat discreetly away from the table, her back to the door, feeling safe, when oh dear, in came Buchanen for lunch. When he realised Nell was feeding, he was acutely embarrassed. He apologised and turned to go.

"Buchanen, no I'm sorry. I shouldn't be in here, feeding Duff. I'm your wife, I can't keep hiding away, Duff needs to be fed. I'm sorry to embarrass you."

She covered herself up and sat the baby up to wind him.

"If you could just take him, Buchanen, I need to reorganise things." He whisked the baby away so Nell could adjust her clothing

Buchanen sat with baby Duff on his knee and rhythmically stroked his back up and down. This baby melted his heart, but he felt he couldn't say anything. Duff was gurgling away, leaning forward to take a chew of Buchanen's jacket sleeve when he suddenly gave a loud burp and sicked up over him.

"Oh Duff." Nell was horrified and went to grab him.

Buchanen could only laugh.

"You bloody little bugger – look what you've done,"

and Duff, looking quite surprised at his achievement, gave Buchanen an angelic smile. They both laughed then and felt a closeness not experienced before.

"I'm so, so sorry; proof that he loves you."

"Yeh, great." Buchanen was rueful. "There'll be a lot more of that, I expect. Better get used to it."

They finally sat for dinner and helped themselves, so they shared holding Duff. It was disconcerting, as he watched every mouthful and opened and closed his mouth like a baby bird. His eyes never left Buchanen's face. It made him laugh.

"Nell, you'll have to come and take this boy, he's watching every mouthful I take."

Later, in the sitting room, Nell nursing a port and Buchanen a brandy, she suddenly said, "Buchanen I must decide what to call you." He looked at her inquiringly. "Well, Mantel Buchanen O'Kyan. What's it to be?"

"You know everyone calls me Buchanen," he said.

"Well, I'm not everyone. From now on, to me, you will be Mantel." She bit her lip. "Is that alright with you?"

Buchanen looked down and extended a finger for Duff to grasp. "Nell, I know it's hard. It's as hard for me as it is for you. I know Eade is still in your mind, I feel it. I can't compare with him, you'll have to take me as you find me."

He shrugged his shoulders and Nell felt a sadness.

She lowered her head. *Don't cry*, she told herself, *it's not fair on Mantel.*

"We will get there?" she inquired.

"Not at the rate we're going," Mantel said dryly.

She stood up, a little indignant. "I think I'd better take Duff up for bed."

Mantel stood also. "Nell, I'm going up to bathe. Bring him in, he needs a wash. He can swim with me; he's a bit smelly, as I am too." He smelled his sleeve and pulled a face.

Goodness, this is a first, thought Nell, but nevertheless, she obeyed.

Mantel finally relaxed and laid back in the hot water. The room was warm and softly lit, towels warming in front of the fire. He'd left the door ajar, but Nell still tapped gently.

"Bring him in, Nell," Mantel called and there he was, baby Duff, naked, legs kicking, arms waving, excited to be immersed in the water.

"Be careful, won't you?" Nell was unable to stop being the fretting mother.

Mantel ignored her. "Pass me the washing cloth"

She did and Mantel carefully washed Duff. He was loving the water, there was much splashing and energetic movements. His face and hair were soaked, but he just blinked the wetness away. He grabbed the cloth and began sucking the water hungrily.

"No, boy," chided Mantel, "don't drink the bath water." This child always made him laugh. "Here, take him."

He held him aloft for Nell to envelope in a warm towel and she whisked him away, knowing full well, that when he realised he was staying out of the water, he would object – and he did.

Back in the bedroom, Nell was aware Mantel had come in wrapped only in a towel, so she concentrated on drying her baby and getting him ready for sleep. He wasn't happy, not until he spied Mantel looking over him and then, his angrily flaying arms turned to friendly waves.

"Nell, I'll finish him, you go and bathe." He never looked at her.

Biting her lip, she left the room and did as she was told, apprehensive as to what this evening held. She was afraid.

She came back and immediately checked Duff. He was lying on his side, thumb in mouth, a picture of contentment, making those soft little baby noises that Nell found irresistible. Her eyes filled with tears. Mantel was watching her. She was trying to avoid getting into bed.

He waited and turned the coverlet back on her side; she knew she had to get in. She couldn't look at him, she couldn't speak to him, but there was a lot of lip-biting going on.

"Mantel."

"Nell," they said together.

He slipped his arms around her and she lay stiff. He drew her head onto his chest and kissed the top of her head.

"Nell, you know I care for you."

"Yes."

"So why this fear?"

She shook her head. How could she tell Mantel how happy Eade made her in bed? She doubted anyone could take her to the levels of sexual bliss that Eade did.

How could she tell him part of her fear was the sheer size of him?

Mantel was a big man. Tall, over six foot. Powerful. Physically solid. Mentally strong.

If only she hadn't listened to Eade.

She tried to extricate herself. It was difficult.

She bit her lip. *Just got to be honest about this.* It was going to be difficult, she knew.

"Mantel, I can't. I just cannot. I'm very sorry."

She thought of Eade and baby Duff. As much as she wanted to keep everything safe and intact for Duff when he came of age, she knew it could not be this way, locked in a useless, loveless, arranged marriage. Mantel had to be free, and so did she. There must be a way of getting out of this mess.

She noticed Mantel had turned his back on her and was feigning sleep. Of course, there would always be the guilt, but tomorrow, they must talk and sort things out. What made it worse was that Nell knew most marriages nowa-days were business arrangements, love didn't come into it, but she had had those few precious weeks with Eade and couldn't contemplate an alliance with someone she had no feelings for. She didn't suppose sleep would come any easier, but with a decision made, she might have a little peace of mind. With that, she turned on her side, away from Mantel, knowing he was not a happy man. He never said a word.

CHAPTER TWENTY-EIGHT

When she awoke, Mantel was up and dressed. He looked exceedingly smart: waistcoat, cravat, shiny black boots; he was dusting down a black Fedora. He looked up at her.

"Have I forgotten something?" she asked. "Who are you meeting? Am I supposed to be there?"

He shook his head. "No, you don't have to be there, Nell. I'm down at the school with the factor. I'm meeting the architect. We're going to try and add the library on to the school, so the children have access to it; so you'll walk through from the school, into the children's library, then into the adults' library, then straight into the reading room. Once this is underway, Nell, then we can go and have a look at your farm. That'll be next, as per Eade's instructions." He finished lacing his boots and stood up. "Right." He pulled on his fob and checked the time. "I must be off."

NO! Nell was alarmed. He hadn't even seen baby Duff. That was a given in the mornings: that precious ritual of Duff's delight on seeing Mantel. His face lit up, there was a lot of dribble and much hand-waving; she was dismayed to see Mantel would not be delayed – he was off, saying he wouldn't be back until later this afternoon. She was more dismayed over this than she cared to admit. Baby Duff was not happy either; he howled and Nell was compelled, after feeding him, to prop him up in the perambulator and walk aimlessly outside to try and distract him. It worked. She took him to see the heifers, then on to see the pigs; they took the two dogs, Ruff and Jess, who spent a lot of time trying to round up the pigs until one of the sows stood her ground.

That was enough: they snuck behind Nell's heels and stayed put.

Eventually, back at the house, Nell ate lunch and fed Duff and asked Tilda to take him to Mrs Fletcher. She was the groundsman's wife. She'd had her baby boy three weeks before Nell had Duff. She was a clean, tidy, respectable woman and, when necessary, she would keep and feed Duff until Nell required him back. This arrangement worked well for both ladies; Mrs Fletcher being paid by Nell in cash. It was to be her money, not her husband's. Nell foresaw this evening would be difficult and she didn't want Duff disturbed by servants coming and going with Mantel's bags and trunks – and if harsh words were to be said, she didn't want him upset. Arguments infected the atmosphere, so best he was tucked with Mrs Fletcher's little baby, safe.

Mid-afternoon, she wandered down to the library, needing tea and an interesting book to read. She checked the other rooms: empty. Obviously Mr Mantel was not back yet. She pursed her lips. Obviously, things were not going quite so smoothly. Approaching the library, she heard a female voice and laughter. Nell was curious and, for some inexplicable reason, slightly annoyed. She entered the room with a flourish and stopped in surprise, to find Mantel in light-hearted conversation with Miss Sorrell. Their chat stopped, Mantel looking very relaxed, leaning against the desk, arms folded and Miss Sorrell seated demurely by the window. The convivial atmosphere changed immediately. Nell was now indignant, and it showed. Miss Sorrell, aware of an undercurrent of antagonism, stood up, discomforted, and announced she should really be leaving – Oh my goodness, was that the time? Mantel pulled the bell cord and Thompson arrived. He was instructed to bring the gig round, and Mantel escorted Miss Sorrell out, leaving Nell fuming, unreasonably, alone in the library. When he arrived back ten minutes or so later, she was quite openly, furious.

"Well, that was very cosy. I shouldn't have to remind you, Mantel, that you are a married man."

"Mrs Mantel, I shouldn't have to remind you, you are a married woman – who promised to love, honour and obey, and so far, you've done none of those things." His voice was dangerously low.

Nell halted in her pacing. How dare he? She always knew he was despicable and here was the proof.

"For better or for worse, Mr Mantel. How dare you bring Miss Sorrell in here and flirt with her! Have you got no morals?" She was biting her lip and trying to contain her jealousy and temper. "I think the sooner you remove yourself from our room, the better."

This stung. "Our room"? Since when had it been "our room"?

"Mrs Mantel, I will just say, that if I wish to speak to someone in the library, male or female, I will do so and you will just have to bloody well put up with it. I suggest you shut up and put up."

Nell was so angry, as she passed him, she raised her hand to slap his face. She hated him. Mantel, aware of what was coming, grabbed her wrist and twisted it, painfully, behind her back.

"No," he said, shaking his head.

She pulled her hand away. "So now we see the real Mr Mantel," she spat. "The sooner you are out of this house, the better; then you can carry on your smutty little liaisons to your heart's content." Oh, if only she was a man… she would punch him, slap him, order him out, never to darken her doors again.

As if reading her mind, he said, "I think the best thing I

can do, is remove myself and from tomorrow, I'll be at the Dower House." He turned and walked out of the room.

Nell stood there, shaking with anger, swallowing down her venom and hatred. She raced upstairs after him; she was ready for the biggest fight of her life. She wasn't going to make it easy for him to just leave. Deep down inside, she was stung and hurt because she knew, she knew, Mantel was right. She had not loved, she had not honoured, she had not obeyed. She was the one in dereliction of her duty. Eade would be ashamed of her. This bought her up short. She didn't want to think of Eade at this moment; but it didn't stop her, though.

She entered the bedroom in a fury, ready to hurl insults and inflict pain, when suddenly, she felt... what did she feel? Eade was there. She could feel his presence. She stopped and looked around. He was telling her, *Stop, Nell, stop*. She looked cautiously at Mantel, who was silently throwing clothes into a trunk. Suddenly, she was overwhelmed with shame. She had to stop. She had to stop this situation; she somehow had to make it good. She had to do something. All the anger was leaving her, she felt deflated. Suddenly, she was near to tears and full of remorse. What could she do?

"Mantel," she said, quietly, hesitantly. He stopped and looked coldly at her. "Mantel, I'm sorry, I'm truly very sorry – I let my anger get the better of me. Please don't go. We made a promise to Eade, didn't we? What about baby Duff? I can't deprive him of you, it's not fair. He loves you – how would I explain to him?"

She became silent. She sank to the floor, in front of the fire; there were no words. What could she say? Hot tears coursed down her cheeks. She was ashamed that Eade had caught her out. Caught her being spiteful, resentful, jealous. She looked sideways at Mantel. Had Eade come to him, she wondered? By the look on his face, most definitely not.

"Mantel." She covered her mouth with her hand. She took a deep breath and decided to start again.

"Mantel." She couldn't look at him. "Mantel, please stop."

He did and flung an armful of clothes over the chair.

"Well?"

"Mantel, you're angry. I know. I'm sorry, I am, I know you'll probably find it hard to forgive me." She stopped, not knowing what more to say. "Please, don't go. Please don't leave us. I will try, I really will. I can't live in this house without you here, just me and Duff. I won't be able to cope." She buried her head in her hands then, so that Mantel would not hear her sobs. She had nothing to lose now. "Mantel, I promise, I will change now. I promise." Hot tears spilled down her face. She couldn't say any more.

She was secretly hoping, Mantel would stop his packing completely and sit on the floor beside her, take her hand and apologise and say how sorry he was, that it had come to this... but he didn't. She sat in silence and he ignored her. Another trunk was dragged out and he began filling it with boots and shoes, endless stuff. She felt dreadful, her hair in disarray, her eyes red and swollen, her mouth sore from her constant biting, snot and saliva running down her chin. She tried, unsuccessfully, to clean herself up and then noticed Mantel was holding a hankie under her face. She took it.

Now he sat beside her, stretching his legs out in front of the fire, folding his arms.

"Well?" he asked again.

"We could start again, couldn't we? Couldn't we? Forget everything that's gone before?" She looked at him sideways. He was very silent. She had to accept that if things were to change, she had to start tonight, after dinner, after brandy. She had to be fragrant, clean, alluring, soft, accommodating, willing even. She closed her eyes; how difficult was this going to be? *Strike while the iron was hot,* she thought.

"We could," she coughed slightly, "we could try now, couldn't we?" Oh! how she was having to humiliate herself.

Mantel was looking at her and smiling. Her heart soared. There was hope!

He stood up and crossed the room to the dressing table and bought back a mirror. "Here, look." He handed her the mirror.

Oh, God in heaven! She covered her face with her hands and started to cry once more. No, it was never going to happen while she looked like this. It was then they heard the gong for dinner.

Mantel stood. "You'd better clean yourself up," he said abruptly and left the room.

Nell sighed. She could only splash her face with water and keep her swollen face averted.

Dinner was awkward. Nell had no appetite, but she drank the wine and had a port while Mantel smoked a cigar. She sat in silence and tried to plan her attack when finally upstairs. Mantel knew she was up to something by the amount of lip-biting going on.

The silence between them in the small eating room was leaden. Mantel deliberately said nothing, knowing full well it would discomfort Nell. He felt a slow, burning anger against this woman. It was not for her to dictate to him whom he could or could not talk to. Her animosity was motivated solely by jealousy. How dare she? Unable to sit brooding any longer, he stood up abruptly, knocked back his brandy in a gulp and puffed the last of his cigar, throwing the stub on the fire. He buttoned his jacket.

"I'm doing the rounds," he said gruffly and was off without another word. Nell knew he would be fifteen minutes or more, checking the empty rooms, the fires, the candles. This was a job usually done by the servants, but Mantel, out of consideration for Nell originally, had taken it on, to give her time to arrange herself for bed and do what women had to do. Of course, it was all unnecessary, as Nell would not co-operate and become his wife.

Nell watched him go and then flew upstairs and rang for Tilda. She wanted to remove herself and sleep in another room, but Tilda was slow in coming. Consequently, Mantel arrived and Tilda, uncomfortable, kept her eyes lowered and said Madame's bath was ready.

"No." Mantel shook his head and shot such a look at Tilda that she removed herself hastily and shut the door behind her quickly.

Nell, standing silent, realised this had to stop.

"Mantel, I can't do this." She felt a desperate need to get away. She didn't actually like Mr Buchanen very much, did she? He did let Eade die, after all. And suddenly, she was filled with a great wave of anger, of resentment, of dislike. Why should she have to put up with him? No. Enough.

"No, I will not do this." She bit her lip as she could see the anger in Mantel's whole stance. She had to show him she was not afraid of his temper and she would not be intimidated by his size or his strength. She was haughty.

"I think we should stop playing games. We've made a terrible mistake and it has to stop." She took a few steps away and turned to look at him.

He finally spoke.

"We made a vow before God, we made a vow to Eade and you have changed your mind." He spoke with contempt. "You have lied, you have deceived, you've misled and never had any intention of committing yourself to holy matrimony."

Saying these words made him furiously angry. He'd

agreed to this because of a promise he'd made. No more, then; he was done.

Nell, stung by his words, completely lost all control.

"How dare you? You! You stupid, useless man, you who let my Eade die! How dare you stand there and lecture me? You are despicable!"

She strode towards him, arm raised and she slapped him as hard as she could. She saw the shock register on his face and emboldened, she raised her hand to do it again. There was no restraint, she no longer cared, she was beyond reasoning. Mantel recovered quickly and caught Nell's wrist in a vice-like grip and twisted it behind her back that made her yelp.

"No." Mantel's voice was ominously low. "You're bloody lucky I don't knock you into next week. Thank God, Eade never got to find out the real woman he married. A cheat, a liar, someone with no moral responsibility at all. You must look to yourself, Mrs Buchanen, you disgust me!"

And with that, he released his grip on her wrist and pushed her away. Unfortunately, Mantel in temper, gave Nell a much more forceful shove than he had originally intended and Nell reeled backwards, losing her balance. She fell heavily.

"Oh my God!" Mantel covered his face with his hands. Shit. He stood for a minute, shocked at what he had actually done. He'd pushed Nell so violently she'd fallen to the floor. He approached her cautiously; she wasn't crying, she was on the floor sitting, in shock, pale, breathing quick shallow breaths.

Mantel sighed. Whatever was he thinking? Why did this woman rouse him to anger so easily? He carefully approached her and lifted her onto a bedroom chair. She offered no resistance, just sat there, silent. For Mantel, the silence was a bigger reproach than if she raged and shouted. He crossed the room and poured a large brandy for Nell.

"Here, drink this. Nell, this has to stop now. No more. This cannot go on." He proffered the glass. She ignored him. He waited. She made no move to take the drink.

"Nell, just a sip. It'll make you feel better, please."

Mantel felt huge shame. He had never been aggressive towards a woman before, not even to the sluts, the camp followers, when he was in the army. He shook his head and sent up a silent apology to Eade.

Nell took a deep breath.

"Mr Buchanen, I have no doubts about how you feel about me; you've now made it plain. You must have no doubts about what I feel about you." She rubbed her wrist, which was very sore looking. "I cannot comply to your wishes, I have no wish to. The arrangement shall cease. I'm sure you realise we could never be compatible. We have to get this marriage annulled and get out of this ridiculous situation."

Oh, silly Nell. Immediately, Mantel was burning with anger. He grabbed her dress by the collar and hauled her out of the chair and dragged her across the room to the bedroom door and pushed her up against it. He shook her violently. God, if he hit her now, he would kill her.

He saw the terror in her eyes. He leant his head on the door, aware of Nell's shallow breathing. He stilled. Nell was so near, so warm, so afraid. He breathed gentle but hot onto her neck; he noticed he'd torn the ruffle on her collar.

"Nell," he whispered softly. He felt her body loosen and she turned her head so that her mouth was as near to his without actually touching. Nell was ashamed to admit to herself, she was now aroused; still frightened, but waiting expectantly. She moved her lips so they brushed against Mantel's; there was still no kiss. He brushed his beard on

Nell's cheek and nuzzled her neck and Nell succumbed then. Mantel knew. He lifted her carefully and took her to their bed and graciously laid her down, all the while, looking at her with eyes dark with desire. Now it was all haste after days of arguments, resentments, hostility, hatred even. Mantel just wanted to get her clothes off, Nell needed him to undress her, so it was fast and desperate; so many clothes to be discarded, they gave up in the end and just fucked as best they could. Mantel enfolded Nell in his arms and kissed her face gently and Nell lifted her head to offer him her neck. She closed her eyes. His soft, warm mouth sent shivers down her spine. Excitingly, Mantel unhooked her dress and slipped it down over her shoulders and removed it entirely. She wouldn't let him remove her shift. That was for later. Mantel didn't need help removing his clothing, but it was erotic and sensuous having Nell touch him and undo buttons. He watched her all the time. She stopped.

"You're looking at me."

He nodded. "Mmm."

"Stop. I'm embarrassed."

"Where should I look then, Nell?"

She gave a little laugh and shrugged. the strap of her shift falling off her shoulder and revealing a goodly part of her breast.

She pulled the strap back up.

"Mantel. An hour ago, I hated you, despised you. Loathed you. Resented you." She bit the inside of her lip. "Now – I don't know." She lowered her head and shed a hot tear.

"Nell, we made a vow, more for Eade than God. I made a promise and I have to keep it. Nell, I'm not mad or insane, but Eade came to me."

"What?" She was shocked.

"Yea. Up at the pavilion. I saw him as clearly as I see you

now. He asked me to take care of you and baby Duff. He died before Duff was born, so he must have been keeping watch all the time. He was so worried about you, Nell. He thought you were vulnerable. Prey to some unscrupulous fortune-hunter because you were sad and low. I promised him."

Mantel shrugged his shoulders and said no more. He noted Nell's mouth had dropped open in shock and she'd gone very pale.

She held her head in her hands as fat tears rolled down.

"Why? Why didn't you tell me? He came to *me*; every time I was alone in the bedroom, he was there. He wouldn't let me touch him. He told me to marry you." She was completely undone then; she felt as if her head would burst. "How could you not tell me? If only I'd known. My Eade." She was desperately sad and sobbing unrestrainedly.

"Nell." Mantel was lost. "Nell, don't. We're doing it, aren't we? No one said it would be easy. We're doing what Eade asked us to do. Now we've got all the shit out of the way. We're married; now, hopefully, we might have reached an understanding." He said this cautiously. "I said I would look after you and baby Duff, and that's what I'm trying to do. Having more luck with Duff than with you," he joked.

"Don't," she choked.

Mantel sighed and retrieved the brandy he'd poured earlier and handed it to Nell. "For God's sake, drink this, woman, or you'll never stop."

He sat down on the bed next to Nell and took a sip of it himself, while she was holding it. She moved to sit on his lap, watching him. She took a large gulp of the brandy and promptly coughed, it was far stronger than she realised. Mantel laughed and kissed her mouth, licking the drink from her lips. Oh! What a sexual, intimate thing to do, Nell felt him shift beneath her. She closed her eyes. *Please*, she silently prayed, *take my shift off now* – and Mantel, as if he'd heard her speak, slowly slipped his fingers along her shoulders and slid the silky fabric down her body. Now he saw Nell naked for the first time and she was lovely. Full breasted, with rosy pink nipples, a rounded belly and hips… hips and bum to die for.

"Mantel," she whispered into his mouth.

He was kissing her everywhere then and it tickled. His beard grazing her skin in unexpected places, suckling her nipples and pulling on the soft skin of her armpits. He was making her laugh and she so wanted him.

"Mantel," she tugged on his beard. "Stop teasing me." She tried to grab his manhood; he was too quick. He had hold of both her hands and he stopped for a moment to examine the red marks on her skin. She felt his tongue on her skin and it sent a bolt of desire through her body.

"Mantel," she said again. "Please!"

He couldn't deny her any longer, nor himself come to that, so he parted her legs and entered her quickly. Nell was more than ready and she rushed him on, coming before him, again and again and Mantel playing "catch-up". He closed his eyes.

"Bloody hell, Nell!" He shook his head in disbelief.

CHAPTER TWENTY-NINE

They lay in sated silence, Mantel's body spooned around Nell's, his hands possessing her soft flesh. She turned to lay on her back, still close to Mantel, his arms around her.

"How can hate turn to love in just a few hours?" she asked.

"Never hate, Nell. Not from me. Every other emotion: frustration, annoyance, impatience, anger and love. I've always loved you, Nell, right from the very beginning. I had no memory, didn't know my own name or what day of the week it was, but I knew a certain female would be walking up the drive. I always tried to stop her and talk to her, but what could I say? She was always very lovely."

"Mantel." Nell was shaking her head and, again, she was crying.

"Nell." He turned her towards him and kissed her wet face. "Stop now. I've got no more nose wipes, you'll have to use one of Duff's muslins. Here." He cuddled her close and pulled her hair away from her face and twirled it in his fist at the back of her neck. "Let everything go now, Nell. Be pleased. Eade has got his way. He doesn't have to worry about you anymore. You're safe, baby Duff's safe, the house and estate are safe..."

"And I'll keep you safe," interrupted Nell.

Mantel laughed. "Yes, Nell, you'll keep me safe. From all those predatory women out there, eager to get their claws into me." He ran a hand up and down her bare back.

"Don't mock me" she warned lightly. "I've seen how they flock round you – and you – you are a bit of a flirt."

"Nell, you do make me laugh." He gripped the cheeks of her bum and kneaded her softly and insistently. "Come on then, Nell, let's have a bit of flirting."

"I don't know how to flirt, but you can kiss me there." She pointed to her neck. He obliged. "And you can kiss me there." She lifted her arm for him to investigate her armpit. "Hey, kiss me here." She stroked her breast. Mantel was very obedient, kissing her everywhere she demanded.

"Is this flirting?" she asked.

Mantel was lost. "I dunno, Nell, don't know what you would call it, but I like it. You do too – where next?"

She indicated her plump belly and deep belly button and Mantel's tickling tongue had her giggling uncontrollably.

"Stop," she gasped, but he could not, so she grabbed his beard. "Please stop, or I'll have an accident." She was serious now. "Flirting's over, now you know what you have to do," she deliberately showed him the tip of her tongue.

Mantel flipped her over, so she was on her knees, bum up in the air; he parted her legs with his knee and entered her from behind, so hard and fast, Nell gasped out loud. He was knocking the breath from her body. Her pleasure was exquisite; she felt herself losing consciousness as wave after wave of orgasm swept through her. She collapsed onto the bed and Mantel rested on his elbows above her. He didn't want to slip away, it was too soon. He brushed his beard on her back and he felt her shiver.

"Lay on me," she whispered. So he did, very gently and rolled over, taking Nell with him, so he was laying on his back and Nell laid on top of him.

"Is that flirting?" she asked, pretending innocence.

Mantel was biting her ear. "No. We got it wrong. That wasn't flirting. Can't believe we got it wrong. We'll just have to keep on practising." He laughed and blew hot breath on Nell's ear and neck.

Ten, twenty minutes later, both quite recovered from their exertions, Nell craftily held her wrist up for Mantel to see.

He looked at her puzzled.

"Look at my wrist. Look at my hand, where I smacked you."

"Yes?"

"It hurts. It's very sore. It needs kissing better."

She pressed her nose against his, so her mouth was over his, not touching, not kissing, just breathing into him. They were hypnotised, Mantel twisting and twisting her hair. He softly took her lip in his mouth and Nell closed her eyes. She needed Mantel this minute, but he was too slow. Out of desperation, she pleasured herself and came immediately, much to her satisfaction and Mantel's amazement, she lay, legs akimbo, unashamed. She took Mantel's hand and covered herself with it. He was warm.

"Sorry. I couldn't wait and you still haven't kissed my hand better," she whispered.

"Nell, I can't believe what you've just done. Have you no shame?" he was laughing. "Ladies don't do that sort of thing."

She bit her lip. "This lady does. I liked doing it with you watching." She closed her eyes. "I could do it again for you, if you like." She moved her legs.

"So you don't need me, then?" he asked. "Well, you carry on, I'll just have a kip!"

He went to turn over, secretly enjoying their game, but Nell was on him, a leg over his hip and her mouth kissing his back, sucking and biting, so that by the morning, he would be covered in love bites. She flung her arms around his neck and began kissing his neck, his ears, pulling on his ear lobes. She would not stop. He turned to her and took her face in his hands, gently slowing her down.

"Nell, you can do that for me anytime you like, but not now."

"Why not?"

"We need to sleep. I need to cuddle you. Turn around."

Only then did she realise, she was exhausted. The tensions, the arguments, the sexing had made her so tired. It was bliss to lay with Mantel's body curved around hers and have him hold her and rub his beard into her neck. She closed her eyes and drifted. Oh Mantel...

Tilda was in early with the tea tray.

"Tilda, can you fetch baby Duff for me?" Nell felt she was at bursting point.

Good Tilda was back within a few minutes.

"He's clean and dry, Ma'am, ready for you." She placed him in his cot and she swiftly left, nervous of Mantel.

Mantel bought him over to Nell.

"He looks hot to me," he commented. "He needs to get some of those layers off."

Nell scrutinized Duff carefully. He was pink; was he hot from a fever or was she being over-protective? She did no more than remove all his clothes, so he was naked and she could examine him closely. Oh! His perfect little body, his smooth, unblemished back and little rounded bum, his chubby legs and fat wrists and his beautiful face. There was no rash, no spots anywhere, so it was with relief, she took him to bed and sat, propped up with cushions and pillows, just holding him. Duff, smelling his MaMa, became fractious.

"Sh, sh, sh," she crooned gently and put him to her breast, Duff never taking his eyes from her face and his little starfish hands clutching at her skin. They were lost in their timeless world of Mother and baby bonding and Mantel, watching, sat silent. A naked Duff, a naked Nell feeding him and him unclothed made him hugely aroused. He wanted to cup Nell's other breast. Nell gave a quiet little laugh.

"Mantel, no," she said. "Don't be sexy with me while I'm feeding the baby."

"Why not?"

"It's not right." She hesitated.

He laughed then and said, "You say? And this baby is the result of what?"

"Patience, Mantel, just a few more minutes."

She shifted Duff from one breast to the other and Duff managed a smile and gleeful wave to Mantel, knowing, in his baby way, it would keep Mantel happy.

"Christ, he's a noisy fella," Mantel commented as Duff slurped away, his tiny hand constantly squeezing Nell's skin. Nell laughed and kissed Duff's warm forehead. Duff halted feeding and caught sight of Mantel and gave him a friendly wave. Nell sat him up and winded him, rubbing his back gently.

"I give up with this boy, he just wants you," and she handed him over to Mantel, who took him cautiously, wary of his nakedness.

He lightly rubbed Duff's back and he began bouncing up and down on Mantel's knee. Nell sat back against Mantel, drinking her tea and enjoying the fun. Baby Duff loved to explore Mantel's face; his fat fingers were always exploring his beard, his nose, his mouth, already swollen from Nell's attentions.

"Nell, take him; he makes me nervous when he has no napkin on. He usually produces something, one end or the other."

Nell chuckled and took him back, just as Duff obligingly burped loudly and farted almost at the same time. His look of surprise was so funny, they both laughed out loud.

Nell dressed him lightly and already, he was rubbing his

eyes and trying to locate his thumb. She sang softly to him while putting him down in his cot.

"Oh hush thee, my baby,
Thy sire was a knight.
The woods and the glens
And the valleys you see
They all, dear baby
Are belonging to thee."

She left him then and came back to sit on the ottoman to talk to Mantel.

"Haven't you got to be out today? Yesterday, you were up and out, no time wasted."

"I might have"

"What do you mean 'might have'?"

He shrugged his shoulders.

"I might just stay here with you today. It might be raining." He waved his hand vaguely at the window.

Nell bit her lip. He was playing a game.

"It's not."

"It might rain later."

"It won't."

He looked pained.

"Nell, I might be changing my mind about going out today. I might stay here with you and Duff. I like watching the two of you together, it makes me hot."

"What? You find me being a mother interesting?"

"I find it very sexy. It makes you even more, even more…" He shook his head. "Um, interesting," he finished lamely. He looked at her meaningfully. "I might have lots to do indoors today." He was biting his lip to mock Nell for constantly biting hers.

"Mantel, I'm getting the feeling you're being a bit naughty. You're playing hookey today, am I right?"

"Might be. "

"Might! Is that all you can say?"

"It might be." And with that, he collapsed on the bed, laughing.

Nell sat on the bed.

"You have no intention of going out today, you haven't even put your boots on."

"Do you know, Nell, you might be right."

He grabbed her and pulled her down on the bed beside him. "I haven't got my boots on, but you haven't got your clothes on, well, not many. You must be cold, best get under the sheets."

He made haste and crawled under the bedding, grabbing Nell and covering the both of them with the covers. He snuggled up close and enclosed Nell in his arms.

"What do you say, Nell, if we stay here all day? This could be our tent, it's nice and cosy."

He ran his tongue over her mouth and she caught him between her teeth She laughed and released him, but she loved his mouth, it was warm, soft and moist and it excited her enormously. He turned on his side, keeping Nell close, resting his head on his hand. She rubbed her thumb lovingly across his lips and he, with his other hand, massaged her bottom, his fingers searching. He loved to feel her body; she was warm, plump and very soft and oh! so kissable and very soon, he was lost in pleasuring Nell. She offered him her body, her beautiful breasts, her rounded belly. He kissed and sucked and tickled and she was helpless with desire, especially when he ran his fingers along the back of her knees. They came together, their bodies in harmony, and Nell gasped as if she was drowning. Mantel could feel her contracting her muscles to try and keep possession of him, but he was slipping away and she gave a great sigh.

"Mantel," she whispered, as she hoicked a leg over his hip; she was not one to hang about.

"Nell," he pushed her hair away from her face, "give me ten minutes to re-load." He ran his hand up her thigh and felt her shiver. Her eyes were closed, so he kissed her eyelids.

"Nell, we've done nothing but fuck and laugh all night. I'm blaming you. You'll have to leave me alone, I need food, I need a bath, I need a rest," he laughed.

"I know, I know." Nell bit her lip.

"Hey!" Mantel ordered, pulling her bottom lip with his fingers. "Stop biting your lip. The only thing you can bite is me!"

She gave a little laugh, but something was on her mind.

"What's up?" Mantel knew immediately she was suddenly preoccupied.

"Mantel, will you leave us one day? "

"Nell, why are you asking me such a question now? Why would I leave you and Duff? What are you thinking?"

"Mantel, when your memory comes back and you discover you have family in Scotland, what will you do? It's only natural you will want to go back and find them. Nothing's certain, is it? What will I do?"

"Nell, through war, surviving that accident, being so close to death and coming through it, you re-evaluate everything. So – I might have an estate in Scotland. Do I care? I have an estate here. My life is here, you are here, Duff is here. Do I want to lose you, do I want to lose everything for an unknown life up there? Maybe I'm a coward, Nell; maybe as I'm getting older, I'm getting softer. I'm not interested, Nell." He shook his head. "You know, there were the highland clearances. The countryside was in turmoil. Then the bloody British government banned the kilt –" He stopped. How did he know this? He didn't want these memories, they were no good to him. They made his head fuzzy; he needed to clear his mind. "I know who I am. Mantel Buchanen

O'Kyan. Do I know how old I am? No. Does it matter? No. Do I want to go back? No. If I ever had to go back, you would have to come with me; I couldn't do it without you. This is my life now: husband, father, landowner, country gentleman – I have an estate to run," he turned to Nell and kissed the top of her head, "and a wife that needs sexing. Try not to worry, Nell. We've got a new life to build together now; nothing else matters." Phew! What a speech.

He pulled on the bell cord for a servant and within minutes, Tilda had appeared.

"We need bath, breakfast, new bed linen."

Tilda bobbed. Secretly, she was appalled. How could they want breakfast this late in the morning? Both of them in a state of dishevelment. It was quite shocking, but maybe this is how the upper classes, newly married, behaved. Who knew?

Within minutes, their bathing room was ready and Mantel insisted Nell bathe first. Slightly embarrassed, she eased herself into the hot, silky water and laid back. Oh! she sighed with satisfaction and closed her eyes. She felt achy and well used. Now she could just relax and let go.

"Hey, want this?" Mantel threw a sponge into the water and splashed her face. "Sorry." He grabbed it and squeezed it over her head.

He was suddenly overcome with need. Nell was naked. Soapy and slippery, her skin pink from the hot bath water. He slipped off his robe.

"Kneel up, Nell," he demanded, and he was in, behind her, the water lapping his thighs.

"Mantel." She had her back to him and tried to turn. He was having none of it. He grabbed her silky bottom and parted her cheeks; he was in quickly and joyously and Nell gripped the edge of the bath as she took him in. How exciting!

"Mantel," she gasped, "stop. Oh, please!" His body was smacking into her; she felt weak; water was splashing everywhere. Nell felt herself quickening, her body beginning to spasm. She came just as Mantel climaxed – it was wonderful. She'd never had sex under water before; he slipped out of her and grabbed her around her waist. He was breathing heavily on her back, rubbing his beard on her skin.

"That was a surprise," he gasped.

"Mantel," she laughed, "I'm trying to get clean."

"Don't bother. I like you dirty. I prefer you dirty. Smelling of me." He sniffed her neck.

"Stop! Here, take this sponge. Control yourself long enough to scrub my back – and my arms – and here, my legs; oh and here," she pointed to her breasts, "and here," she raised her arm so he could see her red, sore wrist. He stilled. He didn't want to be reminded. Nell was immediately contrite.

"Mantel, you don't get it do you?"

"What?"

"I show you my wrist deliberately. I do it to entice you; to make you feel guilty; so you will make it up to me; you will kiss my wrist and I will succumb. It's a game. I didn't want you to be upset. Please."

He didn't say a word, just looked. He shook his head slightly.

"Nell."

"Stop! I'm out now. You wash. I'll go and attend my poor, sore wrist." She made a face of acute pain and then ruined her little act by giggling. She put on Mantel's robe; she thought she could hear Duff.

Sure enough, he was awake and making his presence known. Amazingly, he was standing up in his cot, hanging on to the bar with little fingers.

"Oh my!" she rushed back to the bathing room.

"Mantel, come. Come and see." She waved her hand impatiently. "Quick!"

He was up, out of the bath and wrapping himself in a bath sheet, water going everywhere. "What is it?" he knew it was nothing alarming as Nell was excited. He followed her into the bedroom.

"Look." She pointed to Duff standing. Duff, up until that minute, happy to bounce up and down on his pudgy feet, stopped and sat down with a bump. Tears flowed then. Mantel was straight over to him.

"Nell, you frightened him." He picked him up. "Come and have a bathe with your Pa." He laid him on the bed and with Nell's help, took his clothes off and his wet napkin.

"Poooh! Stinky boy." Mantel pulled a face. "Nell, give him to me when I'm in." So it was back to the bathing room with a fresh, hot pail of water and bubbles and Duff was in with Mantel, baby swimming and splashing, happy to be with his favourite man. Nell sat and watched.

"Mantel, he was standing up. Isn't he marvellous?"

Mantel stopped his play with Duff and laughed.

"Nell, he's doing what babies do. All babies are marvellous to their mothers."

"Mantel." Nell was deflated. "But Duff's more. He *is* more, isn't he?"

"Of course he is, Nell; the most clever, intelligent, most beautiful baby boy in the world. That's about as 'more' as you can get. Come, take him, I'm turning into a prune."

CHAPTER THIRTY

Mantel did not go out on business for three days. He stayed with Nell; breakfast was sent up every morning and Mantel would feed Nell, a mouthful of food for her, then one for him, she even made him chew her food for her and pass it over, into her mouth, which she accepted like a baby bird. For these two, nothing was taboo. Every morning, after feeding and winding Duff, Nell would hand him over to Mantel. One day, this baby would be a force to be reckoned with. He was already like his father, dark-haired, dark-eyed, charismatic, with a forceful personality. There was a strong bond between him and Mantel; Duff had decided Mantel was the man for him. Duff would lock him in his eyes and almost hypnotise Mantel. Nell would watch. Was this a baby survival technique? Duff was doing a good job, teaching Mantel how to be a good father and Mantel, without realising, was a good pupil. He loved to hold Duff when he was tired; he would hold him on his chest and Duff would become frustrated, unable to locate his thumb. Mantel would take hold of his tiny hand and. guide his little thumb into his wet mouth and his eyes would close as he sucked greedily. Mantel laid him gently in his cot.

"He's gone, Nell," Mantel said quietly. He crossed the room and sat on the bed where Nell, in a fresh chemise, was applying lotion to her arms.

Mantel sniffed. "Can I smell that?"

"I expect so." Nell raised an arm for Mantel to scent. "It does have the most wonderful perfume." She watched him, knowing the effect she was having on him.

He indicated to her to pass the bottle to him. "Creamed anywhere else?" She shook her head.

He lifted the hem of her shift and poured a dollop of lotion onto the palm of his hand. He took her foot onto his lap. He then carefully anointed each toe softly and gently. Oh! it was tickly, but Nell didn't want him to stop; then his hand was cupping her heel, pressing her flesh with his thumbs and then over her ankle and up her calf and then, breathtakingly, along the back of her knee.

"Mantel." She looked at him with dark eyes.

He laughed and shook his head. He wasn't going to stop now. Another shake of lotion and his hands were on her thigh, insistent and kneading; he loved to feel her flesh, so soft and fragrant. He was thorough, watching her reaction constantly. He started on her other foot, wisely giving up on her thigh – things could get out of hand. Nell laid back on the bed and succumbed to the tingling sensations coursing through her body. When he arrived at the top of her other leg, Nell was desperate.

"Mantel, please."

He was on top of her then, rifling her chemise over her hips and kissing her there. She could feel his bristly beard on her belly. "Nell," he whispered.

She closed her eyes. If Nell had ever known the effect of massaging her feet and legs would have on her libido, she would have insisted on it every night. She was so ready and willing for Mantel. She clawed his back, bit his shoulder, pulled on his lip, how she wanted him. She'd never been this abandoned, this wanton, this needy. Mantel was taking her higher and higher, she was almost losing consciousness. Oh! Here it was, wave after wave, her body bucked and her thighs convulsed. She tried to call Mantel but realised she was beyond speech. Mantel had hoped to indulge in a slow, passionate encounter, but he realised Nell was far ahead of him. Her excitement bought him on and he shot into her so fast, he took himself by surprise.

"Fuck, Nell, where did that come from?" He collapsed on top of her.

She was beyond words, just pulling on his ear lobes and his beard. It made him laugh.

"Nell, stop." He nuzzled into her neck and they lay in silence, a tangle of limbs They were quite unable to leave each other alone, Nell biting his mouth, and he stroked her, squeezed her, pinched and bit her and suckled her flesh. She held Mantel close and lost herself in him.

Again they asked for food to be sent up, again the bed needed stripping and changing. They fed each other intimately and drank much wine and brandy, with Mantel passing it to Nell via his mouth. It was messy and sexual, and they loved it. They lay in bed, Mantel twisting Nell's hair with one hand and the other softly pinching the skin on her waist. It was delightful and made Nell weak. Mantel whispered in her ear and turned her over, knowing if he ran his fingers along the crease of her bum, they would be away. He couldn't help himself; he parted the cheeks of her buttocks and he was in, strong and rough, his body slapping against Nell's. He was knocking the air from her body and she closed her eyes, feeling faint with need. She arched her back in spasm and pushed hard into Mantel. He had his hands on her hips and he laughed out loud as he came, his release setting him on a high and Nell, only seconds behind, orgasmed spectacularly, her body convulsing and writhing long after Mantel had finished. He watched and waited and wondered at her hungry sexuality. Eventually, she floated back down to earth and he spooned his body around hers, his breathing tickling the back of her neck; she closed her eyes and felt the goosepimples wave through her.

"Mantel," she breathed, biting the top of his arm as that

was the only part of him she could reach. He was going to like this, he knew, the biting and nipping, the hair pulling, his beard, his chest hair, his pubic hair. It was, in its way, a declaration of ownership – *you're mine, look what I can do to you*. He didn't mind being owned by Nell.

Before falling back to sleep, he whispered in her ear, "If you're not pregnant now, Nell, you never will be."

Sanity prevailed the following day, and Mantel was up and out early, in his usual black attire, black fedora, looking formidably handsome and business-like.

He put his hand up to ward off Nell. He shook his head.

"Nell, don't stop me, I have to go. I want to get out before Duff wakes. I can't resist either of you."

She came straight over to him then.

"Will you come back for us later?"

He pulled out his fob.

"In about an hour? Lot to do today. We need to get to your farm, Nell." He put his arm around her waist and pulled her towards him. He looked deep at her and pointed to his cheek. "Kiss?" He looked at her.

"Alright, just the one." She stood on his boots and reached up to plant the most provocative of kisses on his face. He shook his head and chuckled.

"Later then, Nell," and he was off.

True to his word, he was back a few hours later to collect Nell and baby Duff. Work was carrying on apace at Haswell Farm, and Mantel wanted Nell to see what was happening there. Bowling along the valley road, Nell asked Mantel to stop.

She pointed out a derelict hovel. "See that? Granny Oates lived there."

Mantel was astonished. "Surely not? That was never meant to be lived in. It's only a – actually, I'm not sure what it was for. It was never a dwelling. How do you know it was lived in?"

"One of my boys found Granny Oates in there. She'd passed away. I've got her goat. I'm surprised no one has taken it over."

"No, I'll have to get it demolished; we can't have that. I'm surprised it hasn't come to my attention before." He shook his head in disbelief "How could you live there? I'll have to check the inventory. I don't think this has been regarded as a building. It's been overlooked. We'll sort it. I don't want anyone living in there again." He clicked on the horse, but they hadn't got far, when they stopped again.

Mantel whistled low.

"Bloody hell, Nell, we've only got ourselves a gypsy encampment. Shit. We'll have to get them moved on." He stopped the gig and looked.

"What's wrong? They're not doing any harm, are they? Why must you move them on? They'll go on their own accord eventually, won't they?" Nell was fascinated by the brightly painted vardos set in a circle around a campfire, their piebald horses chained, grazing nearby. Children were playing, some gathering wood.

Mantel handed the reins to Nell and without saying a word, jumped down from the gig and crossed the road to speak to them. Nell couldn't hear, but she saw. Mantel was the epitome of authority, his height, towering over the shabbily dressed gypsy man, his decorated vare a signal of his prestige. There were no raised voices but it was clear by Mantel's demeanour, he would have his way.

He returned to the gig and they proceeded, Mantel not saying a word until they were some distance away. He was aware of a slight disapproval emanating from Nell.

"Yes, Nell?"

"Aren't you going to tell me anything?"

"I told them to move on. I want them gone within the next few days. They've to clear any mess." His voice was hard.

"Oh, that seems harsh. Why are you so adamant?"

"Nell, there's not a villager who will sleep easy knowing the gypsies are here. They're thieves, Nell. Dogs, chickens, babies, they'll take whatever they can get." He wanted to deliberately frighten her. "A nice, fair-skinned baby – they'd get a good price." He saw Nell look nervously over her shoulder at baby Duff. "Oh yes. They'd take him if they got the chance. You mustn't be soft, Nell. They know they're not welcome. I don't trust them at all, I don't want them on my land. We must warn them at the farm; I think we need a gate made for the driveway; don't want them camping on your land. They'd be helping themselves to your goat's milk and the chickens' eggs."

Nell was, by now, thoroughly alarmed.

"Mantel, are they really that bad? In the past, I've never really regarded them as a threat. Are you sure they're as bad as you think?"

He looked at her. "Nell, would you say I'm a vindictive man?"

She shook her head, "No."

"Aggressive?"

"No."

"Violent?"

"No"

"When I say the gypsies must go, they must go. I'm not saying it to be spiteful. I'm not saying it out of hatred. I want them gone, Nell, don't question me on it." Nell saw by the set of his jaw he would no longer brook any argument.

"Mantel, I didn't know." And to try and lighten his mood, she joked, "I love you when you're being masterful!"

He laughed then and looked at her. "Watch yourself," he warned with a smile.

CHAPTER THIRTY-ONE

Baby Duff was waking up as they arrived at the farm and Mrs Boswell came out to greet them. She was effusive and had much to tell Nell. Mantel handed Duff down to Nell.

"Excuse me, ladies; got to go and see the workmen. How are you managing, Mrs Bosworth? We'll try and get it all done as quickly as possible; they do have a lot to do." With that, he was off.

"Well," Mrs Bosworth smiled, "come and see. I've put the kettle on. The boys will be up to see you. They've got a lot to tell you; they've had their break this morning already, but they won't mind another. Gives them chance for another slice of cake."

Nell followed her into the kitchen, Nell's favourite place in her old house. She immediately had a memory of Eade, standing by the sink, unaware he was causing her acute discomfort, knowing he had never even been in his own kitchen at Chilworth House. Momentarily, she was very sad and tears welled in her eyes. Her Eade – gone, after only a few short weeks. Oh dear, she was becoming sorrowful.

"Mrs Bosworth, am I safe to feed Duff?"

"Of course, lovey. Oh sorry, forgot myself. In here, look, I've lit the fire. I'll pull the door to – The workman won't be down for their lunch for half an hour or so, so you're quite alright." Mrs Bosworth left her then to make a pot of tea. Nell was back within fifteen minutes with a bouncing Duff. She sat at the table with a cup of tea and a slice of seed cake just as the boys came in. Nell's first thought was how they'd grown. As usual, they filled the kitchen with noise and mess.

There was always a lot of water splashed when they were around.

"Well lads, are you showing me around today?"

Much later, Nell again sat in the kitchen with Mantel and baby Duff, drowsy now from much fresh air.

Mantel stood.

"Nell, we must be on our way." He pulled out his fob. "I need to speak with Mr Fletcher. Mrs Bosworth, carpenters will be over tomorrow, measure for a new gate. Nell, I want to go by the gypsies before dark, so they know we're keeping an eye on them, Mrs Bosworth, be vigilant, tell the boys. Bloody gypos, I…"

Mrs Bosworth shot a glance at Nell and Nell shook her shoulders as if to say she didn't know why Mr Buchanen had such a dislike for the travellers.

Mantel was polite and formal.

"Good day, Mrs Bosworth. Mrs Buchanen will be over after the gypsies have moved on."

Nell rose. "Thank you for everything. The boys are doing marvellously; how things change, don't they?" She didn't expect an answer but smiled. "We must get this baby home."

Back home, a desperately tired Duff was fed and watered and allowed only Mantel to put him down. Mantel loved to have him curled on his chest, making sleepy noises and trying to locate his thumb. Tonight was a first, he managed to find it by himself and Mantel had to resist an urge to run and tell Nell. Get a grip, he told himself. He was always rather scathing when Nell pointed out a new achievement by Duff; Mantel's love for Duff was out of sync with most fathers of that time; but Duff was having a profound effect. He kept Mantel grounded, made him aware of the frailty of human life, that everything Mantel strived for was for him. Duff loved him unconditionally. And if Mantel had to admit it, he loved Duff in the same way.

That night, Nell and Mantel came together in their room, eager and full of love and anticipation and Nell showed Mantel her wrist. Hardly marked now, but finally, Mantel caught on. Her wrist was a signal. As a dutiful, adoring husband, it was his job to kiss it better which he did willingly; those soft and tender kisses led to want and need and lust and they were lost in each other for most of the night. Come the morning, Nell was reluctant to let Mantel go; she always wanted more. The more sexing she had with Mantel, the more she wanted. Her unashamed need drove Mantel on; never let it be said he couldn't satisfy a woman; but worked called. He was reluctant to leave Nell in their nest, but he had to.

"Nell, don't wash. I'll be back lunchtime." He pulled on her lower lip with his mouth.

"Mantel! I can't wait here for you." She laughed.

"Yes you can. Don't get washed, don't get dressed." He left her then and Nell had to wait in a state of sexual arousal until Mantel came back to her at midday.

He was not late, taking his clothes off as he entered the room. Fedora flung, boots kicked off, his Melton coat thrown over the chair; and with Nell's help, he was ready for action within a few minutes.

"Mantel," she breathed, hot and needy. She closed her eyes. To feel him eager was, for Nell, the most wonderful thing. Already, Mantel was lost, suckling a nipple, squeezing her flesh; it didn't take him long.

"Nell," he breathed. He couldn't wait, his need was paramount. Nell knew. She lay still and quiet and waited for Mantel; he just had to touch her and she would succumb – and he did – and Nell came, again and again, her legs twined around Mantel.

"Nell, too quick, too quick," he moaned, burying his head in her neck. Nell sucked on his mouth.

"No control," she laughed.

"No. You're right" he said ruefully. He turned to lay on his back, hand behind his neck. "Can't go back to business until I've got this right, can I?"

"You can, but you're not going to. I've sent Duff to Mrs Fletcher. I know what you're like. Let's have a brandy." This was a signal. Brandy meant Mantel would pass it to Nell from his mouth, which meant only one thing…

Mantel left their bed while Nell was pouring the brandy and he came up behind her and lifted her off her feet. He carried her over to the other side of the bedroom and held her up against the wall, her feet not touching the floor. He bought his knee up to support her while he lifted her shift. Without more ado, he was in, rough and painful, quick, no words of love; this was very basic. He hurt Nell and she was offended.

She never said a word, but Mantel did.

"You know, I used to take a slut up a back alley and fuck her standing up." He laughed. "We'd call it a 'knee trembler'." He looked at Nell. For some reason, he expected her to find this amusing.

Her face fell. "What? How dare you tell me that? Do you honestly think I would want to know something like that?" Secretly she was appalled. Hot tears filled her eyes. "Before, when you were horrible, I slapped you, and what did you do? You twisted my wrist; it was so painful. You're twice my size, I could never fight you off, and here we are again. You are being horrible. You know full well, I can't fight you. What do you want to do to me this time?" she held out her wrists.

"Nell." His voice was pained.

"Well? Would you like to know how many men I fucked before you? How many back alleys I went down? Shall I tell

238

you what they did? Do you want me to make comparisons?"
She was furious.

"Nell! Stop! I know you didn't. Just stop there. I'm
sorry… I'm so sorry." He tapped his forehead.

"Why? Why should I stop? Have you any idea of the hurt?
So – you've had your way with some slack-faced whore,
who's probably given you the pox, which you've now given
to me! You are the most disgusting man." And with that, she
did slap him, and he sat, face down, too ashamed to look at
her. He offered no resistance.

She could have hit him again and again, but she didn't.

Much later, after a fraught dinner, Nell retired to bed,
ostensibly not speaking, as far over her side of the bed as
she could get without falling out. Mantel took some comfort
that, at least, she was still in their bed and not in another
room.

They lay, in silent darkness.

Mantel could not sleep.

"Nell," he murmured. Nothing. "Nell, please." He
reached out to touch her shoulder and she shrugged him
off. He knew then she wasn't asleep. "Nell, I know what
you think of me. Saying sorry is not going to cut it, is it?"
Silence. He was frustrated. "Nell, for God's sake!"

She turned then. "Good job there's no candles alight.
You would see in my face what I think of you. You disgust
me. Leave me alone." But she didn't turn her back on him.
Mantel took this as an encouraging sign. "Do you compare
me?" she asked. "Do you give us trollops marks out of ten?
Swap us around? Eade said you shared things."

She sobbed then. It was too awful. Shame swept over her:
first Eade, now Mantel. These were real tears now, not cries
to elicit sympathy, real, heart-rending sobs.

Mantel sat up. This was terrible.

"Nell." He held his hands up in supplication. "I dare not

touch you. I can explain. I know you don't want to hear, but I can explain. I'm sorry, really. Please stop."

He grabbed a muslin cloth from a pile kept on the bedside table for Duff. Instead of handing it to Nell, he kept it so she turned to him to take it and he wouldn't give it to her. He gently wiped her face, the snot and the tears. He was used to this; Nell never had a handkerchief.

"Nell." He slipped his arms around her. He kissed the top of her head. He could feel the resentment in Nell's body.

"Nell." He was humble.

"Nell, I have such a lot to learn. Don't hate me; I had a memory. It just came out. I didn't think. I must learn to keep quiet, not say anything. I am so, so sorry Nell."

How could Nell not soften? She sobbed.

"Mr Mantel Buchanen O'Kyan," she cried.

"Nell." He pulled her close and felt the mess on her face transfer onto his shoulder. He handed her the muslin.

"Wipe your face. Then, if you wouldn't mind, wipe my shoulder." She gave a little laugh.

That's it, thought Mantel. Now he could start to make amends. He pulled her hair away from her face and twisted it in his hand.

No more talking. They were as close as they could possibly be. No sexing either. They just lay. Every now and again, Mantel would shake his head as if in disbelief at his own stupidity.

Much, much later, Nell awoke to find Mantel wide-awake, laying on his back, looking up at the ceiling.

"What is it?" she asked, but she knew it was shame.

He shook his head. He couldn't answer.

"No," he said and went to turn away from her.

"Mantel, don't turn away from me. No, don't," as she felt him resist. She put her face up against his, feeling his hot breath.

She stroked his beard.

"Let's be sorry. You be sorry. I'll be sorry. Mantel, I'm sorry." In those few seconds, Mantel was elated.

"Nell, sorry, sorry, sorry," he nuzzled into her neck. He breathed a sigh of relief.

With all the sorrowful sorries out of the way, Mantel and Nell got down to doing what they did best and what they loved to do; this time with love and gentleness. It would be another morning where Mantel would reluctantly have to tear himself away.

For the next few days Mantel's main concern was moving the gypsies on. He and a few of the men, on horseback (he thought they looked more intimidating than in a carriage), approached their encampment. Mantel could see they had made no attempt to clear the site; in fact, there was more mess. There were wood shavings everywhere. They were creating carved woodland folk and faces of green men and huge mushrooms with red painted tops and white spots. Mantel was furious. All this with wood stolen from his land. He carefully walked his horse through the encampment, looking, not saying a word. Then he walked around the outer circle, noting paraphernalia everywhere, piled under the vardos. He signalled to his men to stay put. Things must not be allowed to get out of control. Back into the circle, and he was aware of the women, looking at him with hostility, the children dirty and silent and suspicious; the men – ah, here were the men – finally got themselves together to face him *en masse*.

Mantel pointedly looked around. "So when are you thinking of leaving?" he asked sarcastically.

Their leader doffed his cap; he was subservient. "Well, sire, three days an' we be off. No harm done, see, sir; we jus' uses the fallen wood, like." He was aware of Mantel's disapproval of their carvings.

Mantel was silent, the encampment was silent, all sound was from the crackling fire.

He shifted in his saddle and adjusted his fedora.

"I want you out by tomorrow."

"Ah, but sire, see, it's…"

"Out! By tomorrow, or else we'll be back to burn your vardos. You understand me? You've got until mid-day – understand?" His face was grim. He turned his horse to go, knowing he was doing a dangerous thing, turning his back on them. It signalled one of two things. Either he was naïve, or he knew he had complete authority and they would not dare to touch him. He and the men rode off without a backward glance and not a word being said until they were some distance away.

"Right, we will be here tomorrow, 12 o'clock. We'll hold back if they're moving. If they're not, we must chivvy them along. No violence – unless they get arsy." He doffed his fedora. "Thank you, boys. Back to work, then." And Mantel went off to see Mr Fletcher.

He eventually found him in one of the hot houses.

"Mr Fletcher! Nice place to be on a chilly morning. All well?"

"Ay, sir, ay. You be wanting fruit?" This was unusual. The *hoi polloi* from the house don't come into the hot house as a rule.

"No, no. Just wanted a word. Mr Fletcher, how would you feel about moving house? Mrs Buchanen has suggested to me, seeing as your wife is looking after Master Duff, it would be a better arrangement if you were nearer the main house. She also thinks your wife might need assistance with laundry and domestic work, seeing as she has the two babes to look after. Also, her ladyship wants you to have a garden so that they can play outside in safety. Her ladyship will also send over – baby clothes, napkins, bedding and another cot.

I'll have a word with the factor as to your move. Would you like to go and see your wife? Let her know? What do you think?"

"Ay, sir, you do us a great honour. I'll go tell the missus now, sir. She'll be that made up. Thank you." He took his cap off and bowed his head.

Well, I've made someone happy today, at least, Mantel thought.

Mr Fletcher rushed off to tell the good news to his wife. Quite frankly, he was amazed. Occasionally, she looked after her ladyship's baby. She fed him. She kept him overnight sometimes. And for that, they were going up in the world. Glory be – who would have thought it? Not through his own hard work and efforts either, but because his wife was a mother, clean and wholesome and a goodly wet nurse. Mr Fletcher was a good man; he cared for his wife, but maybe from now on, he would care for her a little more assiduously. Whoever would have thought her mothering skills, her love of babies and her abundance of milk would have bought about this?

The gypsies might have felt anger and resentment and even hatred, but Mr and Mrs Fletcher felt only overwhelming happiness at their good fortune.

Later, over dinner, he told Nell about the Fletchers.

"I told them it was your idea and that you would send baby stuff over. What do you think?"

"Mantel, I think it's a wonderful idea. You are so kind. I might get the boys to deliver goat's milk and butter once a week. Ultimately, Duff will benefit. Of course, any more babies that come along will also benefit."

Mantel gave a smile. "Any more babies?"

"Well," Nell shrugged her shoulders, "you never know, do you? I'd like to think there would be a few more."

"D'know, Nell, I'd like to think so too. Maybe three or four."

Nell looked alarmed. "Well, one more would be nice. Duff was hard work. He made my eyes water a bit."

"Don't forget, I was there. You made quite a fuss as I remember." He laughed, being deliberately provocative.

"Mantel, I think you know, having a baby is no easy thing." She crossed the room to sit on his lap. "They're worth it, though. Where would be without Duff? He's so lovely."

"He is," agreed Mantel. There was a silence between them, then Mantel suggested hopefully: "So, do you fancy going upstairs and making a baby?"

The following morning, Mantel was up early and out, looking extremely dark and so foreboding. It was gypsy day and also, destruction day of the hovel. The last thing he wanted was some tramp living there; so the men were rounded up and they were all in high spirits. They were looking forward to having a showdown with the travellers.

CHAPTER THIRTY-TWO

Mrs Fletcher was busy in her little house, humming away, a very happy lady, knowing she and her husband would be moving into a bigger house and all because of baby Duff. She loved that boy, almost as much as she loved her own, and now it was about to pay dividends. What a step up in the world it would be for their son to be the companion and playmate of such a high born. She sighed with happiness; life couldn't get any better.

Nell, looking out of the eating room window, decided as it was such a lovely morning, she would take Duff out in the gig. Mantel would be out best part of the day, so they could browse through the estate and they would go and see the animals. That always caused great excitement with Duff. She wrapped him warmly, collected the two dogs, Jess and Ruff (they were only there because the men were out expelling gypsies), and they were off, the dogs running behind the gig and Duff gurgling with... happiness.

The pigs caused much laughter; the fat old sows lying in the mud and basking in the sun, besieged by squealing piglets. They were a delight.

Then it was on to see the heifers. They were in calf.. and to Nell, looked enormous. Not as big as Mantel's shire, though. When they arrived at the stables, the blacksmith was there and Nell and Duff watched, fascinated, as one great hoof after another was fitted with a new shoe.

Then back round to see the hens. A few had just laid, as they were making such a noise. Pity Nell didn't have a basket with her; otherwise, she would have sneaked in and collected a few eggs to give to Mrs Fletcher,

Back in the gig the pair of them, and on down to the woods. Sometimes, if you were quiet, you could see the deer. Usually, they were silent and secretive, but Nell remembered once coming across a stag: enormous and very intimidating. He stood his ground and so did Nell, only because she was too frightened to move away. A few tense moments passed before he turned and fled and only then did Nell notice the other deer, hidden so well, who followed him.

Oh! It was beautiful in the dappled shade of the woods, the birds singing and Duff, perfectly content, propped up in his little travelling cot. He was crooning away and waving at everything. Nell stopped the gig to enjoy the moment. It was perfect. Only then, did she hear the cry. At first, she thought it was an animal. There it was again, surely not? Vixens cried like that at night sometimes, but not usually during the day. There it was again. Intrigued and a little apprehensive, Nell climbed down from the gig. She bought Duff with her, mindful of Mantel's warning that the gypsies would steal him. Naturally, now she was searching, the crying – stopped. How frustrating. Nell looked around suddenly. Was someone spying on her? Watching for an unguarded moment to attack her and steal baby Duff? She was suddenly alarmed and turned to go back to the gig when she saw it. A rush basket, at the base of a tree. Intrigued, she cautiously approached and peeped in. She almost lost her breath. There was a baby, tiny, wrapped in a rough cloth. Nell stood upright and looked around.

"Hello? louder "Hello? Is there anyone here? Show yourself!" she demanded. "Show yourself NOW!" She looked around. All was suddenly silent except for the baby which gave a pathetic wail. To say Nell was confused and baffled would be an understatement. She called again and again, very imperious. "If you do not reveal yourself, I will have

246

my men come and detain you. It will not be pleasant. This is your last chance. Show yourself!"

She waited. Nothing. Now what should she do? The woods, so perfect only a few minutes ago, were now sinister and frightening. Nell knew, deep inside, she couldn't leave the baby where it was. Maybe someone had left it there deliberately, hoping it would be found. Resigned, Nell, with great difficulty, somehow dragged the rush basket back to the gig, while roughly holding Duff under her right arm. He didn't like it and protested, but she didn't dare put him back in the gig and leave him while she collected the basket.

She strapped Duff in his travel cot, then lifted the basket in by her feet and carefully made her way out of the woods and back up the drive to the house and round to the stables.

"Boy," she called to the stable lad sweeping the cobbles, "go to the kitchen and ask for Tilda. She's to make haste. Come immediately, tell her." She unstrapped Duff and hugged him and kissed his cheek. Suddenly he was very precious to her.

Thank God Mantel was getting rid of the gypsies today. Her thoughts were entirely irrational. If they had wanted to steal a baby, why, they could have stolen this one. Tilda arrived, breathless and somewhat alarmed.

"Tilda, take Duff to Mrs Fletcher. Tell her not to let the babies out of her sight, not for one minute. Tell her there's gypsies around. If she could keep him overnight…"

"Yes Ma'am.' She bobbed, took Duff and was off.

Nell had stood in front of the rush basket and fortunately, the baby hadn't made a sound. Nell hastily grabbed the basket and sped through the back kitchen and into the house. She was up the stairs and into their room in a flash. She rang for a servant immediately.

"Hot water, please. Leave it in the bathing room."

The little maid bobbed and went.

While Nell waited, she unwrapped the baby. My goodness, she noticed how tiny it was. A girl, so new, she still had the umbilical cord attached. Nell was panicked now. She searched her mind. She looked around. in the woods. There was no girl or woman newly birthed. How could this be? She heard the maid with the water and caught her.

"Send for Doctor Murray. Say he must come straight away. It's an emergency. He's not to delay."

Nell knew instinctively this baby was hungry; her pitiful wails tugged at her heart. She swaddled her in a towel and sat on the bed. Somehow, she managed to remove her gown and she put the baby to her breast. Oh, that was Nell's undoing. This baby was so tiny, so helpless, so fragile, she sucked greedily. Nell shook her head. Whatever was she going to do? She sat her up and winded her and put her on the other side. My goodness, she was perfect. Just performing these normal, motherly jobs calmed Nell. She held the baby on her shoulder, while sorting out a napkin and warm vest. Would it be better to bathe her before Doctor Murray arrived or after he'd seen her? Before, she decided. This baby needed washing. Nell gently sponged her olive skin and washed her greasy hair and the baby made soft mewling noises. She didn't cry. Nell lifted her carefully out of the warm water and laid her on an equally warm towel, when she heard commotion in the corridor.

Doctor Murray.

"Doctor, in here," she called.

The door opened slowly and Doctor Murray cautiously put his head round. On seeing Nell, he was concerned. Then he saw the baby. He stopped in surprise. "What's this?" he asked. His mind was racing. There wasn't time for another baby. Ten months hadn't passed. His perplexity showed.

"Doctor, just look at this baby. It's not mine, no. You will never believe it. I found her."

"What?"

He had picked her up with one hand and was examining her carefully. He turned her over, checked her fingernails, her ears, her legs. Nell was amazed to see one of her legs wasn't as big as the doctor's finger.

"Well Mrs Buchanen, she's not forty-eight hours old. I'll have to remove the umbilical cord," he indicated to Nell that she hold the baby where she was while he got his bag.

To Nell watching, it seemed quite brutal and Doctor Murray saw her look of alarm. "Not to worry, it doesn't hurt. Just have to clean her up a bit now. There, all done. Now, you have clothes for her?"

"Yes. Yes, follow me"

Back in the bedroom, Nell dressed the baby and swaddled her and held her close.

"Doctor, will you stay for lunch? I can tell you everything then. I'm awfully hungry. Maybe it's the excitement." She looked questioningly at him.

He smiled. "I would love lunch. That's something I don't usually have time for."

They made their way down to the eating room and the doctor, after helping himself to a good lunch, looked searchingly at Nell.

"Well, Mrs Buchanen, would you like to tell me?"

Nell put down her cutlery.

She told the good doctor about her and Duff's outing in the gig. Viewing the pigs, seeing the blacksmith, coming through the woods because it was such a lovely day and then coming across the basket.

"Doctor, it was just there at the foot of the tree. I looked all around. I called and called. I was a little frightened, actually. I thought it was some sort of a trap to steal Duff from me. I mean – why? A new baby – it could have died, couldn't it? Do you think they wanted that? For it to die? How terrible."

Doctor Murray shook his head. "I don't know. I have no woman on my list ready for confinement. As I said, this baby is less than two days old. She couldn't have lasted much longer, certainly not another night." He breathed heavily. "Now we have a problem; we must try and find the mother."

"But surely, any mother who abandons her baby like that doesn't want it, does she?"

"Mmm," Doctor Murray inclined his head. "Sometimes there are strange forces at work in a new mother's mind. I must do all I can to find her. If she hasn't seen anyone since giving birth, she will need help. Meanwhile, the baby – I can get her cared for if you give me a day or two to sort something out."

"Doctor, please, can I look after her? I found her, I feel a responsibility for her. I also have Mrs, Fletcher, she's Duff's wet nurse occasionally. A good woman, respectable; please Doctor?"

He was silent for a moment "You mustn't get too attached, Mrs Buchanen. It will be hard for you when she goes."

"Oh Doctor, I do know that, but please, it just seems fate that I found her and I can care for her. Maybe that's what the mother wanted, maybe?" Nell was anxious. Already she felt – what? – something for this tiny, helpless mite.

Doctor Murray inclined his head and nodded.

"Right, Mrs Buchanen. You're sure? I will make inquiries and get back to you. Do not worry if you do not hear from me for a day or two. I will be in touch. Keep an eye on her tummy button, any worries, send for me. I'll leave you now. And thank you for lunch. Oh and by the way, I've heard about the improvements to the school, the library and reading room. Wonderful." He paused. "And things are well with you and Mr Mantel?" He had been informed by Mr Mantel himself that they were to be married. Proposals could be made, but they didn't always go to plan, as the good doctor knew.

"Doctor, you know how I was after losing my Eade. Lost, I was completely lost, nothing to live for and I was full of resentment, I think you knew. Well, it took a bit of time to come round, but Mantel's a good man. He made me realise."

"What will he have to say about this baby?"

"Oh, Doctor Murray, he's a good man, he will be fine, promise you, he won't mind."

"Well," the doctor bowed his head, "I'll leave you now then. I will speak to you soon. Good day."

Within minutes of him leaving. Nell was racing upstairs to the bedroom to look at her baby. She was still sleeping. Nell gently touched her to make her move and she did, moving her head and pursing her tiny mouth. *Oh my goodness*, thought Nell, *she's lovely*. Dark hair and lashes, not fair-skinned like her Duff, but slightly darker. *Goodness knows what Mantel will think*. She bit her lip. Inwardly, she had doubts. Well, she was resolved. She would keep this baby until things were sorted. She shook her head. She couldn't expect Mantel to have the same kind of feelings that she had. She had to bring him round. She rang for Tilda.

"Tilda, I need a bath drawn now – and – Tilda," she beckoned with her hand, "come." She took Tilda into the bedroom and showed her the baby.

Tilda was astonished. "Ma'am? What? What is this?" she was bewildered.

So once again, Nell told the story.

"Tilda, do you know of anyone? Anyone who might try and hide a pregnancy?"

"Ma'am," Tilda shook her head, "no Ma'am, no one. Really, no one." She turned to look at Nell "What are you going to do, Ma'am?"

"Well, I've told Doctor Murray and he's going to conduct a search for the mother. Until she's found, we will care for her. I will see Mrs Fletcher in the morning. Now, I will feed her while you draw me a bath. Let me know when it's ready." She smiled at Tilda to dismiss her.

The baby was fretting in the cot and Nell went over to pick her up. Oh poor little mite, she was so, so tiny.

"Tilda," she called in the corridor, just as she was filling the last water in the bath.

"Tilda, undo my dress, I must take it off."

"Yes Ma'am." Tilda obliged and Nell was soon ensconced in the bedroom, in a state of undress, but now able to feed the baby.

She sat on the bed and enveloped the baby in her arms and just gazed at her. As Duff was becoming more independent of her and learning to eat and drink, a step Nell acknowledged as inevitable, here, now, was another dependent little one, and she was secretly pleased. She settled herself comfortably on the bed and slipped the strap of her chemise down off her shoulder. She looked softly at this tiny baby. *You are a perfect pearl*, she thought. *A tiny pearl. That's what I'm going to call you.*

Unexpectedly, into this intimate world, came Mantel. Huge, noisy, smelling of the outdoors. Loud. On a high. Ready to tell Nell about what a day they'd had. He crossed the room in a few short strides, ready to kiss Nell and Duff and stopped short. Nell saw confusion cross his face.

"Nell? What? Where's Duff?" Before she replied, she put the frantic baby to her breast. "Nell?" Mantel looked at her.

"Duff is with Mrs Fletcher. He's safe. She is keeping him

until tomorrow. Now, sit on the bed," she patted the cover-let, "and I'll tell you about this little one."

Mantel was not to be easily taken in.

"No, no, you carry on. I've got to take all this stuff off." And he sat on the stool to unlace his boots, all the while, looking at Nell. So, boots off, Melton coat off, waistcoat and cravat off and thrown on the chair. Only then did he come over to Nell. He watched her intently. He always liked to watch Nell breastfeed. It stirred something inside him. He sat on the bed. He was aware that Nell was apprehensive and, deep within him, was a little worm of anger. What was going on? "Well?" he asked ominously.

Oh dear. Nell closed her eyes. Why was this going to annoy Mantel, she wondered. *Here goes,* she thought, and for the third time that day she told the story about finding the baby in the woods. She watched for Mantel's reaction when she finished. He leaned back, shook his head, pursed his lips and never said anything. She knew, for some reason, he was very cross.

"I've told Doctor Murray. He says she's not two days old. He says she wouldn't have survived another night. Mantel – you're angry. I know. I can tell." She took the sleepy baby off her breast and covered herself and rubbed the baby's back, before putting her on the other nipple. "Mantel, what could I do? I couldn't leave her there."

Nell's eyes filled with tears. To her, this was a simple problem, easily remedied. Abandoned baby, you take it in, care for it, feed it until the mother is found. Is that so terrible? Is it anything to get angry about? To lose your temper? Really, what was it about Mantel that he turned a molehill into a mountain?

Nell was working herself up. She looked very vulnerable, naked shoulder and breast, her hand cupping a tiny head, a defenceless baby.

"Well?" she took the baby off her breast and pulled the strap up over her shoulder.

The baby she held in one hand and patted her with the other. Little Pearl obligingly burped and sicked up excess milk which Nell wiped away with a muslin cloth. She felt her chin begin to wobble and her eyes filled. *For God's sake,* Nell told herself, *be strong, don't be intimidated by Mantel.* Don't let him be a bully. She swallowed. She shook her head.

"Mantel, I can tell, you are cross. I don't understand why." Again her eyes filled with tears. *No! No crying,* she told herself. She looked at him, holding Pearl up to her shoulder.

"Well? Here, take her." Nell held her out to Mantel "Go on, take her. There's her basket. Go and put her back in the woods." She was biting the inside of her lip until it bled. There was such a silence- and Nell allowed a hot tear to roll down her face. She watched Mantel carefully. He wouldn't look at her. "Take her, Mantel. You're the one that doesn't want her. If you leave her in the woods, the foxes will have her, won't they? There won't be anything to show for her in the morning, just a few bones."

Nell, intending to shock Mantel, shocked herself and she began to cry in earnest.

"Nell," Mantel closed his eyes, "Nell, I give in. Stop. I give in, you win. No more, no need to over-egg the omelette" he joked weakly. He moved nearer to give her a cuddle. He enveloped her in his arms and they sat in silence, repairing fences without either of them saying a word.

Eventually, Nell spoke.

"Look Mantel, when I found her, she still had her umbilical cord. Doctor Murray had to remove it, that's how he knew she was only hours old." Nell unswaddled her and showed her to Mantel, "Look how tiny she is."

"My God, Nell, how does something so small survive? My thumb is bigger than her foot."

"Now, perhaps you understand why I couldn't just leave her."

Mantel slipped his arm around Nell's waist and they sat as close as they could. Mantel holding Nell and Nell holding baby Pearl. They sat on the bed in silence and Nell heard, through the slightly opened bedroom window, the song of the nightingale.